全国英语等级考试系列丛书

全国英语等级考试全真模拟试题

ETS

PETS研究小组编写　　第**3**级

主　　编　　张顺生

副 主 编　　李　磊　丁亚军　姜　烨

编写组成员　　（按姓氏拼音顺序排列）

丁亚军　董　嫣　郝艳娥　姜　烨　李　杰

李　磊　练稳山　毛婉洁　浦　鹏　沈　俐

王　锋　吴广珠　杨　婳　张荣伟　张顺生

张晓生　周建军

北京航空航天大学出版社

图书在版编目(CIP)数据

全国英语等级考试全真模拟试题. 第 3 级 / PETS 研究
小组编. —北京:北京航空航天大学出版社,2009.7
ISBN 978-7-81124-842-5

Ⅰ. 全… Ⅱ. P… Ⅲ. 英语—水平考试—习题 Ⅳ.H319.6

中国版本图书馆 CIP 数据核字(2009)第 113780 号

全国英语等级考试全真模拟试题第 3 级
PETS 研究小组编写
责任编辑 姜伟娜

*
北京航空航天大学出版社出版发行
北京市海淀区学院路 37 号 (100191) 发行部电话:010-82317024 传真:010-82328026
http:// www.buaapress.com.cn Email:bhpress@263.net
北京市松源印刷有限公司印装 各地书店经销
*
开本:787×1092 1/16 印张:10.75 字数:280 千字
2009 年 7 月第 1 版 2009 年 7 月第 1 次印刷
ISBN 978-7-81124-842-5 定价:20.80 元

前 言

　　全国英语等级考试(Public English Test System,简称PETS)是教育部考试中心设计并实施的全国性英语水平考试体系。作为中、英两国政府的教育交流合作项目,在设计过程中它得到了英国专家的技术支持。PETS共分五个级别:PETS 3是中间级,其考试要求相当于我国学生高中毕业后在大专院校又学了2年公共英语或自学了同等程度英语课程的英语水平。

　　全国英语等级考试是面向社会的、开放的、以全体公民为对象的非学历性的英语等级考试,是测试应试者英语交际能力的水平考试。PETS的设计有助于鞭策社会人员的英语学习,促进英语爱好者不断提高自己的英语水平。

　　基于社会的需要,我们特组织编写了一套《全国英语等级考试全真模拟试题》供广大应试者复习使用。我们出版的这套书是根据2009年全国英语等级考试PETS大纲编写的。每册均由试题评析及应试技巧、模拟试题、专家预测试题、历年真题、参考答案与解析和口试真题与提示六个部分组成。本书编写的特点如下:

　　一、试题真实　本册的笔试题目共9套,其中5套模拟试题、2套专家预测试题、2套历年真题。模拟试题和专家预测试题均经过调研,与真题难度相当且具有代表性。同时,我们还特意准备了两份口试真题,供备考人员应考。对于口语试题的分析和建议为切身经验之谈,既可信,又可操作,对备考人员来说非常有帮助。

　　二、解析透彻　本书对各类题型进行了详细、到位的解释。与同类书相比,讲解全面、具体。特别在完形填空和写作方面,我们更是精心设计。完形填空方面,我们本着"以人为本"的理念,每一篇文章都提供了参考译文或文章概述,以利于自学者更好地理解,有时我们还提供了一些拓展性知识以开阔学习者的眼界。至于写作,我们不仅提供了精彩的范文,而且提供了切实可行的写作技巧,力求"授人以鱼"与"授人以渔"并举。

　　三、选材经典　本书的试题均选自国家题库,而且经过了精心筛选,并征求了有相关经验师生的意见。本书的选材不仅能让考生学习到英语知识,而且可以拓展自身的文化知识。

　　四、版式醒目　本书每道题都有答案、解析等内容,便于学习者能清楚知道答案是什么,也能知道为什么,同时也方便学习者归纳和总结。我们还提供了口试真题,这对没有参加过口试或者参加过而没有通过的人来说无疑很有参考价值。

　　当然,真正的学习没有什么秘诀,只有努力。建议学习者每天坚持看英语文章,每周坚持至少做一套试题,帮助自己寻找考试的感觉。接近考试前一个月,每周坚持做两份以上试题。每次做完试题之后要及时总结,将自己的错误记录下来。有毅力的话,每天坚持写100—200词左右的英语日记或者英语评论。滴水穿石。我坚信,只要大家能够坚持不懈,什么考试都难不倒自己。

　　本书中如有疏漏、错误和不足之处,敬请广大同仁和读者批评指正,以便我们再版时进一步改进。最后,祝广大考生考试顺利!

编者

2009年5月

目 录

第1章

试题评析及应试技巧

考试大纲与内容解读

全国英语等级考试(Public English Test System,简称 PETS)是教育部考试中心设计并负责的全国性英语水平考试体系。PETS 3 是五个级别中的中间级,通过该级考试的考生,其英语可以达到高等教育自学考试非英语专业本科毕业水平或符合普通高校非英语专业本科毕业的要求,基本符合企事业单位行政秘书、经理助理、初级科技人员、外企职员的工作,以及同层次其他工作在对外交往中的基本需要。

该级考生应能适当运用基本的语法知识,掌握 4,000 左右的词汇以及相关词组。PETS 3 考试由笔试试卷和口试试卷组成。笔试试卷(120 分钟)分四部分:听力理解、英语知识运用、阅读理解和写作。口试试卷(10 分钟)分三节考查考生的口语交际能力。下面从试卷组成、题型概述、试卷结构三方面为大家全面解读 PETS 3 考试大纲。

一、试卷组成

笔试试卷(120 分钟)分四部分:听力理解、英语知识运用、阅读理解和写作。

口试试卷(10 分钟)分三节考查考生的口语交际能力。

笔试试卷和口试试卷都使用英文指导语。

二、题型概述

(一) 听力理解

该部分由 A、B 两节组成,考查考生理解英语口语的能力。

A 节(10 题):通常考查考生理解事实性信息的能力。要求考生根据所听到的 10 段简短对话(总长约 400 词,总时长约为 3′30″),从每题所给的 4 个选项中选出最佳选项。每题有 15 秒答题时间 (5 秒用做听前读题,10 秒用做听后答题)。

B 节(15 题):考查考生理解总体和特定信息的能力。要求考生根据所听到的 4 段对话或独白(每段平均约 200 词,时长约为 1′40″—2′10″,总长约 800 词,总时长约 8′30″),从每题所给的 4 个选项中选出最佳选项。每题有 20 秒答题时间(5 秒用做听前读题,10 秒用做听后答题。每篇对话或独白的听前读题和听后答题时间,都按题数累计给出)。

每段录音材料只播放一遍。问题不在录音中播放,仅在试卷上印出。听力考试进行时,考生将答案标在试卷上;听力部分结束后,考生有 3 分钟的时间将试卷上的答案转涂到答题卡 1 上。该部分所需时间约为 25 分钟(含转涂时间)。

(二) 英语知识运用

该部分考查考生对语法结构、词汇知识和表达方式的掌握情况。在一篇 200—250 词的短文中留出 20 个空白,要求考生从每题所给的 4 个选项中选出最佳选项,使补足后的短文意思通顺、语法正确、前后连贯、结构完整。其中有13—15道题考查词汇和表达方式,5—7道题考查语法结构。该部分所需时间约为15分钟。

(三) 阅读理解

该部分由 A、B 两节组成,考查考生理解英语阅读材料的能力。

A 节(15题):A节一般为三篇文章,考查考生理解总体和特定信息的能力。要求考生根据所提供的 3 篇文章的内容(平均长度为 350 词左右)从每题所给的 4 个选项中选出最佳选项。

B 节(5题):B节一般为一篇文章,主要考查考生理解文章(约长 350 词)的主旨要义的能力。考生须从七个选项中排除两个干扰项,将正确的概述与五段文字逐一搭配成对。

该部分所需时间约为 40 分钟。考生在答题卡 1 上作答。

(四) 写作

该部分由 A、B 两节组成,考查考生的书面表达能力。

A 节:考生根据所给情景(英/中文)写出约 100 词(不计算标点符号)的简单信件、便笺等。

B 节:考生根据所给情景,写出一篇不少于 120 词(不计算标点符号)的文章,通常为议论文和说明文。提供情景的形式有图画、图表、文字等。

该部分所需时间约为 40 分钟。考生在答题卡 2 上作答。

(五) 口试

口试分 A、B、C 三节,测试考生用英语进行口头交际的能力。每次口试采取两名口试考官和两名考生的形式。一名考官不参与交谈,专事评分;另一名主持口试,随时与考生交谈并评分。专事评分的考官所给分数的权重占考生口试成绩的三分之二,主持口试的考官所给分数的权重占考生口试成绩的三分之一。

A 节:考查考生提供个人信息、回答有关他们日常生活、家乡、家庭、工作、学习等问题的能力。该节约需 3 分钟。

B 节:考查考生就信息卡上的图片或文字讨论有关问题的能力。该节约需 3 分钟。

C 节:要求考生就信息卡上的图片或文字作简短描述,之后另一考生就同一话题阐述个人观点。该节约需 4 分钟。

三、试卷结构表

表一 笔试结构表

部分	节	为考生提供的信息	考查要点	题型	题数	原始分	权重	时间(分钟)
I 听力*(接受)	A	10 段简短对话(约400 词)(只放一遍录音)	事实性信息	多项选择题(4 选 1)	10	10	30%	25
	B	4 段长对话或独白(约 800 词)(只放一遍录音)	总体与特定信息	多项选择题(4 选 1)	15	15		
II 英语知识运用(接受)		1 篇文章(200—250 词)	语法和词汇	完形填空 多项选择题(4 选 1)	20	20	15%	15

续表

部分	节	为考生提供的信息	考查要点	题型	题数	原始分	权重	时间（分钟）
III 阅读理解（接受）	A	3篇文章（每篇约350词）	总体与特定信息	多项选择题（4选1）	15	30	30%	40
	B	一篇文章（约350词）	理解主旨要义	搭配题	5	5		
IV 写作（产出）	A	中/英文提示信息	写简单信件与便笺等	应用文	1	10	25%	40
	B	英文提示信息	写短文	议论文或说明文	1	20		
总计					67	110	100%	120

* 问题不在录音中播放，仅在试卷上印出。

表二　口试结构表

节	时间（分钟）	形式	为考生提供的信息	考查要点	考生需提供的信息	分数
A	3	口试教师与考生对话	口试教师提出的问题（使用标准语言）	* 回答询问 * 提供个人信息	回答有关个人信息的问题	5
B	3	两考生对话	信息卡（图片或文字）	* 与他人交流 * 讨论一般性质问题	* 交换信息 * 表达观点 * 提出建议	
C	4	考生连续表达	信息卡（图片或文字）	* 描述事物 * 阐述观点或论证	* 事物的描述 * 观点的阐述或论证	

* 观点的阐述或论证。

试题透视与技巧点拨

一、听力理解

三级听力理解部分在100分的原始分中占20分，而其加权占了30%，可见PETS 3对听力的重视。三级的听力理解部分由A(10段简短对话，4选1)和B(4段对话或独白，4选1)部分组成，考查考生理解英语口语的能力。

从听力信息上讲,考生应该学会理解主旨要义、获取事实性具体信息、理解明确表达的概念性含义、进行有关的判断、推理和引申、理解说话者的意图、观点或态度等。要在听力部分得到高分,平时的训练技巧和考试的良好发挥都是不容忽视的。考生在平时的训练中,要从语感、技能两方面入手,着力提高语言知识水平,提高学习者利用非语言知识分析、归纳获取语言信息的能力。

1. 试题透视

短对话部分:这一部分是日常生活中的一般对话,即衣、食、住、行、工作、学习等话题,可分为校园、公共场所、家庭等方面。对话部分常见的及应注意的题型有以下几种:

(1) 关系判断题:听力对话题中会测试一些包括说话者的身份、职业以及两个说话者之间的关系等的题目。考生要根据说话内容确定人物关系,通常有家长和孩子、老师和学生、医生和病人、售货员和顾客等常见关系。

【典型例题】

What is the most probable relationship between the two speakers?

[A] Teacher and student.　　　　[B] Doctor and patient.

[C] Boss and worker.　　　　　[D] Mother and son.

【听力原文】

W: We are going to hold our evening party at the weekend, would you join us, sir?

M: Since it's the first evening party of your class, I'd very much like to attend it.

【答案与解析】　根据男子的回答"既然这是你们班首次举行的晚会,我很乐意去。"结合选项,可以推断是老师和学生的关系。

(2) 地点推断题:人物的对话都是发生在一定的场合或地点,因此,关于地点或场合类的题目是常见的。那么考生一定要抓住对话中提到的一些词或内容来判断对话发生的地点或场合。这种题型既考查考生捕获细节的能力,又考查其综合判断能力。

【典型例题】

Where is the dialogue most likely taking place?

[A] In a post office.　　　　　[B] In a restaurant.

[C] In a bank.　　　　　　　[D] In a police station.

【听力原文】

M: Excuse me! I just need to send this letter the fastest way possible.

W: Let's see. We have overnight business service. That takes just two days.

【答案与解析】　根据 send this letter 我们就可以判断对话是发生在邮局,所以答案为 A。

(3) 数字计算题:对话中经常会涉及到时间、价钱、号码、人或物的数量等与数字有关的信息,有时还要进行简单的计算。答题时要注意记下听到的数字,以便核查计算。

【典型例题】

When does school begin?

[A] At 7:00.　　　　[B] At 7:30.　　　　[C] At 8:00.　　　　[D] At 8:30.

【听力原文】

M: Does school begin at eight o'clock?

W: No. It begins half an hour earlier.

【答案与解析】　本题是有关时间的问题。这道题的难点是 It begins half an hour earlier. 这说明对方是早到了半个小时,因此把 8:00 向前推半个小时,我们应该选择 7:30。

(4) 言外之意题:对话中的含蓄性试题较多,所以,不仅要理解说话人的表层意义,还需体会言外之意。这类题型往往要注意说话者的"转折",如 I'd love to, but ...等。

【典型例题】

What does the man mean?

[A] He went mountain climbing last year.　　[B] He doesn't want to go at all.

[C] He hasn't traveled around the world yet.　　[D] He wants to go very much.

【听力原文】

W: Jack, we will go to mountain climbing this weekend, would you join us?

M: That's the last thing in the world I ever want to do.

【答案与解析】　女士问男士是否愿意一起爬山,男子说:"这是我这辈子最不愿做的事。"说明自己不喜欢爬山。所以答案为 B。

短文理解部分:由一篇短文组成,每篇约为150词。短文后有3—4个问题,所选取的短文以英语国家有关的材料为主,与对话相比,本部分信息量大、题材广泛,主要包括叙事、说明、议论、讲座、新闻等类型。常见题型有以下几种:

(1) 事实细节题:主要考查辨认文中具体事实细节的能力以及对短文中人名、地名、时间、原因、数据、目的等细节信息的把握。

问题类型:Who did ... ? / When (Where, What, Why or How) did... ? / What is... ? / What are the causes of the accident? / Which of the following is true / mentioned? / Why was...? / What is the reason / purpose... ?

(2) 综合推断题:主要测试考生根据文章所提供的信息进行判断、推理、综合和归纳的能力。主要涉及说话人的态度、观点以及原因、结果等。

问题类型:What can be inferred from the passage?/What does the speaker think about the problem... ?/ What was the speaker most concerned about?/How does the writer feel about... ?

(3) 主旨大意题:主要考查理解和概括文章主要内容的能力,涉及文章的主题、标题以及中心思想等。

问题类型:What is the main idea(topic) of the passage? / What can we learn from this passage? / What is the best title for this passage?/What is the passage mainly about?/What does the passage tell us?

2. 技巧点拨

【平时训练技巧】

(1) 熟悉语音语调,多听多读。众所周知,英语听说不分家。平时练习时不只是为了做题,更要从做题中积累经验,要仔细分析听力原文,跟读,这样能强化语音语调,自然适应和熟悉地道的发音规则,如失去爆破、连读、弱读等等;跟读还能培养语感,增强记忆。通过多听,我们还可以熟悉各种讲话人的语音,并使自己的思维反应能力跟上,只有这样,才能听懂材料内容并快速做出正确的选择判断。

(2) 强化速记能力,多听多记。听力考试要求考生在很短的时间内记住听到的重要信息,这需要很强的短期记忆能力。为加强记忆,考生可以掌握一些速记的方法,如利用缩略词、符号、首字母等记下重要的数字、时间、地点、中心词等。

(3) 全面提高英语各方面水平。提高英语听力的水平单靠"听"是不能解决理解能力问题的,个人的听力水平的高低与其掌握的词汇量、语法点、知识面、理解能力甚至阅读理解能力等都密切相关。因此,考生应注意全面提升自己听、说、读写的能力,尤其是语法和词汇量方面的积累,还要注意了解一些英美国家文化习俗。

【考场应试技巧】

(1) 力争主动,带着问题听。听力考试开始前的几分钟,老师会先发试卷,这时有些同学就会很着急的开始做选择题或者阅读理解题,其实这个时候,你应该好好把听力的题目浏览一遍,熟悉一下听力题的选项,充分的准备工作对听力考试有很大的好处。而且听力理解中的每一个问题都留有 15 秒的答题时间。考生可充分利用这段时间去阅读试卷上各题的问题。这样,考生基本上可以预测出下一个对话的大致内容,带着问题答题。

(2) 最大化地获取信息。听力测试要求考生能分清主次,边听边想,抓住重要信息,排除次要信息。在听懂大意的基础上,抓住所听内容的主旨与有关细节,同时利用在预读中得到的潜在信息,并用自己熟悉的形式把关键信息、数字等迅速记录下来。做到耳眼并用,一边听录音信息,一边浏览书面信息,边听边想。采取抓信息词、关键词,用预测法、排除法等各种方法进行判断和选择。另外,在录音中某些词的重读、声调的高低、语调的变化都暗示这些是重要信息,考生在此基础上做综合归纳、判断推理。

(3) 注意答题策略,有"舍"才有"得"。正式开始做题之后,要严格控制答题时间,根据自己听懂的内容,尽快确定并标出答案。剩下的 5 秒钟用于浏览下一题的问题和选项。如果遇到没听清楚的题目,则可考虑放弃该题,专心听下一题,不要死盯着一道题目,以致影响后面的发挥。

二、英语知识运用

该部分首先复习语法知识、搭配知识和语篇知识,在练习中要复习掌握词汇手段、语法手段和逻辑手段,提高在词汇辨析、习惯用法、固定搭配、逻辑推理和语篇理解等方面的能力。

1. 试题透视

完形填空侧重于对文章上下文联贯性的理解能力,以及语法上对句型结构、固定搭配、习惯用法和同义词辨析的认知能力。针对此种题型,我们应分别从词汇、语法和语篇层次上学习应对方法,提高对连贯性和一致性等语段特征的掌握和对一定语境下规范的语言成分的掌握。常见题型有以下五种:

(1) 推理判断题。对一篇文章进行综合填空,当然要考查对整篇文章的理解。拿到文章之后,首先应该通读全文以了解文章的中心思想和主要内容。

(2) 固定搭配题。这种题目在该部分考试中出现得比较多,而且无论是否有选项实际上对考生做这类题目来说影响并不大,因为对付这类题目只需要记往常用的固定搭配,特别是一些动词短语,所以平时要注意积累记忆。

(3) 关联词语题。关联词语有时会成对出现,有时会单独使用。它们在整个句子中起着非常重要的作用,因为它们连接着一句话中不同的分句,并告诉读者这些分句之间的关系。

(4) 名词代词题。这类题目与其说是对名词的考查,不如说是对代词的考查。众所周知,代词是用来代替名词的,而且,在文章中,有时为了避免重复,不宜过多地使用名词,这时,只有使用代词来充当名词的角色。无论使用代词还是选择代词,我们都应该注意名词和代词的一致性问题。

(5) 细节连贯题。考生一定要有全局意识,即语篇意识。在做有些题目时,我们可以直接或间接地从上下文中找到答案。这样的题目又可以分为两类:一类是能够从上下文中直接找到。另一类是不能直接从原文中找到,但是可以根据上下文的意思来做判断。有时,我们可以从上下文中找到该单词的反义词或者近义词,然后根据连接词的意思,来做出相应的选择;有时,我们可以根据上下文中的有关信息来判断此处填的单词。

【典型例题】

What would life be like without television? Would you spend more time ___26___, reading, or studying? Well, now it's your chance to turn off your TV and ___27___ ! TV-Turnoff Week is here.

The goal of TV-Turnoff Week is to let people leave their TV sets ___28___ and participate in activities ___29___ drawing to biking. The event was founded by TV-Turnoff Network, a non-profit organization which started the event in 1995. In the ___30___, only a few thousand people took part. Last year more than 7.6 million people participated, ___31___ people in every state in America and in more than 12 other countries!　This is the 11th year in which ___32___ are asking people to "turn off the TV and turn on ___32___."

...

26. [A] drinking　　　[B] sleeping　　　[C] washing　　　[D] playing outside
27. [A] find out　　　[B] go out　　　　[C] look out　　　[D] keep out
28. [A] away　　　　[B] off　　　　　[C] on　　　　　[D] beside
29. [A] like　　　　[B] as　　　　　[C] from　　　　[D] such as
30. [A] end　　　　[B] event　　　　[C] beginning　　[D] total
31. [A] besides　　　[B] except for　　[C] including　　[D] except
32. [A] governments　[B] parents　　　[C] organizers　　[D] businessmen

...

【答案与解析】

26. D 【解析】推理题。从文章大意可知是希望人们有健康的生活方式,参加一些 activities (第二小节中),因此 playing outside 最合适。后面的 reading 和 studying 都是室内活动。

27. A 【解析】细节题。根据上下文考查合适的动词。上文提出了一个问题,所以选 find out "发现,找到(答案)"。

28. B 【解析】固定搭配。leave ... off "关掉"。此句中 let 为动词,people 为宾语,而 leave ... and participate ... 作 people 的宾补。

29. C 【解析】固定搭配。由后文的 to,可见这里只能填 from。

30. C 【解析】细节题。这两句话讲的是参与这个活动的人数的变化,因此先说的是"一开始" in the beginning。

31. C 【解析】细节题。这句话是对前一句话的补充说明,根据后文 的... and in more than 12 other countries. 可见是对所有参与者的一个说明,用 including "包括"。

32. C 【解析】名词代词题。考查符合上下文的名词,进一步陈述组织者的目的。

...

2. 技巧点拨

(1) 做题前:要有语篇意识。在做题之前一定要通读全文,把握全文的大意和作者的写作思路;一般来说,文章的开头会包含重要的提示和基本的背景信息。把握了这个文章大意,我们在作选择填空题时,就能做出最符合主题意思的选择。

(2) 做题时:要联系上下文,从语法、词汇、逻辑等各个角度进行考虑。语法题,要使补充完整后的句子在时态、语气、语态、单复数、主谓一致、主从关系以及句际关系等方面都是正确的;词汇题,要先看是受词语搭配的支配还是受上下文意思的支配,每道题所在的句子以及前一句和后一句都是重要的判断依据。此外,有的题目需要我们运用常识进行判断。

(3) 做完后:再读一遍文章,看语法是否正确、上下文是否意义连贯、词语搭配是否恰当,以保证补充后的文章是一篇语法正确、逻辑严密、主题突出、意思连贯的文章。

(4) 建议没有较大的把握不要随便改变自己的选项。通常,在没有十分把握的情况下,往往第一印象正确率更高。

三、阅读理解

该部分是考查考生理解文章主旨要义的能力。

1. 试题透视

A 节:全面介绍了大纲规定的阅读能力的构成和培养,包括:(1)理解主旨要义;(2)理解文中具体信息;(3)根据上下文推测生词的词义;(4)进行有关的判断、推理和引申;(5)理解文中的概念性含义;(6)理解文章的结构以及单词之间、段落之间的关系;(7)快速阅读较长的文字材料,获取有关信息;(8)理解作者的意图、观点或态度;(9)区分观点、论点和论据;(10)与作者形成有意识的交流。

B节:考查考生理解文章的主旨要义的能力,它需要考生根据所读材料进行判断、推理和引申,并理解文中的概念性含义,学会抓住文章的主旨要义,理解作者的意图、观点或态度以及区分观点、论点和论据的关系。内容一般是选自报刊或杂志或访谈节目中的就某一专题对不同人进行的调查访问。内容比较新颖、生活化,语言比较口语化。

【典型例题A】

My parents have always raised me to be very money-conscious, so I guess, in that sense, they are rather untraditional. Since I was a little girl, if I ever wanted to purchase anything, my parents would sternly remind me of the value of every cent, prompting me to spend my pocket money only when necessary. My mom actually came up with a system that we strictly abide by in regards to money-spending. She gives me a certain amount of allowance every month, and whenever I buy anything with my accumulated money, I keep track of my receipts and record it in a little notebook, essentially a tiny version of my mom's own accounting booklet.

...

What happened when the author bought anything with her accumulated money?

A. She asked her parents to give her a large amount.

B. She controlled her own money without using it.

C. She kept track of her receipts and recorded it in a little notebook.

D. She wanted to go out and find a job at typical American occupation locales.

【答案与解析】 C 细节题。根据第一段最后一句 She gives me a certain amount of allowance 判断答案为 C。

【典型例题B】

Mark Lily

Young consumers often have not established their credit ratings. Many do not have steady incomes. They might have difficulty borrowing money from an agency in business to make loans. Parents or relatives are usually their best source of loans. Of course, the parents or relatives would have to have money available and be willing to lend it. You might even get an interest-free loan. However, a parent or relative who lends should receive interest the same as any other lender.

Chris John

For most consumers the cheapest place to borrow is at a commercial bank. Banks are a good source of installment loans which may run for 12 months or up to 36. Most banks also make single payment loans to consumers for short periods—30, 60, or 90 days. A typical interest rate is 3 cents per \$100 per day. Suppose that you used \$100 of your credit and repaid it in 30 days. The cost would be 90 cents.

Karen Barber

Another possible source of loans is a life insurance policy. Anyone who owns this type of insurance may borrow up to the amount of its cash value. The amount the insurance company will pay in case of death is reduced by the amount of the loan. For example, suppose that someone with \$10,000 of insurance borrows \$2,000 and dies leaving the loan unpaid. The insurance company would pay only \$8,000 to the person entitled to receive the money.

Louise Richard

Borrowing from pawnbrokers is both easy and expensive. In exchange for a loan the borrower leaves some item of value such as jewelry, a camera, a musical instrument, or clothing. Usually the amount of money received is far less than the actual value of the item left. When a borrower repays the loan plus interest, the pawnbroker returns the item. If the loan is not paid within a year, the pawnbroker gets his or her money by selling the item.

Jodie Morse

When money is urgently needed, people may agree to pay any price for a loan. Too late, they may find themselves in the clutches of loan sharks. A loan shark is an unlicensed lender because their rates are higher than the law allows, sometimes 1,000 percent or more a year. Borrowers are hardly ever able to repay their loans. It is all they can do to pay the interest. Borrowers who fail to pay the interest on time have been threatened with injury.

Now match each of the persons to the appropriate statement.

Note: there are two extra statements.

Statements

61. Mark Lily   [A] A person can borrow as much as his life insurance's cash value.

[B] The lender gets huge profits.

62. Chris John   [C] The borrowers may not take as long as they want to repay their loans.

[D] If the loan is not paid in a year, the item belongs to the lender.

63. Karen Barber   [E] Borrowing from their parents or relatives is the easiest or the best loan source for the young consumers.

64. Louise Richard   [F] The consumers without good credit can borrow money from their parents or relatives.

65. Jodie Morse   [G] The interest rate of the commercial bank is the lowest. For example, the cost would be 360 cents if you borrowed $200 and repaid it in 60 days.

【答案与解析】 抓主旨要义最简单的方式就是找主题句,值得注意的是:在做这类题目的时候,不要将段落的局部信息或者其中的某一个例子误以为是这段话的中心论点,要正确理解作者的意图、观点或态度以及区分观点、论点和论据的关系。本例题中,各人观点如下:Mark Lily:主要围绕年轻人借债谈,父母、亲人是最简单的来源,故选E;Chris John:第一句即为主旨句,the cheapest place to borrow is at a commercial bank. 因为这里的利率较低,所以选G;Karen Barber:他提出了另一个借贷来源:a life insurance policy,其中提到 borrow up to the amount of its cash value,选项A符合;Louise:第一句即为主旨句,Borrowing from pawnbrokers is both easy and expensive,他所说的这个也就相当于中国古代的"当铺",如果借款人在一年内不能赎买物品,则当物就属于"当铺"了,所以选D;Jodie Morse:当急需钱的时候,人们不得不向"黑市"借钱,而这些未经注册的黑商,利率远远高于法律所规定的,相当赚钱,所以选B。

2. 技巧点拨

PETS 3 的阅读理解,主要有三种题材:记叙文、说明文、议论文。针对不同的文章,考生在做阅读理解题时要把握不同的解题技巧:记叙文考试的重点是考生对故事情节、事件的结局、人物的性格等的把握,在应试的过程中,考生应当密切注意记叙文的六要素。在阅读说明文时,由于有大量的专业术语,这些专业术语并不能在很大程度上影响考生对整篇文章的理解,所以千万不要被这些生词吓倒。阅读议论文时,要特别注意作者的态度观点以及论证方法,尽量揣摩作者的真正观点和言外之意。

每篇文章的五个问题,一般都会涉及以下四种题型:细节题、主旨题、词汇题、推理引申题。

(1) 细节理解题:这种问题是最基本的考试题目,主要目的是考查学生对文章中某些事实和数据的掌握,例如:时间、地点、人物、数量、事件。这类问题的答案一般都能够在原文中找到,因为这类题目的某些结构、词语和表达方式与原文中的某些句子结构是一致的。

(2) 主旨判断题:要想理解文章的主旨,就必须从文章中找出主题句。主题句在文章中有时直接可以找到,有时需要考生自己总结和归纳。一般来说,主题句的位置比较灵活,需要仔细阅读进行理解。

（3）相关词汇题：一定数量的词汇是提高阅读能力的必要条件，而阅读理解中的词语问题并非是单纯地考查词汇量，而是考查学生在上下文中辨认和推测词义的能力。

（4）推理引申题：这种题目的解答不仅要靠对上下文相关信息的理解，更重要的是在理解的基础上做出合理的逻辑推断。这样，推理问题就要求考生不仅要有良好的理解能力，更要具有较强的逻辑分析能力。

四、写作

PETS 3 写作部分由 A、B 两节组成，旨在考查考生的书面表达能力。

1. 试题透视

A 节：考生根据所给情景（英/中文）写出约 100 词（不含标点符号）的简单信件、便笺等，常考的有书信、通知和便条三种，主要考查写作信件、通知、便条等简单应用文的能力，包括应用文的固定格式，如信件的称呼、署名、结尾套语等。分值为 10 分。

B 节：考生根据所给情景，写出一篇不少于 120 词（不含标点符号）的文章。提供情景的形式有图画、图表、文字等，主要考查写说明性或议论性文章的能力。分值为 20 分。

【典型例题 A】　Write a note of asking for leave to your boss Mr. Smith. You have got a bad cold and high fever, and want to ask for 3 days off from work. You should write about 100 words. Do not sign your own name at the end of your note. Use "Nancy" instead.

【答案与解析】　本例要求考生写一个请假条。因为感冒发烧，向老板请三天假，需要注意的是，下面四个方面不可缺：请假的日期、请假原因、请假期限、签名。

第一步：确定题材——便条，注意格式；

第二步：列出要点——请假时间、原因、证明等；

第三步：列出关键词——I am sorry to tell that I … ; have a high fever; ask for a sick leave; the medical certification of sick leave, etc.

第四步：落笔成文

July 22nd, 2009

Dear Mr. Smith,

　　I'm terribly sorry to tell you that I have caught a bad cold. The doctor suggests that I ask for three days' sick leave as I also have a high fever. I would be very grateful if you are kind enough to grant me a sick leave from July 23rd to July 25th.

　　I am sorry if I cause you any inconvenience but I promise that I will go back to work as soon as I have recovered.

　　Attached is the medical certification of sick leave written by the doctor.

Yours sincerely,

Nancy

【典型例题 B】

Below is a graph showing the numbers of the overseas Chinese who returned to Shanghai between 1978 and 2007. Study the graph and write an essay of about 120 words making reference to the following points:

1）a description of the graph;

2）the causes of it.

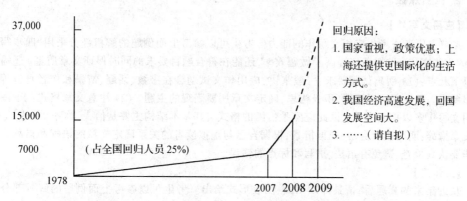

上海出国人员回归统计图

【答案与解析】　本题是近年来 PETS 3 的常考题型:图表题,要注意描述图中数据的变化,并正确根据提示分析原因。

第一步:审题

1. 题型:图表作文

2. 文体:论述说明文

第二步:框架分析

1. 说明图表内容,点出每个要点;

2. 分析图表现象的原因。

第三步:列出写作思路

1. 根据题干提示,改革开放以来,上海地区海外华人归国情况的变化,可以发现,2007 年来,数量大幅提高;

2. 分析原因:图中给出了两点,还需自己写一点,这可从当前经济危机分析,国内形势相对更加稳定,海外华人回国创业更有安全感等。

第四步:列出关键词和词组

a reversal of; account for; come up to; it is estimated that … ; mainly three causes; value overseas Chinese talents; preferential policies; warmly encourage them, etc.

第五步:落笔成文

There has been a reversal of the brain drain since 1978 across the country. Between 1978 and 2007, about 7,000 overseas Chinese returned to Shanghai after completing their further studies abroad. They accounted for about 25% of all returnees nationwide. The year 2008 witnessed a boom. The number of returnees came up to 15,000. It is estimated that by the end of 2010, a further 22,000 will have returned to this city.

There are mainly three causes for the reversal of the brain drain. First, our government values overseas Chinese talents and always warmly encourages them to return home to start their own careers and has worked out a series of preferential policies. In Shanghai, the famous international city, they can enjoy an equally modern lifestyle. Second, China's economy has been developing at a high speed, which provides them with a vast space of development. Third, the current global financial crisis leaves many overseas chinese talents out of work or at the edge of being laid off. They feel more secure at home because the economy here is more stable.

I believe that, with time going by, more and more overseas Chinese are coming home as our motherland is growing increasingly powerful in economy and increasingly influential in culture.

2. 技巧点拨

【应用文写作】

A节主要考查考生应用文写作的能力。考生可以参考上面例题的解析部分采用"四步写应用文"的方法完成。这样不仅提高了做题效率,还能在符合题目要求的同时保证文章质量。还需要注意以下几点:(1) 明确试题要求:一般来讲,应用作文试题会在字数、话题、情景和作者身份等方面提出要求。考生应认真阅读,积极构思,确定文章所要表现的主题。(2) 注意文章格式:PETS 3 的应用文写作多以信函为主。因此应熟悉信函的格式。其基本结构主要是信头、称呼、结尾。(3) 规范文章措辞:明确读者身份,根据情景,根据自己与虚拟读者的关系确定文章的语气和措辞。写作完毕要认真检查,避免有语法、拼写和标点的错误。

【大作文】

从近年来的真题看,情景都以图画、图表形式给出。考生可以参考上面例题的解析部分采用"五步大作文"的方法完成:考生平时要注意多读一些文章,记忆一些常用的句式等,提高自己运用语言的能力,这样在考试时才能"得心应手",写出高分作文。

五、口试

一般来说,走进口试考场的时候,一些问题可能是在考生的准备之中,那么怎样才能取得更好的成绩呢?

1. 克服紧张心理:在口试中,考生的心理素质非常重要。一般来说,考生都是有备而来,大多数问题可能都在考生的准备之中。当然,有时候,主考官的问题也可能出于考生的意料之外。这时,考生也要放松,可以缓一缓,只要保持镇定,持续对话即可。

2. 和伙伴形成良性互动:由于口试一般都要与伙伴合作,因而形成良性互动也比较重要。不管对方口语胜于自己或不如自己,自己都要认真互动,要能够持续与对方进行对话。

3. 言谈大方,不要患得患失:始终保持微笑和保持眼神接触,要放松,放开,配合自己的动作及面部表情,及时转换话题,转到自己所熟悉的话题,更有利于自己的发挥。

4. 一般而言,考官都非常人性化,因此考生不必紧张,即使有些地方一时语塞,可以通过其他方式,即更换个别语词进行交流,甚至可以求助于考官,使用"Excuse me, ..." "Pardon?"和"Will you please explain it a little bit to us?"等,让对方解释一下。

总之,口语考试重在交流,因此,只要能够有效地交流即可。

第②章 模拟试题

模拟试题（一）

Section I Listening Comprehension

Directions: *This section is designed to test your ability to understand spoken English. You will hear a selection of recorded materials and you must answer the questions that accompany them. There are two parts in this section, Part A and Part B.*

Remember, while you are doing the test, you should first put down your answers in your test booklet. At the end of the listening comprehension section, you will have 3 minutes to transfer your answers from your test booklet onto your ANSWER SHEET 1.

If you have any questions, you may raise your hand NOW as you will not be allowed to speak once the test has started.

Now look at Part A in your test booklet.

Part A

You will hear 10 short dialogues. For each dialogue, there is one question and four possible answers. Choose the correct answer A, B, C or D, and mark it in your test booklet. You will have 15 seconds to answer the question and you will hear each dialogue ONLY ONCE.

Example:

You will hear:

W: Could you please tell me if the Beijing flight will be arriving on time?

M: Yes, Madam. It should be arriving in about ten minutes.

You will read:

Who do you think the woman is talking to?

[A] A bus conductor.　　　　　[B] A clerk at the airport.

[C] A taxi driver.　　　　　　[D] A clerk at the station.

From the dialogue, we know that only a clerk at the airport is most likely to know the arrival time of a flight, so you should choose answer [B] and mark it in your test booklet.

Sample Answer: [A] ■ [C] [D]

Now look at question 1.

1. What would the woman most probably do?

　　[A] She will go without dessert.　　　[B] She will take a look at the menu.

　　[C] She will prepare the dinner.　　　[D] She will have some chocolate cake.

2. What doesn't the woman do on the Internet?

　　[A] Playing games.　　　　　　　　[B] Making friends.

　　[C] Booking tickets.　　　　　　　　[D] Searching for information.

3. What's the weather like today?

　　[A] Cloudy.　　　[B] Sunny.　　　[C] Rainy.　　　[D] Windy.

4. When should the woman return the book?

　　[A] Next Monday.　　　　　　　　　[B] Next Sunday.

　　[C] Next Friday.　　　　　　　　　　[D] Next Tuesday.

5. What will the man do first after class?

　　[A] Meet the woman.　　　　　　　　[B] See Professor Smith.

　　[C] Go to the library.　　　　　　　　[D] Have a drink in the bar.

6. When is the woman's hospital appointment?

　　[A] 2:00.　　　[B] 2:30.　　　[C] 3:30.　　　[D] 3:00.

7. What will the man probably do next?

　　[A] Ask a policeman for help.　　　　[B] Turn left.

　　[C] Stop for a while.　　　　　　　　[D] Get back onto the main highway.

8. Where does the conversation take place?

　　[A] In a post office.　　　　　　　　[B] In a hotel.

　　[C] In a bank.　　　　　　　　　　　[D] In the restaurant.

9. What does the man mean?

　　[A] He went mountain climbing last year.

　　[B] He doesn't want to go at all.

　　[C] He hasn't traveled around the world yet.

　　[D] He wants to go climbing.

10. Who has taken the stamps?

　　[A] The woman.　　　　　　　　　　[B] The woman's sister.

　　[C] The man's classmates.　　　　　　[D] The man himself.

Part B

You are going to hear four passages or conversations. Before listening to each conversation, you will have 5 seconds to read each of the questions which accompany it. After listening, you will have time to answer each question by choosing A, B, C or D. You will hear each passage or conversation ONLY ONCE. Mark your answers in your test booklet.

Questions 11—14 are based on the following conversation. You now have 20 seconds to read the questions 11—14.

11. What is the man most probably?

　　[A] A tour guide.　　　　　　[B] A teacher.

　　[C] A driver.　　　　　　　　[D] The woman's husband.

12. What places does the woman especially want to visit?

　　[A] The Summer Palace and the Great Wall.

　　[B] The Water Cube and the National Stadium.

　　[C] The Temple of Heaven and the Former Imperial Palace.

　　[D] The Great Wall and the Temple of Heaven.

13. How long does it take to go to the Great Wall by car from where they are?

　　[A] One hour.　　　　　　　　[B] Half an hour.

　　[C] One and a half hours.　　　[D] Two hours.

14. Which of the following is not mentioned?

　　[A] The Temple of Heaven.　　　[B] The Former Imperial Palaces.

　　[C] The Winter Palace.　　　　[D] The Ming Tombs.

You now have 40 seconds to check your answers to questions 11—14.

Questions 15—18 are based on the following passage. You now have 20 seconds to read the questions 15—18.

15. Which car was badly damaged?

　　[A] The sports car.　　　　　　[B] A car at the bottom of the hill.

　　[C] A car outside the supermarket.　　[D] Paul's car.

16. Where was the driver of the sports car when the accident happened?

　　[A] In the supermarket.　　　　[B] In the garage.

　　[C] At the foot of the hill.　　　[D] Inside the car.

17. Who did Paul think was to blame for the accident?

　　[A] The salesman from London.　　[B] The two girls inside the car.

　　[C] The man standing nearby.　　[D] The driver of the sports car.

18. Who was injured in the accident?

　　[A] Nobody.　　　　　　　　[B] The bus driver.

　　[C] Paul.　　　　　　　　　[D] The two girls.

You now have 40 seconds to check your answers to questions 15—18.

Questions 19—22 are based on the following passage. You now have 20 seconds to read the questions 19—22.

19. What is the characteristic of learners of special English?

　　[A] They want to change the way English is taught.

　　[B] They want to have an up-to-date knowledge of English.

　　[C] They know clearly what they want to learn.

　　[D] They learn English to find well-paid jobs.

20. Who needs ESP courses most?

[A] Professionals.   [B] Beginners.

[C] College students.   [D] Intermediate learners.

21. What are the most popular ESP courses in Britain?

[A] Courses for reporters.   [B] Courses for doctors.

[C] Courses for lawyers.   [D] Courses for businessmen.

22. What is the speaker mainly talking about?

[A] Three groups of learners.

[B] The importance of business English.

[C] Features of English for different purposes.

[D] English for Specific Purposes.

You now have 40 seconds to check your answers to questions 19—22.

Questions 23—25 are based on the following conversation. You now have 15 seconds to read the questions 23—25.

23. Why is the woman here?

[A] To meet Jack.   [B] To have a test.

[C] To have a dinner.   [D] To see her school once more.

24. How does the woman feel about the test?

[A] She is not worried about it.   [B] Not mentioned.

[C] She is not sure about the test.   [D] She is sure it will be too hard.

25. Which of the following is not true?

[A] She has studied hard all week.

[B] This is the woman's first term of school.

[C] The man wishes her good luck.

[D] She has failed in a test.

You now have 30 seconds to check your answers to questions 23—25.

Now you have 3 minutes to transfer your answers from your test booklet to the ANSWER SHEET 1.

That is the end of the listening comprehension section.

Section II   Use of English

Directions: *Read the following text. Choose the best word or phrase for each numbered blank and mark A, B, C, or D on ANSWER SHEET 1.*

On May 30, 2009, a speeding car hurtled (猛冲，飞驰) towards an open top bus __26__ the Queen of the Netherlands today __27__ smashing (撞开) into a crowd and killing four people who were __28__ the royal parade.

A 38-year-old Dutchman, who was driving a black hatchback, has been 　29　 on suspicion 　30　 carrying out an attack on the Royal Family.

Thirteen people were 　31　, five of whom 　32　 in a serious condition, but the Queen and 　33　 members of the Dutch royal family were not hurt. The black Suzuki(铃木) 　34　 through the crowd during a parade to mark the Queen's Day national holiday in the city of Apeldoorn. Princess Maxima, wife of heir Willem-Alexander, watched in 　35　, with her hand 　36　 her mouth, as the vehicle sped a few meters past the royal bus. Footage of the incident shows the damaged car continuing to be driven at high-speed after crashing into members of the crowd. People were thrown up 　37　 the air as the car swerved across police railings, 　38　 hundreds were waiting to see the Queen. The car was only 　39　 once it had 　40　 into a stone monument in the center of the city, about 50 miles 　41　 of Amsterdam.

Queen Beatrix responded to the attack in a 　42　 broadcast that afternoon. "What started as a beautiful day has 　43　 in terrible drama, which has shocked us 　44　," she said.

A spokesman from the Dutch prosecutor's office said the 　45　 was believed to have purposely targeted the Royal Family. "We have reason to believe that this was a deliberate act," said Ludo Goossens, a public prosecutor. He said there were no indications of terrorist links nor were there signs of explosives.

26. [A] carrying   [B] carried   [C] carry   [D] to carry

27. [A] after   [B] before   [C] when   [D] since

28. [A] seeing   [B] viewing   [C] watching   [D] looking

29. [A] arresting   [B] arrest   [C] arrested   [D] imprisoned

30. [A] for   [B] with   [C] at   [D] of

31. [A] hurt   [B] injured   [C] wounded   [D] killed

32. [A] maintain   [B] stay   [C] remain   [D] were

33. [A] the other   [B] following   [C] fellow   [D] another

34. [A] rushed   [B] ploughed   [C] headed   [D] crushed

35. [A] horror   [B] honor   [C] danger   [D] fear

36. [A] in front of   [B] over   [C] covering   [D] hiding

37. [A] to   [B] towards   [C] into   [D] in

38. [A] which   [B] when   [C] as   [D] where

39. [A] ceased   [B] stopped   [C] halted   [D] paused

40. [A] smashed   [B] slammed   [C] crunched   [D] crashed

41. [A] east   [B] the east   [C] at east   [D] eastern

42. [A] international   [B] local   [C] nation   [D] national

43. [A] stopped   [B] ended   [C] finished   [D] closed

44. [A] deep   [B] intense   [C] deeply   [D] intensive

45. [A] suspicion   [B] suspect   [C] suspicious   [D] suspected

Section Ⅲ　Reading Comprehension

Part A

Directions: *Read the following three texts. Answer the questions on each text by choosing A, B, C or D. Mark your answers on the ANSWER SHEET 1.*

Text 1

David Beckham is the king of the football world, but it is his wife Victoria, former "Posh Spice" girl, who makes it possible. She was the person who turned him from a footballer into a global attractor. Even now that he has left Manchester United for Royal Madrid, instead of Barcelona or Milan, it might be because of her.

"Posh Spice" has become a name for Victoria. The Collins Dictionary even has the term "Posh and Beckham" (Victoria and Beckham).

Before meeting Victoria Adams, Beckham was a good-looking and likeable footballer with a bright future at Manchester United, but that was about all.

Since he married her in 1999, he has become the most famous player British sports have ever produced, and, some say, the most influential man in the country. "When they got together, she was clearly the more popular of the two." said Andrew Parker, a sports expert at Warwick University in Britain. "She certainly introduced him to a new circle of people and, all of a sudden, he was a top list celebrity."

It's believed that, behind the high walls and iron gates of their "Beckingham Palace", it is Victoria who decides everything.

When their baby boy, Brooklyn, fell in 2000, Beckham left a United training session to look after him, and this led to his being dropped from the team. Many were sure it was Victoria who has asked her husband to stay at home. During a trip to the United States this year, Victoria has worked hard to push her husband to the US public. They would not have recognized him if they met him in a car park.

She may appear to have taken a back seat, but Victoria is still at the forefront of the "Posh and Back" project.

46. From the passage, we can conclude that at home _____.

    [A] Beckham listens to his wife

    [B] Victoria listens to her husband

    [C] Beckham and Victoria discuss and do everything together

    [D] Beckham has no mind of his own

47. Before meeting Victoria Adams, Beckham _____.

　　[A] had become world-famous 　　[B] was completely unknown

　　[C] was an ordinary football player 　　[D] was not so influential

48. Which of the following is best supported by the fourth paragraph?

　　[A] People still like Victoria better than Beckham.

　　[B] People liked to see Beckham and Victoria together.

　　[C] To a large degree, Beckham owes his popularity to Victoria.

　　[D] Sports experts used to think little of Beckham.

49. Which of the following is NOT true according to this passage?

　　[A] Beckham is the most influential man in Britain.

　　[B] In 2000, Beckham was dropped from his team because he spent a holiday in the United States.

　　[C] Beckham is now playing for Real Madrid.

　　[D] Brooklyn was born in 2000.

50. Which of the following might be the best title of the text?

　　[A] The Posh Power

　　[B] A Perfect Couple

　　[C] Who Is More Influential—Beckham or Victoria

　　[D] "Posh and Back" Project

Text 2

The black robin is one of the world's rarest birds. It is a small, wild bird, and it lives only on the island of Little Mangere, off the coast of New Zealand. In 1967 there were about fifty black robins there; in 1977 there were fewer than ten. These are the only black robins left in the world. The island has many other birds, of course, of different kinds, large and small; these seem to multiply very happily.

Steps are being taken to preserve the black robin. Detailed studies are going on, and a public appeal for money has been made. The idea is to buy another island nearby as a special home for threatened wild life, including black robins. The organizers say that Little Mangere should then be supplied with the robin's food — it eats only one kind of seed. Thousands of the required plants are at present being cultivated in New Zealand. The public appeal is aimed at the conscience of mankind, so that the wild black robin will not die out and disappear from the earth in our time at least.

Is all this concern a waste of human effort? Is it any business of ours whether the black robin survives or dies out? Are we losing our sense of what is reasonable and what is unreasonable?

In the earth's long, long past hundreds of kinds of creatures have evolved, risen to a degree of success — and died out. In the long, long future there will be many new and different forms of life. Those creatures that adapt themselves successfully to what the earth offers will survive for a long time. Those that fail to meet the challenges will disappear early. This is Nature's proven method of operation.

The rule of selection — the survival of the fittest — is the one by which human beings have themselves arrived on the scene. He, being one of the most adaptable creatures the earth has yet produced, may last longer than most. You may take it as another rule that when, at last, man shows signs of dying out, no other creature will extend a paw to postpone our departure. For Nature, though fair, is a hard-hearted mistress. She has no favorites.

Life seems to have grown too tough for black robins. I leave you to judge whether we should try to do something about it.

51. The black robins are getting fewer and fewer because _____.
    [A] there are too many other kinds of birds on the island
    [B] of lack of food
    [C] they can't multiply
    [D] there is no room for them on the island

52. A public appeal for money has been made to _____.
    [A] protect some rare wild creatures
    [B] plant the kind of seed
    [C] awake the conscience of mankind
    [D] make a home for the organizers

53. The creatures that _____ can survive.
    [A] come across some challenges in their lives
    [B] don't come across any challenges in their lives
    [C] grow tough
    [D] fit the surroundings perfectly

54. Which of the following statements is true?
    [A] Nature is unfair to man.
    [B] What the earth offers makes man survive.
    [C] Everything will be selected by Nature including man.
    [D] Small animals will certainly survive for a longer time than man.

55. Creatures will _____ when man is dying out.
    [A] not help him   [B] not step on him
    [C] also be dying   [D] hurry out

Text 3

In Japan many workers for large corporations have a guarantee of lifetime employment. They will not be laid off during recessions or when the tasks they perform are taken over by robots. To some observers, this is capitalism at its best, because workers are treated as people not things. Others see it as necessarily inefficient and believe it cannot continue if Japan is to remain competitive with foreign corporations more concerned about profits and less concerned about people.

Defenders of the system argue that those who call it inefficient do not understand how it really works. In the first place not every Japanese worker has the guarantee of a lifetime job. The lifetime employment system includes only "regular employees". Many employees do not fall into this category, including all women. All businesses have many part-time and temporary employees. These workers are hired and laid off during the course of the business cycle just as employees in the United States are. These"irregular workers" make up about 10 percent of the nonagricultural work force. Additionally, Japanese firms maintain some flexibility through the extensive use of subcontractors. This practice is much more common in Japan than in the United States.

The use of both subcontractors and temporary workers has increased markedly in Japan since the 1974—1975 recession. All this leads some to argue that the Japanese system is not all that different from the American system. During recessions Japanese corporations lay off temporary workers and give less business to subcontractors. In the United States, corporations lay off those workers with the least seniority. The difference then is probably less than the term "lifetime employment" suggests, but there still is a difference. And this difference cannot be understood without looking at the values of Japanese society. The relationship between employer and employee cannot be explained in purely contractual terms. Firms hold on to the employees and employees stay with one firm. There are also practical reasons for not jumping from job to job. Most retirement benefits come from the employer. Changing jobs means losing these benefits. Also, teamwork is an essential part of Japanese production. Moving to a new firm means adapting to a different team and at least temporarily, lower productivity and lower pay.

56. The observers are divided with regard to their attitudes towards _____.

    [A] the guarantee of employment

    [B] the consequence of recessions and automation

    [C] the effect of lifetime employment

    [D] the prospects of capitalism

57. It is stated in the second paragraph that _____.

    [A] defenders themselves do not appreciate the system

    [B] about 90% of "irregular workers" are employed in agriculture

    [C] the business cycle occurs more often in Japan and in the US

    [D] not all employees can benefit from the policy

58. During recessions those who are to be fired first in the US corporations are _____.

    [A] regular employees   [B] part-time workers

    [C] junior employees   [D] temporary workers

59. According to the passage, Japanese firms differ strikingly from American firms in that the former _____.

    [A] use subcontractors more extensively

[B] are less flexible in terms of lifetime employment

[C] hold on to the values of society

[D] are more efficient in competition than the latter

60. Which of the following does NOT account for the fact that a Japanese worker is reluctant to change his job?

[A] He will probably be underpaid.

[B] He will not be entitled to some job benefits.

[C] He has been accustomed to the teamwork.

[D] He will be looked down upon by his prospective employer.

Part B

Directions: *Read the texts from an article in which five people talked about their depression and ways to deal with it. For questions 61 to 65, match the name of each person (61 to 65) to one of the statements (A to G) given below. Mark your answers on ANSWER SHEET 1.*

Grose

My family wanted me home every other weekend, but I didn't fit in there anymore. I'd argue constantly with my father, who still treated me like a child. My sister thought I was "uppity". Everyone was miserable, and I felt guilty. I decided to try treatment when my friends got fed up with me. They didn't want to talk about my problems any more, but my problems were the major focus of my life. I needed someone who could help me understand what was happening to me. I'd seen ads for the counseling center and decided to give it a try.

Kwanzaa

When I took a part-time job and started living off-campus, my course work fell apart. I couldn't concentrate or sleep, and I was always irritable and angry. When I began considering suicide, I knew I needed serious help. My resident advisor helped me call a local hotline where I got some good referrals. It was just a phone call, but it was the starting point that got me to the professional help I needed.

Cheever

I've always been anxious and never had much confidence. College was harder than I had expected, and then my parents divorced, which was traumatic for me. After a while, all I did was cry, sleep, and feel waves of panic. Actually while the depression was painful, working to get better has taught me a lot about who I am and how to stay healthy.

Colbert

After two years of straight A's, I couldn't finish assignments anymore. I felt exhausted but couldn't sleep, and drank a lot. I couldn't enjoy life like my friends did anymore. I kept asking myself, "How could I be depressed? I'd had a normal family life, had been getting good grades, and hadn't experienced any big trauma — where did my depression come from?" I knew I was depressed but thought I could pull out of it by myself. Unfortunately, friends reinforced this attitude by telling me to just toughen up. When that didn't work, I felt even worse because I had "failed" again. When a friend suggested I talk to his counselor, I resisted at first. In my mind, professional help was for weak, messed up people. But then, I hit a bottom so low that I was willing to try anything. Getting treatment definitely changed my life for the better and helped me avoid flunking a semester.

Fenty

During a manic episode, I stayed awake for five days straight, but had a lot of energy. I spent my tuition money on a major shopping spree (购物狂欢) and long distance phone calls. I also played around with several guys that I hardly knew. At the time, I felt so great that I couldn't see that there were serious problems with what I was doing. Now that I've gotten some treatment, I'm back from the edge, I know how to keep from being out there again.

Now match each of the people (61 to 65) to the appropriate statement.

Note: There are two extra statements.

Statements

61. Grose　　[A] I never changed the opinion that professional help was for weak, messed up people.

62. Kwanzaa　[B] Getting professional treatment can really pull me out of depression.

63. Cheever　[C] At first I didn't know where my depression came from and resisted professional help.

64. Colbert　[D] When my friends were impatient with me, I decided to go to the counseling center for help.

65. Fenty　　[E] A phone call got me to the professional help.

　　　　　　[F] Everyone can be full of energy for five days without sleep.

　　　　　　[G] I learned a lot about myself and to stay healthy through the way of working to get better.

Section IV　Writing

Directions: *You should write your responses to both Part A and Part B of this section on ANSWER SHEET 2.*

Part A

You have had a dinner in a very famous restaurant, but the service was terrible. The food was cold and soup was too salty, the table was wet and the waiter was very rude. Write a letter of complaint with approximately 100 words to the manager of the restaurant.

Do not sign your own name at the end of your letter. Use "Michael" instead. You do not need to write the address.

Part B

Below is a graph showing the change in family consumption in your city between 1998 and 2008. Look at the graph and write an essay of about 120 words making reference to the following points:

    1. a description of the graph;

    2. a conclusion of the change.

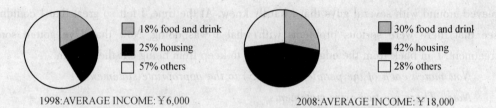

18% food and drink
25% housing
57% others

1998: AVERAGE INCOME: ￥6,000

30% food and drink
42% housing
28% others

2008: AVERAGE INCOME: ￥18,000

模拟试题(二)

Section I Listening Comprehension

Directions: *This section is designed to test your ability to understand spoken English. You will hear a selection of recorded materials and you must answer the questions that accompany them. There are two parts in this section, Part A and Part B.*

Remember, while you are doing the test, you should first put down your answers in your test booklet. At the end of the listening comprehension section, you will have 3 minutes to transfer your answers from your test booklet onto your ANSWER SHEET 1.

If you have any questions, you may raise your hand NOW as you will not be allowed to speak once the test has started.

Now look at Part A in your test booklet.

Part A

You will hear 10 short dialogues. For each dialogue, there is one question and four possible answers. Choose the correct answer A, B, C or D, and mark it in your test booklet. You will have 15 seconds to answer the question and you will hear each dialogue ONLY ONCE.

Example:

You will hear:

W: Could you please tell me if the Beijing flight will be arriving on time?

M: Yes, Madam. It should be arriving in about ten minutes.

You will read:

Who do you think the woman is talking to?

[A] A bus conductor.　　　　　[B] A clerk at the airport.

[C] A taxi driver.　　　　　　[D] A clerk at the station.

From the dialogue, we know that only a clerk at the airport is most likely to know the arrival time of a flight, so you should choose answer [B] and mark it in your test booklet.

Sample Answer: [A] ■ [C] [D]

Now look at question 1.

1. What time is it now?

　　[A] Nine o'clock.　　　　　　[B] Eight o'clock.

　　[C] Seven thirty.　　　　　　[D] Eight thirty.

2. What will the woman probably do?

　　[A] She will drink some coffee.　　[B] She will get some tea for the man.

　　[C] She will meet her friend.　　　[D] She will drink what she has with her.

3. What size does the woman want?

    [A] Size 8.　　　[B] Size 12.　　　[C] Size 11.　　　[D] Size 10.

4. What does the man mean?

    [A] He can help the woman.

    [B] No one can help her.

    [C] The machine was just repaired.

    [D] The clerk doesn't like to be troubled.

5. What does the man mean?

    [A] Do as well as you can.　　　　[B] It's difficult to do something important.

    [C] Nobody can be the best.　　　　[D] Leave the task behind.

6. Where are the man and the woman probably talking?

    [A] Outside an art museum.　　　　[B] Inside a bookstore.

    [C] In the restaurant.　　　　　　[D] Outside a sports center.

7. What's the man now?

    [A] A student.　　　　　　　　　[B] A teacher.

    [C] An engineer.　　　　　　　　[D] An official.

8. What were the two speakers going to do?

    [A] Go bicycle-riding.　　　　　　[B] Go sailing.

    [C] Swimming.　　　　　　　　　[D] Playing tennis.

9. What will the woman tell the man?

    [A] Her new address.　　　　　　[B] Her company's name.

    [C] Her email.　　　　　　　　　[D] Her phone number.

10. What is the relationship between the two speakers?

    [A] Student and teacher.　　　　　[B] Patient and nurse.

    [C] Wife and husband.　　　　　　[D] Lawyer and client.

Part B

You are going to hear four passages or conversations. Before listening to each conversation, you will have 5 seconds to read each of the questions which accompany it. After listening, you will have time to answer each question by choosing A, B, C or D. You will hear each passage or conversation ONLY ONCE. Mark your answers in your test booklet.

Questions 11 — 13 are based on the following conversation. You now have 15 seconds to read the questions 11—13.

11. What kind of color TV did the man plan to buy?

    [A] A cheaper one.　　　　　　　[B] A bigger one.

    [C] A smaller one.　　　　　　　[D] A black and white one.

12. Why does the woman suggest that the man buy a smaller TV?

    [A] Because it's bad for his eyes.

[B] Because the man can't afford an expensive TV.

[C] Because a smaller TV is on sale.

[D] Because his sitting-room isn't very big.

13. What may the relationship be between the two speakers?

[A] They are teacher and student. [B] They are husband and wife.

[C] They are classmates. [D] They are shop assistant and customer.

You now have 30 seconds to check your answers to questions 11—13.

Questions 14—17 are based on the following conversation. You now have 20 seconds to read the questions 14—17.

14. Where is Tom now?

[A] At the college. [B] At TV studio.

[C] At the hospital. [D] In the classroom.

15. Which day is Tom's birthday?

[A] Sunday. [B] Monday. [C] Saturday. [D] Tuesday.

16. What's the woman going to do?

[A] To think about a good idea for Tom.

[B] To give up the chance of helping Tom.

[C] To help Tom leave the hospital as soon as possible.

[D] To go out for a birthday party with her classmates.

17. Why does the woman ask Tom to put on his clothes?

[A] She is afraid that Tom may catch a bad cold.

[B] She'll take Tom to see other children who'll have their tonsils (扁桃体) out.

[C] She knows Tom used to wear more clothes in autumn.

[D] He is very careless and will lose his clothes.

You now have 40 seconds to check your answers to questions 14—17.

Questions 18—21 are based on the following passage. You now have 20 seconds to read the questions 18—21.

18. What does the speaker think are the causes of automobile accidents?

[A] The causes are very complicated. [B] The causes are obvious.

[C] The causes are familiar. [D] The causes are not well understood.

19. What has helped to reduce car accidents?

[A] Regular driver training. [B] Improved highway design.

[C] Stricter traffic regulations. [D] Better public transportation.

20. What remains an important factor for the rising number of road accidents?

[A] Highway crime. [B] Poor traffic control.

[C] Confusing road signs. [D] Drivers' errors.

21. What's the focus of people's attention today according to the passage?

[A] Designing better cars.

　　[B] Building more highways.

　　[C] Increasing people's awareness of traffic problems.

　　[D] Enhancing drivers' sense of responsibility.

You now have 40 seconds to check your answers to questions 18—21.

Questions 22—25 are based on the following conversation. You now have 20 seconds to read the questions 22—25.

22. What does Jane think of Potter's course?

　　[A] Very good.　　　　　　　　　　[B] Too general.

　　[C] Clear and interesting.　　　　　[D] Meticulous and too specialized.

23. What is true of Potter's first lecture?

　　[A] There was an interesting start and a well-organized end.

　　[B] There was a natural transition from its introduction to the following part.

　　[C] The plan about the Western development was good.

　　[D] The whole lecture was over-detailed and formless.

24. Which of the following is true about Potter?

　　[A] He is a postgraduate.

　　[B] He is qualified for teaching postgraduates.

　　[C] He is an expert in town planning.

　　[D] He has only given one undergraduate course so far.

25. What can we learn from the interview?

　　[A] Jane and Helen are sisters.

　　[B] Jane and Helen are postgraduates.

　　[C] Jane and Helen are undergraduates.

　　[D] Jane and Helen are teachers.

You now have 40 seconds to check your answers to questions 22—25.

Now you have 3 minutes to transfer your answers from your test booklet to the ANSWER SHEET 1.

That is the end of the listening comprehension section.

Section Ⅱ　Use of English

Directions: *Read the following text. Choose the best word or phrase for each numbered blank and mark A, B, C, or D on ANSWER SHEET 1.*

On Friday nights when her friends are deciding which film to see, Karina Wood ___26___ to a recreational club where she ___27___ after adults with learning difficulties. Karina has been ___28___ at the club in Stonehaven for two years. She helps organise social events for a group of 30, ___29___ in age from young adults to the ___30___ .

Now Karina is one of 70 young people being ___31___ for her work with a Diana Award, an honor ___32___ upon children and teenagers who have made an outstanding or selfless ___33___ to their community.

The awards, ___34___ to the memory of the Princess of Wales, will be ___35___ at the Scottish parliament tomorrow in the first ceremony north of the border. Karina, a sixth-year pupil at Mackie Academy, is going to the event with her ___36___ teacher, Ewen Ritchie, who ___37___ her for the award. Karina, who is studying advanced chemistry, maths and biology and hopes to become a doctor, insists that she doesn't seek ___38___ for her work.

"It is a fantastic experience," she says. "I get to meet new people and learn new skills." She isn't ___39___ that she is the only one of her friends who ___40___ volunteer work, and she says she doesn't ___41___ their Friday night get-togethers.

"I don't know what they think but I ___42___ the volunteer work. It is good fun." Although Karina was only seven when the ___43___ of Wales died, she says: "I know she was very ___44___ in charity work. She was the people's royal and people could relate to her. I am glad the award is ___45___ her name."

26. [A] headed [B] head [C] heads [D] heading
27. [A] looks [B] takes [C] attends [D] cares
28. [A] volunteer [B] volunteered [C] voluntary [D] volunteering
29. [A] ranging [B] arranging [C] varying [D] varied
30. [A] elders [B] elderly [C] olders [D] olderly
31. [A] encouraged [B] recognized [C] admitted [D] complimented
32. [A] bestowed [B] feel [C] given [D] reserved
33. [A] effort [B] endeavor [C] contribution [D] sacrifice
34. [A] dedicated [B] designed [C] aimed [D] intended
35. [A] given out [B] presented [C] delivered [D] handed out
36. [A] guiding [B] instructing [C] guidance [D] instruction
37. [A] introduced [B] nominated [C] encouraged [D] recommended
38. [A] praise [B] acknowledge [C] admission [D] recognition
39. [A] worried [B] concerned [C] afraid [D] sorry
40. [A] do [B] have done [C] does [D] has done
41. [A] miss [B] think of [C] think about [D] dream of
42. [A] love [B] choose [C] like [D] prefer
43. [A] Princess [B] Queen [C] King [D] Prince
44. [A] exhausted [B] involved [C] devoted [D] busy
45. [A] by [B] after [C] in [D] at

Section III Reading Comprehension

Part A

Directions: *Read the following three texts. Answer the questions on each text by choosing A, B, C or D. Mark your answers on the ANSWER SHEET 1.*

Text 1

Why do men die earlier than women? The latest research makes it known that the reason could be that men's hearts go into rapid decline when they reach middle age.

The largest study of the effects of aging on the heart has found that women's <u>longevity</u> may be linked to the fact that their hearts do not lose their pumping power with age.

"We have found that the power of the male heart falls by 20—25 percent between 18 and 70 years of age," said the head of the study, David Goldspink of Liverpool John Moores University in the UK.

"Within the heart there are millions of cells that enable it to beat. Between the age of 20 and 70, one-third of those cells die and are not replaced in men," said Goldspink. "This is part of the aging process."

What surprises scientists is that the female heart sees very little loss of these cells. A healthy 70-year-old woman's heart could perform almost as well as a 20-year-old one's.

"This gender difference might just explain why women live longer than men," said Goldspink. They studied more than 250 healthy men and women between the ages of 18 and 80, focusing on healthy persons to remove the confusing influence of disease. "The team has yet to find why aging takes a greater loss on the male heart," said Goldspink.

The good news is that men can improve the health of their heart with regular exercise. Goldspink stressed that women also need regular exercise to prevent their leg muscles becoming smaller and weaker as they age.

46. The underlined word "longevity" in the second paragraph probably refers to "_____".

    [A] health   [B] long life   [C] aging   [D] effect

47. The text mainly talks about _____.

    [A] men's heart cells   [B] women's aging process
    [C] the gender difference   [D] hearts and long life

48. According to the text, the UK scientists have known that _____.

    [A] women have more cells than men when they are born
    [B] women can replace the cells that enable the heart to beat
    [C] the female heart loses few of the cells with age
    [D] women never lose their pumping power with age

49. If you want to live longer, you should _____.

    [A] enable your heart to beat much faster

[B] find out the reason for aging

[C] exercise regularly to keep your heart healthy

[D] prevent your cells from being lost

50. We can know from the passage that _____.

[A] the reason why aging takes a greater loss on the male heart has been found out

[B] scientists are on the way to find out why the male heart loses more of the cells

[C] the team has done something to prevent the male from suffering the greater loss

[D] women over 70 could lose more heart cells than those at the age of 20

Text 2

The Man of Many Secrets — Harry Houdini — was one of the greatest American entertainers in the theater this century. He was a man famous for his escapes — from prison cells, from wooden boxes floating in rivers, from locked tanks full of water. He appeared in theaters all over Europe and America. Crowds came to see the great Houdini and his "magic" tricks.

Of course, his secret was not magic or supernatural powers. It was simply strength. He had the ability to move his toes as well as he moved his fingers. He could move his body into almost any position he wanted.

Houdini started working in the entertainment world when he was 17, in 1891. He and his brother Theo performed card tricks in a club in New York. They called themselves the Houdini Brothers. When Harry married in 1894, he and his wife Bess worked together as magician and assistant. But for a long time they were not very successful. Then Harry performed his first prison escape, in Chicago in 1898. Harry persuaded a detective to let him try to escape from the prison, and he invited the local newspapermen to watch.

It was the publicity (宣传) that came from this that started Harry Houdini's success. Harry had fingers trained to escape from handcuffs and toes trained to escape ankle chins. But his biggest secret was how he unlocked the prison doors. Every time he went into the prison cell, Bess gave him a kiss for good luck — and a small skeleton key, which is a key that fits many locks, pass quickly from her mouth to his.

Harry used these prison escapes to build his fame. He arranged to escape from the local prison of every town he visited. In the afternoon, the people of the town would read about it in their local newspapers, and in the evening every seat in the local theater would be full. What was the result? World-wild fame and a name remembered today.

51. According to the passage, Houdini's success in prison escapes depends on _____.

[A] his special tricks and supernatural powers

[B] his unusual ability and a skeleton key

[C] his magic tricks and unhuman powers

[D] his wisdom and magic tricks

52. In the fourth paragraph, the underlined word "this" refers to _____.

[A] his first prison escape　　　　　　[B] the year 1898

[C] the publicity　　　　　　　　　　[D] Harry Houdini's success

53. Which of the following statements is true?

[A] Houdini was put into prison for several times because of crime.

[B] Houdini achieved great success once he entered entertainment world.

[C] Houdini performed prison escape in an effort to draw people's attention.

[D] Houdini had super magic power to twist his body into almost any position he wanted.

54. It can be inferred from the passage that Houdini became famous _____.

[A] in 1894   [B] before he married

[C] at the age of 17   [D] when he was about 24

55. Which of the following is the best title for the passage?

[A] A Skeleton Key   [B] A Man of Many Secrets

[C] World-wild Fame   [D] Great Escape

Text 3

You're busy filling out the application form for a position you really need. Let's assume you once actually completed a couple of years of college work or even that you completed your degree. Isn't it tempting to lie just a little, to claim on the form that your diploma represents a Harvard degree? Or that you finished an extra couple of years back at State University? More and more people are turning to utter deception like this to land their job or to move ahead in their careers, for personnel officers, like most Americans, value degrees from famous schools. A job applicant may have a good education anyway, but he or she assumes that chances of being hired are better with a diploma from a well-known university.

Registrars at most well-known colleges say they deal with deceitful claims like these at the rate of about one per week. Personnel officers do check up on degrees listed on application forms, then. If it turns out that an applicant is lying, most colleges are reluctant to accuse the applicant directly. One Ivy League school calls them "impostors(骗子)"; another refers to them as "special cases". One well-known West Coast school, in perhaps the most delicate phrase of all, says that these claims are made by"no such people". To avoid outright (彻底的) lies, some job-seekers claim that they "attended" or "were associated with" a college or university. After carefully checking, a personnel officer may discover that "attending" means being dismissed after one semester. It may be that"being associated with" a college means that the job-seeker visited his younger brother for a football weekend. One school that keeps records of false claims says that the practice dates back at least to the turn of the century—that's when they began keeping records, anyhow. If you don't want to lie or even stretch the truth, there are companies that will sell you a phony diploma.

One company, with offices in New York and on the West Coast, will put your name on a diploma from any number of nonexistent colleges. The price begins at around twenty dollars for a diploma from "Smoot State University". The prices increase rapidly for a degree from the "University of Purdue". As there is no Smoot State and the real school in Indiana is properly called Purdue University, the prices seem rather high for one sheet of paper.

56. The main idea of this passage is that _____.

    [A] employers are checking more closely on applicants now

    [B] lying about college degrees has become a widespread problem

    [C] college degrees can now be purchased easily

    [D] employers are no longer interested in college degrees

57. According to the passage, "special cases" refers to cases that _____.

    [A] students attend a school only part-time

    [B] students never attended a school they listed on their application

    [C] students purchase false degrees from commercial firms

    [D] students attended a famous school

58. From the sentence "job-seeker visited his younger brother for a football weekend" (Para.2), we can infer that _____.

    [A] the job-seeker is a student in that college

    [B] the job-seeker's brother is a student in that college

    [C] neither the two are students in that college

    [D] both A and B

59. We can infer from the passage that _____.

    [A] performance is a better judge of ability than a college degree

    [B] experience is the best teacher

    [C] past work histories influence personnel officers more than degrees do

    [D] a degree from a famous school enables an applicant to gain advantage over others in job competition

60. The underlined word "phony" (Para. 2) means _____.

    [A] thorough   [B] false   [C] ultimate   [D] decisive

Part B

Directions: *Read the texts from an article in which five economists talked about the recession. For questions 61 to 65, match the name of each person(61 to 65) to one of the statements (A to G) given below. Mark your answers on ANSWER SHEET 1.*

Simpson

The global financial crisis of 2008—2009 began in July 2007 when a loss of confidence by investors in the value of securitized mortgages in the United States resulted in a liquidity crisis that prompted a substantial injection of capital into financial markets by the United States Federal Reserve, Bank of England and the European Central Bank. The TED spread, an indicator of perceived credit risk in the general economy, spiked up in July 2007, remained volatil(反复无常的) for a year, then spiked even higher in September 2008, reaching a record 4.65% on October 10, 2008.

Amy

In September 2008, the crisis deepened, as stock markets worldwide crashed and entered a period of high volatility, and a considerable number of banks, mortgage lenders and insurance companies failed in the following weeks. For many months before September 2008, many business journals published commentaries warning about the financial stability and risk management practices of leading US and European investment banks, insurance firms and mortgage banks consequent to the **subprime mortgage crisis** (次贷抵押危机).

Oliver

The ultimate point of origin of the great financial crisis of 2007 — 2009 can be traced back to an extremely indebted US economy. The collapse of the real estate market in 2006 was the close point of origin of the crisis. Beginning with failures caused by misapplication of risk controls for bad debts, collateralization(附带,并行) of debt insurance and fraud, large financial institutions in the United States and Europe faced a credit crisis and a slowdown in economic activity.

Wright

The crisis rapidly developed and spread into a global economic shock, resulting in a number of European bank failures, declines in various stock indexes, and large reductions in the market value of equities and commodities. Moreover, the de-leveraging of financial institutions further accelerated the liquidity crisis and caused a decrease in international trade. World political leaders, national ministers of finance and central bank directors coordinated their efforts to reduce fears, but the crisis continued.

Judith

By March 9, 2009, the Dow had fallen to 6440, a percentage decline exceeding the pace of the market's fall during the Great Depression and a level which the index had last seen in 1996. On March 10, 2009, a countertrend Bear Market Rally began, taking the Dow up to 7900 by March 26, 2009. Financial stocks were up more than 60% during this rally. By April 14, financial stocks had rallied more than 90% in just over a month.

Now match each of the persons to the appropriate statement.

Note: there are two extra statements.

Statements

61. Simpson　[A] After financial stocks hit the lowest on March 9, 2009, a countertrend Bear Market rally began.

62. Amy　　　[B] In September 2008, the crisis deepened, mortgage lenders and insurance companies failed in the following weeks.

63. Oliver　　[C] The crisis rapidly developed and spread into a global economic shock, because of the failures of a number of European banks.

64. Wright　　[D] The crisis rapidly developed and spread into a global economic shock, leading to a number of European bank failures.

65. Judith　　[E] The beginning of the global financial crisis is a loss of confidence by investors in the value of securitized mortgages in the US in July 2007.

　　　　　　[F] Many business journals published commentaries warning about the financial stability because they were able to predict the future economy.

　　　　　　[G] The ultimate point of origin of the great financial crisis of 2007 — 2009 can be traced back to an extremely indebted US economy.

Section IV   Writing

Directions: *You should write your responses to both Part A and Part B of this section on ANSWER SHEET 2.*

Part A

You have read the following magazine advertisement in which a company is looking for a secretary.

Secretary Needed

At least three years' experience to work in an office. Ability to type 120 to 150 words per minute. Fluent in spoken and written English. Good at teamwork. Send your resume and a latest photo to the company address by the end of this week.

Write an application letter of approximately 100 words to the company. Do not sign your own name at the end of your letter. Use "Xiao Tao" instead. You do not need to write the address.

Part B

Below is a table showing the growth in the number of people who prefer to travel abroad in your city between 1998 and 2008. Look at the table and write an essay of about 120 words making reference to the following points:

1. a description of the table;
2. the causes and impacts of it.

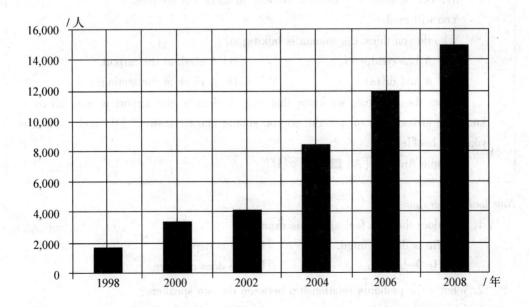

模拟试题（三）

Section I Listening Comprehension

Directions: *This section is designed to test your ability to understand spoken English. You will hear a selection of recorded materials and you must answer the questions that accompany them. There are two parts in this section, Part A and Part B.*

Remember, while you are doing the test, you should first put down your answers in your test booklet. At the end of the listening comprehension section, you will have 3 minutes to transfer your answers from your test booklet onto your ANSWER SHEET 1.

If you have any questions, you may raise your hand NOW as you will not be allowed to speak once the test has started.

Now look at Part A in your test booklet.

Part A

You will hear 10 short dialogues. For each dialogue, there is one question and four possible answers. Choose the correct answer A, B, C or D, and mark it in your test booklet. You will have 15 seconds to answer the question and you will hear each dialogue ONLY ONCE.

Example:

You will hear:

W: Could you please tell me if the Beijing flight will be arriving on time?

M: Yes, Madam. It should be arriving in about ten minutes.

You will read:

Who do you think the woman is talking to?

[A] A bus conductor.　　　　　[B] A clerk at the airport.

[C] A taxi driver.　　　　　　[D] A clerk at the station.

From the dialogue, we know that only a clerk at the airport is most likely to know the arrival time of a flight, so you should choose answer [B] and mark it in your test booklet.

Sample Answer: [A] ■ [C] [D]

Now look at question 1.

1. How does the man feel about his exam?

　　[A] He is disappointed.　　　　[B] He is happy.

　　[C] He feels so-so.　　　　　　[D] He does not care.

2. What's the probable relationship between the two speakers?

　　[A] Father and daughter.　　　　[B] Husband and wife.

　　[C] Doctor and patient.　　　　　[D] Teacher and doctor.

3. Where does the conversation most probably take place?

    [A] In the booking office.   [B] At the airport.

    [C] In the restaurant.   [D] In the reception office.

4. Where does this conversation take place?

    [A] At home.   [B] At a hotel.

    [C] In a restaurant.   [D] In a hospital.

5. What contributes to the woman's high score?

    [A] Doing lots of homework.   [B] Attending every lecture.

    [C] Using test-taking strategies.   [D] Reading very extensively.

6. What does the woman suggest the man do?

    [A] Give his ankle a rest.   [B] Go to a doctor.

    [C] Be careful when walking.   [D] Continue his regular activity.

7. What does the man imply?

    [A] The woman has a natural for art.

    [B] Women have a better artistic taste than men.

    [C] He doesn't like abstract paintings.

    [D] He isn't good at abstract thinking.

8. When can the woman get the computer?

    [A] On Wednesday.   [B] On Tuesday.

    [C] On Thursday.   [D] On Sunday.

9. Who is the woman talking to?

    [A] A painter.   [B] A porter.   [C] A mechanic.   [D] A carpenter.

10. What gift will the woman probably get for Mary?

    [A] A school bag.   [B] A book.   [C] A theater ticket.   [D] A record.

Part B

You are going to hear four passages or conversations. Before listening to each conversation, you will have 5 seconds to read each of the questions which accompany it. After listening, you will have time to answer each question by choosing A, B, C or D. You will hear each passage or conversation ONLY ONCE. Mark your answers in your test booklet.

Questions 11—14 are based on the following passage about Halloween. You now have 20 seconds to read the questions 11—14.

11. How often is Halloween?

    [A] Monthly.   [B] Every other year.

    [C] Once a year.   [D] Weekly.

12. What day is Halloween?

    [A] December 31st.   [B] October 31st.

    [C] November 4th.   [D] November 1st.

13. Why did people dress strangely?

[A] They wanted to frighten away spirits.

[B] They wanted to frighten their neighbors.

[C] They wanted to have fun.

[D] They wanted to have a celebration.

14. How did people act on Halloween?

[A] They hid their houses.　　　　[B] They had a dinner together.

[C] They acted wild.　　　　[D] They handed out gifts.

You now have 40 seconds to check your answers to questions 11—14.

Questions 15—18 are based on the following conversation. You now have 20 seconds to read the questions 15—18.

15. Where does this conversation take place?

[A] At the airport.　　　　[B] In the classroom.

[C] In a restaurant.　　　　[D] On the street.

16. Why does the woman like San Francisco?

[A] People there are friendlier.　　　　[B] It has the best food and music.

[C] It has less traffic.　　　　[D] It is advanced.

17. Where does the woman come from?

[A] Pennsylvania.　　[B] Boston.　　　　[C] San Francisco.　　　　[D] China.

18. What does the woman think of the man's English?

[A] Terrible.　　[B] Strange.　　[C] Excellent.　　　　[D] Acceptable.

You now have 40 seconds to check your answers to questions 15—18.

Questions 19—21 are based on the following news report. You now have 15 seconds to read the questions 19—21.

19. The Chinese satellite is _____.

[A] functioning properly　　　　[B] two tons

[C] totally out of control　　　　[D] going to hit the Atlantic Ocean

20. The Chinese satellite is supposed to return to the earth _____.

[A] within 16 months　　　　[B] soon

[C] in 6 months' time　　　　[D] on Thursday

21. When is part of the satellite likely to splash down?

[A] On Tuesday.　　　　[B] On Wednesday.

[C] On Thursday.　　　　[D] On Friday.

You now have 30 seconds to check your answers to questions 19—21.

Questions 22—25 are based on the following passage. You now have 20 seconds to read the questions 22—25.

22. Why are London taxi drivers very efficient?

    [A] Because they have a driving license.

    [B] Because they have received special training.

    [C] Because the traffic system of the city is not very complex.

    [D] Because the traffic conditions in London are good.

23. How long does the training period last?

    [A] About three weeks.   [B] At least half a year.

    [C] Two years or more.   [D] Two to four months.

24. Why does the speaker think the driving test is a terrible experience?

    [A] Government officers are hard to please.

    [B] The learner usually fails several times before he passes it.

    [C] The learner has to go through several tough tests.

    [D] The driving test usually last two months.

25. Why do learner drivers have to keep their present jobs?

    [A] They don't want their present bosses to know what they're doing.

    [B] They cannot earn money as taxi drivers yet.

    [C] They want to earn money from both jobs.

    [D] They look forward to further promotion.

You now have 40 seconds to check your answers to questions 22—25.

Now you have 3 minutes to transfer your answers from your test booklet to the ANSWER SHEET 1.

That is the end of the listening comprehension section.

Section II   Use of English

Directions: *Read the following text. Choose the best word or phrase for each numbered blank and mark A, B, C, or D on ANSWER SHEET 1.*

    An elderly carpenter was ready to retire. He told his employer of his plans to __26__ the house-building business to live a more __27__ life with his wife and enjoy his __28__ family. He would miss the paycheck (工资) each week, but he wanted to retire. They could __29__ . The employer was __30__ to see his good worker go and asked if he could build just one more house as a personal favor. The carpenter said yes, __31__ over time it was easy to see that his heart was not in his work. He used bad workmanship and __32__ materials. It was an unfortunate way to __33__ a dedicated (献身的) career.

    When the carpenter finished his work, his employer came to __34__ the house. Then he handed the front-door __35__ to the carpenter and said, "This is your house—my __36__ to you." The carpenter was shocked! What a __37__ ! If he had only known he was building his own house, he would have done it all so differently.

 38 it is with us. We build our lives, a day at a time, often putting 39 than our best into the building. Then, with a shock, we 40 we have to live in the house we have built. If we could do it 41 , we would do it much differently.

But, you cannot go back. You are the carpenter, and every day you hammer a nail, place a board, or build a wall. Someone 42 said, "Life is a do-it-yourself project." Your 43 , and the choices you 44 today, help build the "house" you will live in tomorrow. Therefore, build 45 !

26. [A] continue   [B] start   [C] leave   [D] find

27. [A] leisurely   [B] lonely   [C] orderly   [D] friendly

28. [A] expend   [B] expanded   [C] extended   [D] extensive

29. [A] go off   [B] get by   [C] pass on   [D] work away

30. [A] polite   [B] nervous   [C] proud   [D] sorry

31. [A] but   [B] while   [C] which   [D] before

32. [A] perfect   [B] inferior   [C] superior   [D] tough

33. [A] satisfy   [B] improve   [C] meet   [D] end

34. [A] buy   [B] repair   [C] inspect   [D] sell

35. [A] roof   [B] window   [C] key   [D] design

36. [A] gift   [B] promise   [C] salary   [D] words

37. [A] disappointment   [B] shame   [C] pleasure   [D] success

38. [A] So   [B] Yet   [C] As   [D] Such

39. [A] worse   [B] more   [C] rather   [D] less

40. [A] realize   [B] explain   [C] think   [D] admit

41. [A] up   [B] over   [C] out   [D] around

42. [A] never   [B] again   [C] once   [D] nearly

43. [A] attitude   [B] experience   [C] skill   [D] advantage

44. [A] learn   [B] take   [C] see   [D] make

45. [A] badly   [B] wisely   [C] early   [D] confidently

Section III   Reading Comprehension

Part A

Directions: *Read the following three texts. Answer the questions on each text by choosing A, B, C or D. Mark your answers on the ANSWER SHEET 1.*

Text 1

The struggle against malnutrition and hunger is as old as man himself, and never across the face of our planet has outcome been more in doubt. Malnutrition caused much suffering to an estimated 400 million to 1.5 billion of the world's poor. Even in the wealthy US poverty means undernourishment for an estimated ten to twenty million. Hardest hit are children, whose growing bodies demand two and a half times more protein, pound for pound, than those of adults. Nutrition experts estimate that 70 percent of the children in low-income countries are affected.

Badly shaped bodies tell the tragic story of malnutrition. Medical science identifies two major types of malnutrition which usually occur in combination. The first, kwashiorkor (恶性营养不良), is typified by the bloated look. The opposite of what we associate with starvation. Accumulated fluids pushing against wasted muscles account for the plumpness of hands, feet, belly, and face. Lean shoulders reveal striking thinness. Caused by an acute lack of protein kwashiorkor can bring brain damage, anemia, diarrhea, irritability, apathy, and loss of appetite.

On the other hand, stick limbs, a bloated belly, wide eyes, and the stretched skin face of an old person mark victims of marasmus, a word taken from the Greek "to waste away". Lacking calories as well as protein, sufferers may weigh only half as much as normal. With fat gone, the skin hangs in wrinkles or draws tight over bones. With marasmus comes anemia, diarrhea, dehydration, and a very hungry appetite. Children, whose growing bodies require large amounts of protein, have to suffer in greatest numbers, but perhaps only three percent of all child victims suffer the extreme stages described.

Scientists are doing best to develop new weapons against malnutrition and starvation. But two thirds of the human population of 3.9 billion live in the poorest countries which also have the highest birth rates. Thus, of the 74 million people added to the population each year, four out of five will be born in a country unable to supply its people's nutritional needs.

46. Malnutrition has caused much suffering to millions of people all over the world for a long time _____.

   [A] but the problem is not as serious now as before

   [B] and the problem is as serious now as at any time before

   [C] but the future looks quite promising

   [D] but the problem is likely to become less serious

47. According to the author, children _____.

   [A] suffer more than adults because they eat less food

   [B] suffer less than adults because they are physically smaller

   [C] are affected more than adults since their food contains less protein

   [D] are affected more than adults simply because they need more protein

48. Children suffering from "kwashiorkor" will look _____.

   [A] plump in feet and hands, as well as faces and bodies, but their shoulders are very thin

[B] bloated all over their bodies

[C] plump in feet and hands, as well as faces and bodies, especially in shoulders

[D] swollen, an appearance that we associate with starvation

49. Children suffering from "marasmus" will _____.

[A] look like old men and lose their appetite

[B] have extremely thin arms and legs, but big bellies, and they will easily get angry at small things, and they may suffer from brain damage

[C] have extremely thin arms and legs, but big bellies

[D] have long, thin faces like old men, and feel hungry all the time

50. Of the 74 million people added to the population each year _____.

[A] four out of five will be born in countries that do not have a large population

[B] 80% will be born in countries which do not have problems of malnutrition

[C] 80% will be born in developed countries

[D] four fifths will be born in underdeveloped countries

Text 2

For years there have been endless articles stating that scientists are on the verge of achieving artificial intelligence, that it is just around the corner. The truth is that it may be just around the corner, but they haven't yet found the right clock.

Artificial intelligence aims to build machines that can think. One immediate problem is to define thought, which is harder than you might think. The specialists in the field of artificial intelligence complain, with some justification, that anything that their machines do is dismissed as not being thought. For example, computers can now play very, very good chess. They can't beat the greatest players in the world, but they can beat just about anybody else. If a human being played chess at this level, he or she would certainly be considered smart. Why not a machine? The answer is that the machine doesn't do anything clever in playing chess. It uses its blinding speed to do a brute-force search of all possible moves for several moves ahead, evaluates the outcomes and picks the best. Humans don't play chess that way. They see patterns, which computers don't.

This wooden approach to thought characterizes machine intelligence. Computers have no judgment, no flexibility, no common sense. So-called expert systems, one of the hottest areas in artificial intelligence, aim to mimic the reasoning processes of human experts in a limited field, such as medical diagnosis or weather forecasting. There may be limited commercial applications for this sort of thing, but there is no way to make a machine think about anything under the sun, which a teenager can do. The hallmark of artificial intelligence to date is that if a problem is severely restricted, a machine can achieve limited success. But when the problem is expanded to a realistic one, computers fall flat on their display screens. For example, machines can understand a few words spoken individually by a speaker that they have been trained to hear. They cannot understand continuous speech using an unlimited vocabulary spoken by just any speaker.

51. From the passage we know that the author _____.

　　[A] thinks that scientists are about to achieve artificial intelligence

　　[B] doubts whether scientists can ever achieve artificial intelligence

　　[C] does not think that scientists have found real artificial intelligence

　　[D] is sure that scientists have achieved artificial intelligence

52. We learn from the second paragraph that _____.

　　[A] the writer thinks that the specialists' complaints have some reasons

　　[B] anything that the computer does can be regarded as thought

　　[C] it is not very difficult to define thought

　　[D] computers play chess in exactly the same way as humans

53. The advantage of the computer in playing chess lie in its _____.

　　[A] cleverness in thinking out original moves

　　[B] ability to pick up the best out of all possible moves very quickly

　　[C] flexibility in choosing several different moves

　　[D] ability to see patterns

54. The characteristic of machine intelligence is its _____.

　　[A] correct judgment　　　　　　　　[B] high flexibility

　　[C] ability to think about anything　　　[D] rigid approach to thought

55. Which of the following statements about computers is true according to the passage?

　　[A] Computers can beat any chess player in the world.

　　[B] Computers can never be used to forecast weather.

　　[C] Computers can be trained to understand some words spoken by a speaker.

　　[D] Computers can be made to think as a teenager does.

Text 3

　　Thierry Daniel Henry (born on 17 August 1977) is a French football striker currently playing for Spanish La Liga club FC Barcelona and the French national team.

　　Henry was born and brought up in the tough neighborhood of Les Ulis, Essonne — a suburb of Paris — where he played for an array of local sides as a youngster and showed great promise as a goal-scorer. He was spotted by AS Monaco in 1990 and signed instantly, making his professional debut in 1994. Good form led to an international call-up in 1998, after which he signed for the Italian defending champions Juventus. He had a disappointing season playing on the wing, before joining Arsenal (兵工厂) for 10.5 million in 1999.

　　It was at Arsenal that Henry made his name as a world-class footballer. Despite initially struggling in the Premiership, he emerged as Arsenal's top goal-scorer for almost every season of his tenure there. Under long-time mentor and coach Arsène Wenger, Henry became a prolific striker and Arsenal's all-time leading scorer with 226 goals in all competitions. The Frenchman won two league titles and three FA Cups with the gunners shoulder to shoulder; he was twice nominated for the FIFA World Player of the Year, was named the PFA Players' Player of the Year twice, and the Football Writers' Association Footballer of the Year three times. Henry spent his final two seasons with Arsenal as club captain, leading them to the UEFA Champions League final in 2006. In June 2007, after eight years with Arsenal, he transferred to FC Barcelona for a fee of 24 million.

Henry has enjoyed similar success with the French national squad, having won the 1998 FIFA World Cup and Euro 2000 (the Delaunay Cup). In October 2007, he surpassed Michel Platini's record to become France's top goal-scorer of all time. Off the pitch, as a result of his own experience, Henry is an active spokesperson against racism in football. His footballing style and personality have ensured that he is one of the most commercially marketable footballers in the world; he has been featured in advertisements for Nike, Reebok, Renault, Pepsi and Gillette.

56. When did Thierry Henry first appear in a professional football game?

    [A] 1990.   [B] 1994.   [C] 1998.   [D] 1999.

57. Which position does Thierry Henry usually like to play in a football game?

    [A] Wing.   [B] Striker.   [C] Goalkeeper.   [D] Captain.

58. According to the passage, "the gunners" (Para. 3, Line 5) probably means _____.

    [A] the enemies of Arsenal   [B] the coaches of Arsenal

    [C] the supporters of Arsenal   [D] the footballers of Arsenal

59. Which of the following honors does Thierry Henry NEVER get?

    [A] The Premiership League champion.   [B] The FIFA World Cup.

    [C] The Delaunay Cup.   [D] The France Cup.

60. According to the passage, which one is true?

    [A] Thierry Henry is always a prolific striker from AS Monaco to FC Barcelona.

    [B] Juventus is where Thierry Henry's splendid football life started.

    [C] Arsene Wenger is not only a teacher but also a friend as to Thierry Henry.

    [D] Michel Platini is France's top goal-scorer of all time.

Part B

Directions: *Read the texts from an article in which five people talked about the future life. For questions 61 to 65, match the name of each person (61 to 65) to one of the statements (A to G) given below. Mark your answers on ANSWER SHEET 1.*

Michael

The future will not determine itself. The future is determined by the action of the present day. The future is not something imposed upon us by fate or other forces beyond our control. We ourselves build the future both through what we do and what we do not do.

Tony

The future will see more unbelievable things. In the future, people will be able to predict their performance from the strength of the brain's electrical activity. Doctor Kramer has found that the strength of the brain's electrical activity can be measured through the scalp. Bosses would measure brain activity through the scalp and tell whether a worker is performing well, working hard, or too tired to do the job properly.

Mary

In the new century, things around us will be more fascinating. The chemical gelatin in the brain is said to increase your desire for fat, when it is stimulated. This means that disturbances of this chemical gelatin can lead to overeating. Doctor Sarah Leibowits presented an academic paper suggesting that the appetite for fat-rich food can be controlled through drugs that block the effects of gelatin.

David

In the future our life will change dramatically. It is quite certain that computers will play an important part in our life. You will visit your doctor, and find that he uses a computer screen and visual information about your condition, instead of his text books. Computers in your home will enable you to answer interactive question about your health and show the alternative results which will affect you if you act in a certain way.

Kate

In the future, computers will change the way the doctors diagnose and treat their patients. Also doctors will change their traditional notion of medicine. Although pills for tension, heart conditions, being overweight and other life-threatening conditions are prescribed by Western doctors, most doctors now require patients to focus on a healthy way of living by changing diets and using more exercise as a means to keep well.

Now match each of the people (61 to 65) to the appropriate statement.

Note: There are two extra statements.

Statements

61. Michael   [A] We create our own future.

62. Tony   [B] Changing diets and having exercise is a good way to stay healthy.

63. Mary   [C] Computers will play an essential role in our life.

65. David   [D] Pills for tension, overweight will no longer be prescribed by doctors.

65. Kate   [E] Your brain waves may be used to check out your work performance.

[F] People no longer need to see doctors.

[G] Chemical gelatin, once stimulated, can increase our desire of eating fat-rich food.

Section IV Writing

Directions: *You should write your responses to both Part A and Part B of this section on ANSWER SHEET 2.*

Part A

Suppose you are Li Hua, your father called you and said your mother is now in hospital. Write a short note to your English teacher Professor Zhang in about 100 words and tell him you have to ask for two days' leave and can't attend his class this afternoon and you'll make up the missed class right after you come back.

Do not sign your own name at the end of your letter; use Li Hua instead. You do not need to write the address.

Part B

Below is a picture showing the improvement of the air quality in your city between 1998 and 2008. Look at the graph and write an essay of about 120 words making reference to the following points:

1. a description of the graph;

2. the cause and effect of it.

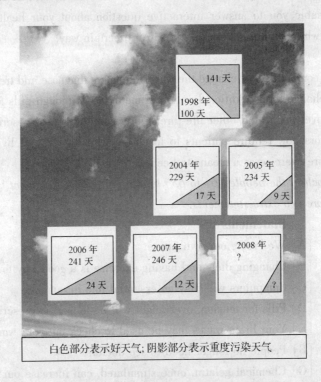

白色部分表示好天气; 阴影部分表示重度污染天气

模拟试题（四）

Section Ⅰ   Listening Comprehension

Directions: *This section is designed to test your ability to understand spoken English. You will hear a selection of recorded materials and you must answer the questions that accompany them. There are two parts in this section, Part A and Part B.*

Remember, while you are doing the test, you should first put down your answers in your test booklet. At the end of the listening comprehension section, you will have 3 minutes to transfer your answers from your test booklet onto your ANSWER SHEET 1.

If you have any questions, you may raise your hand NOW as you will not be allowed to speak once the test has started.

Now look at Part A in your test booklet.

Part A

You will hear 10 short dialogues. For each dialogue, there is one question and four possible answers. Choose the correct answer A, B, C or D, and mark it in your test booklet. You will have 15 seconds to answer the question and you will hear each dialogue ONLY ONCE.

Example:

You will hear:

W: Could you please tell me if the Beijing flight will be arriving on time?

M: Yes, Madam. It should be arriving in about ten minutes.

You will read:

Who do you think the woman is talking to?

[A] A bus conductor.   [B] A clerk at the airport.

[C] A taxi driver.   [D] A clerk at the station.

From the dialogue, we know that only a clerk at the airport is most likely to know the arrival time of a flight, so you should choose answer [B] and mark it in your test booklet.

Sample Answer: [A] ■ [C] [D]

Now look at question 1.

1. What does the man mean?

    [A] They want to go downtown.

    [B] He doesn't know where to park the car.

    [C] He wants to go to the park, but she doesn't.

    [D] He wants to find out where the park is.

2. At what time does the train to Leeds leave?

[A] 3:00.　　　　[B] 3:15.　　　　[C] 5:00.　　　　[D] 6:10.

3. What are the two speakers talking about?

[A] A football player.　　　　　　　[B] A football team.

[C] A football match.　　　　　　　[D] None of the above.

4. Where does this conversation probably take place?

[A] In a bookstore.　　　　　　　　[B] In a reading room.

[C] In a furniture store.　　　　　　[D] In the man's study.

5. What are they talking about?

[A] A holiday.　　[B] Luck.　　[C] Work.　　[D] An accident.

6. Why does the woman refuse to go the party?

[A] Because she has got an appointment.

[B] Because she doesn't want to.

[C] Because she has to work.

[D] Because she wants to eat in a new restaurant.

7. What's the woman doing?

[A] Visiting the Browning.　　　　　[B] Writing a postcard.

[C] Looking for a postcard.　　　　　[D] Filling in a form.

8. What is the probable relationship between the two speakers?

[A] Librarian and student.　　　　　[B] Operator and caller.

[C] Boss and secretary.　　　　　　[D] Customer and repairman.

9. What can we learn from the dialogue?

[A] The man didn't want the woman to have her hair cut.

[B] The woman followed the man's advice.

[C] The woman is wearing long hair now.

[D] The man didn't care if the woman had her hair cut or not.

10. How does the woman feel?

[A] Worried.　　[B] Angry.　　[C] Surprised.　　[D] Sad.

Part B

You are going to hear four passages or conversations. Before listening to each conversation, you will have 5 seconds to read each of the questions which accompany it. After listening, you will have time to answer each question by choosing A, B, C or D. You will hear each passage or conversation ONLY ONCE. Mark your answers in your test booklet.

Questions 11—14 are based on the following conversation. You now have 20 seconds to read the questions 11—14.

11. Where does the conversation probably take place?

    [A] In an office.   [B] At the doctor's.

    [C] At home.   [D] None of the above.

12. What can we know about the two speakers?

    [A] The woman is a nurse.

    [B] The man doesn't know how to take care of himself.

    [C] The woman is having a cold.

    [D] The man is sick in bed.

13. What does the woman do about the man's headache?

    [A] She calls the secretary.   [B] She calls the doctor at last.

    [C] She tells him to go to bed.   [D] She takes some hot water for him.

14. Which of the following is not mentioned by the woman to help the man?

    [A] Put the cigarrette out.

    [B] Drink some hot water.

    [C] Wrap a piece of cloth around his neck.

    [D] Put his nose over the hot water.

You now have 40 seconds to check your answers to questions 11—14.

Questions 15—18 are based on the following conversation. You now have 20 seconds to read the questions 15—18.

15. Why doesn't Peter drive a car to work?

    [A] His car is broken.

    [B] His car is stolen.

    [C] His working place is not far from his home.

    [D] The road is full of small stones.

16. How many years have Peter been driving to work?

    [A] 2 year.   [B] 3 years.   [C] 4 years.   [D] 5 years.

17. Which of the following can we infer from the passage?

    [A] The woman goes to work on foot.   [B] The woman goes to work by car.

    [C] The woman goes to work by bike.   [D] The woman goes to work by plane.

18. What's the possible relationship between the two?

    [A] Classmates.   [B] Husband and wife.

    [C] Brother and sister.   [D] Colleagues.

You now have 40 seconds to check your answers to questions 15—18.

Questions 19—22 are based on the following news report. You now have 20 seconds to read the questions 19—22.

19. How many kinds of travel books are mentioned in the passage?

    [A] 2.   [B] 3.   [C] 4.   [D] 5.

20. What is the characteristic of the second kind of travel books?

[A] It gives an objective description of things.

[B] It gives an analysis to the information.

[C] It gives a subjective description of things.

[D] It gives interpretation to the information.

21. Why should you pay attention to the publication of the book?

[A] Because it shows what kind of travel book it is.

[B] Because it is a sign of good quality.

[C] Because it is easy to find.

[D] Because things change quickly.

22. You won't buy a travel book that _____.

[A] contain both positive and negative accounts

[B] is well-presented

[C] has a publication date

[D] describes everything as "fabulous"

You now have 40 seconds to check your answers to questions 19—22.

Questions 23 — 25 are based on the following passage. You now have 15 seconds to read the questions 23—25.

23. According to this passage, which factor influenced the Roman way of communication most?

[A] The amount of weapons.   [B] The tower height.

[C] The weather condition.   [D] The voice volume.

24. What was the similarity between the Roman and African way of communication?

[A] People had to shout.

[B] People could send complicated messages.

[C] The messages could be sent out over a long distance within a time.

[D] Both of the ways relied on messages in the form of sound.

25. What can be inferred about the French way of communication?

[A] It could send speech sounds.

[B] It could send complicated messages.

[C] It could be understood by any French person.

[D] It could carry messages over a long distance in just a few seconds.

You now have 30 seconds to check your answers to questions 23—25.

Now you have 3 minutes to transfer your answers from your test booklet to the ANSWER SHEET 1.

That is the end of the listening comprehension section.

Section II   Use of English

Directions: *Read the following text. Choose the best word or phrase for each numbered blank and mark A, B, C, or D on ANSWER SHEET 1.*

I was parked in front of the mall wiping off my car. Coming my way from across the parking lot was __26__ society would consider a bum(无业游民). From the __27__ of him, he had no car, no home, no clean clothes, and no money. He sat down in front of the bus stop but didn't look like he could have enough money to even __28__ the bus. "That's a very pretty car," he said. He was __29__ but he had a (n) __30__ of dignity around him. I said, "thanks," and __31__ wiping off my car. He sat there __32__ as I worked. The __33__ beg for money never came. As the silence between us widened something inside said, "ask him if he needs any help." I was __34__ that he would say "yes". "Do you need any help?" I asked. He answered in three __35__ but profound（深远的）words that I shall never __36__. "Don't we all?" he said.

I had been feeling high, successful and important __37__ those three words __38__ me like a shotgun. Don't we all? I needed help. Maybe not for bus fare or a place to sleep, but I needed help. I __39__ my wallet and gave him not only enough for bus fare, but enough to get a warm meal and __40__ for the day. Those three little words still ring __41__. No matter how much you have, no matter how much you have __42__, you need help too. No matter how __43__ you have, no matter how __44__ you are with problems, even without money or a place to sleep, you can __45__ help.

26. [A] that   [B] what   [C] which   [D] how
27. [A] expressions [B] manners   [C] looks   [D] attitudes
28. [A] ride   [B] buy   [C] drive   [D] stop
29. [A] generous   [B] disappointed [C] modern   [D] ragged
30. [A] air   [B] atmosphere [C] appearance   [D] figure
31. [A] finished   [B] stopped   [C] continued   [D] began
32. [A] quietly   [B] casually   [C] aimlessly   [D] eagerly
33. [A] intending   [B] expected   [C] boring   [D] supposed
34. [A] afraid   [B] glad   [C] doubtful   [D] sure
35. [A] simple   [B] complex   [C] strange   [D] rigid
36. [A] accept   [B] forget   [C] respond   [D] choose
37. [A] unless   [B] after   [C] until   [D] while
38. [A] frightened   [B] moved   [C] wounded   [D] hit

39. [A] reached in   [B] searched for   [C] looked up   [D] exposed to

40. [A] shelter   [B] clothes   [C] reward   [D] blanket

41. [A] nice   [B] ridiculous   [C] true   [D] proper

42. [A] submitted   [B] devoted   [C] applied   [D] accomplished

43. [A] few   [B] many   [C] little   [D] enough

44. [A] loaded   [B] puzzled   [C] angry   [D] unsatisfied

45. [A] receive   [B] give   [C] need   [D] seek

Section III Reading Comprehension

Part A

Directions: *Read the following three texts. Answer the questions on each text by choosing A, B, C or D. Mark your answers on ANSWERSHEET 1.*

Text 1

Everyone chases success, but not all of US want to be famous. South African writer John Maxwell Coetzee is well-known for keeping himself to himself.

When the 63-year-old was named the 2003 Nobel Prize winner for literature earlier this month, reporters were warned that they would find him "particularly difficult to catch".

Coetzee lives in Australia but spends part of the year teaching at the University of Chicago. He seemed shocked by the news that he won the US$1.3 million prize. "I wasn't even aware they were due to make the announcement," he said.

His love of privacy led to doubts as to whether Coetzee will attend the prize-giving in Stockholm, Sweden, on December 10.

But despite being described as difficult to track down the critics agree that his writing is easy to get to know.

Born in Cape Town South Africa to all English-speaking family, Coetzee made his breakthrough in 1980 with the novel *Waiting for the Barbarians*. He took his place among the world's leading writers with two Booker prize victories, Britain's highest honor for novels. He first won in 1983 for the *Life and Times of Michael K*, and his second title came in 1999 for *Disgrace*.

A major theme in his work is South Africa's former apartheid (种族隔离) system, which divided whites from blacks. Dealing with the problems of violence, crime and racial division that still exist in the country, his books have enabled ordinary people to understand apartheid from within.

"I have always been more interested in the past than the future." he said in a rare interview. "The past casts its shadow over the present. I hope I have made one or two people think twice about whether they want to forget the past completely."

In fact this purity in his writing seems to be mirrored in his personal life. Coetzee is a vegetarian, a cyclist rather than a motorist and doesn't drink alcohol.

But what he has contributed to literature, culture and the people of South Africa is far greater than the things he has given up. "In looking at weakness and failure in life," the Nobel Prize judging panel said, "Coetzee's work expresses the divine spark in man."

46. When the news came that he won the 2003 Nobel Prize for literature, Coetzee was _____.

    [A] excited   [B] surprised   [C] frightened   [D] satisfied

47. People wonder if he will come to the prize-giving in December because _____.

    [A] he lives in Australia not in South Africa

    [B] he likes to be left in peace without being bothered

    [C] he is busy teaching at the University of Chicago

    [D] he is particularly difficult to find

48. John Maxwell Coetzee is a person who _____.

    [A] prefers riding a bike to driving a car   [B] likes eating meat very much

    [C] ever drinks wine   [D] often accepts interviews

49. According to the passage, which of the following information is _____ right?

    [A] he became famous for the novel *Waiting for the Barbarians*

    [B] racial division still exists in South Africa

    [C] he won British highest honor for novels

    [D] he wanted to forget the past completely

50. What's the author's attitude towards John Maxwell coetzee?

    [A] Critical.   [B] Positive.   [C] Skeptical.   [D] Not clear.

Text 2

Many a young person tells me he wants to be a writer. I always encourage such people, but I also explain that there's a big difference between "being a writer" and writing. In most cases these individuals are dreaming of wealth and fame, not the long hours alone at a typewriter. "You've got to want to write," I say to them, "not want to be a writer."

The reality is that writing is a lonely, private and poor-paying affair. For every writer kissed by fortune there are thousands more whose longing is never rewarded. When I left a 20-year career in the US Coast Guard to become a freelance writer (自由撰稿人), I had no prospects at all. What I did have was a friend who found me my room in a New York apartment building. It didn't even matter that it was cold and had no bathroom. I immediately bought a used manual typewriter and felt like a genuine writer.

After a year or so, however, I still hadn't gotten a break and began to doubt myself. It was so hard to sell a story that barely made enough to eat. But I knew I wanted to write. I had dreamed about it for years. I wasn't going to be one of those people who die wondering, "What if?" I would keep putting my dream to the test — even though it meant living with uncertainty and fear of failure. This is the Shadowland of hope, and anyone with a dream must learn to live there.

51. The passage is meant to _____.

[A] show young people it's unrealistic for a writer to pursue wealth and fame

[B] advise young people to give up their idea of becoming a professional writer

[C] warn young people of the hardships that a successful writer has to experience

[D] encourage young people to pursue a writing career

52. Why did the author begin to doubt himself after the first year of his writing career?

[A] He wasn't about to produce a single book.

[B] He hadn't seen a change for the better.

[C] He wasn't able to have a rest for a whole year.

[D] He found his dream would never come true.

53. What can be concluded from the passage?

[A] The chances for a writer to become successful are small.

[B] A writer's success depends on luck rather than on effort.

[C] Famous writers usually live in poverty and isolation.

[D] Genuine writers often find their work interesting and rewarding.

54. "... people who die wondering, 'What if?'" (Para. 3) refers to "those _____".

[A] who think too much of the dark side of life

[B] who regret giving up their career halfway

[C] who think a lot without making a decision

[D] who are full of imagination even upon death

55. "Shadowland" in the last sentence refers to _____.

[A] the bright future that one is looking forward to

[B] the wonderland one often dreams about

[C] the state of uncertainty before one's final goal is reached

[D] a world that exists only in one's imagination

Text 3

Disposing（处理）of waste has been a problem since humans started producing it. As more and more people choose to live close together in cities, the waste-disposal problem becomes increasingly difficult.

During the eighteenth century, it was usual for several neighboring towns to get together to select a faraway spot as a dumpsite. Residents or trash haulers（垃圾托运者）would transport household rubbish, rotted wood, and old possessions to the site. Periodically（定期的）some of the trash was burned and the rest was buried. The unpleasant sights and smells caused no problem because nobody lived close by.

Factories, mills, and other industrial sites also had waste to be disposed of. Those located on rivers often just dumped the unwanted remains into the water. Others built huge burners with chimneys to deal with the problem.

Several facts make these choices unacceptable to modern society. The first problem is space. Dumps, which are now called landfills, are most needed in heavily populated areas. Such areas rarely have empty land suitable for this purpose. Property is either too expensive or too close to residential (住宅区的) neighborhoods. Long-distance trash hauling has been a common practice, but once farm areas are refusing to accept rubbish from elsewhere, cheap land within trucking distance of major city areas is almost nonexistent.

Awareness of pollution dangers has resulted in more strict rules of waste disposal. Pollution of rivers, ground water, land and air is a price people can no longer pay to get rid of waste. The amount of waste, however, continues to grow.

Recycling efforts have become commonplace in recent years, and many towns require their people to take part. Even the most efficient recycling programs, however, can hope to deal with only about 50 percent of a city's reusable waste.

56. The most suitable title for this passage would be _____.

　　[A] Places for Disposing Waste　　　[B] Waste Pollution Dangers
　　[C] Ways of Getting Rid of Waste　　[D] Waste Disposal Problem

57. During the 18th century, people disposed their waste in many ways EXCEPT for _____.

　　[A] burying it　　　　　　　　[B] recycling it
　　[C] burning it　　　　　　　　[D] throwing it into rivers

58. Which of the following is NOT a factor that leads to the disposing of waste in modern society a problem?

　　[A] Strict rules of waste disposal.
　　[B] Shortage of cheap land.
　　[C] Farm areas' refusal of accepting waste from city.
　　[D] Recycling efforts.

59. What can be inferred from the fourth paragraph?

　　[A] Farm areas accept waste from the city in modern society.
　　[B] There is cheap land to bury waste in modern society.
　　[C] It is difficult to find space to bury waste in modern society.
　　[D] Ways to deal with waste in modern society is similar to that of the past.

60. The main purpose of writing this article is to _____.

　　[A] warn people of the pollution dangers we are facing
　　[B] draw people's attention to waste management
　　[C] tell people a better way to get rid of the waste
　　[D] call on people to take part in recycling programs

Part B

Directions: *Read the following article in which five people talk about their ideas of education. For questions 61 to 65, match name of each person (61 to 65) to one of the statements (A to G) given below. Mark your answers on your ANSWER SHEET 1.*

Bernal

Well, there are a lot of different views on this, but I think it is probably wrong to imagine that there was some golden age in the past when everything was perfect. It all depends, of course, on what you measure and how you measure it. Some people might be surprised that there has not been an obvious and dramatic increase in the standard of education, given the vast amounts of money spent in this area by successive governments in recent years. Unfortunately, most improvements in education are intangible.

Carlos

Many people talk about how to improve education and a lot suggest raising the salaries of teachers and professors. Of course, this is very important to education. However, increasing the salary of teachers is just one way to improve education. It will not work without the cooperation of the other determinants, such as student's interest in gaining knowledge and in reading. Even if the teachers are devoted, it won't make any difference if the students are not willing to learn.

Stevens

Well, if you asked me, it's all these modern methods that is the problem. In the old days you sat in rows at desks and you did as you were told. You knew what you had to do and you follow the way as the teachers instructed and you kept quiet. Nowadays, my god, the noise in most schools is deafening especially in primary schools. As far as I am concerned the children wander around—do whatever they would like to. The teacher just sits there or wanders around with them, talking to them. Informal teaching they call it. Discovery methods sounds more like a recipe for discovering disaster to me.

Ingersoll

The criticism that what students learn today is not adapted to present-day society is utterly wrong because education can never be seen only in terms of how useful the subjects are when students leave school. We ought to evaluate education in terms of how much the students enjoy those subjects and how much they mean to those students. Instead of being trained to be utilitarian, students should be encouraged to do things for their own sake, and study what they are interested in.

Jessica

I think it's a great shame people don't learn anything today. I mean, good heavens, when you think of all the millions of pounds the Government have spent on education—new schools, more teachers, new equipment. And yet still you find people who can't read properly, can't even write their names and don't know what two and two is without a calculator. I think it's downright disgraceful. Think of the time when we were young, we went to school to learn and did as the teachers told and respected our teachers. Nowadays we get long-haired kids who aren't interested in anything. No wonder they don't learn anything.

Now match each of the persons to the appropriate statement.

Note: there are two extra statements.

Statements

61. Bernal   [A] The modern methods of teaching should be responsible for the deafening noise in primary schools.

62. Carlos   [B] It's shameful of some people not to learn anything with provided conditions.

63. Stevens   [C] We should evaluate education from the students' aspect, how much they enjoy is what counts most.

64. Ingersoll [D] Raising salary of teachers and professors is the only way to improve education.

65. Jessica   [E] Students' own willingness to learn really matters in terms of education.

[F] There is no improvement in education.

[G] Most of the improvements in the standard of education are intangible.

Section IV   Writing

Directions: *You should write your responses to both Part A and Part B of this section on ANSWER SHEET 2.*

Part A

Write a short letter to your friend Liu Yang, who is a freshman in another college and doesn't know how to prepare for the CET-4. Tell him:

1. You have passed the CET-4;

2. what you have done in preparation for the test;

3. encourage your friend to be confident and work hard for the test in the next term.

Do not sign your own name at the end of your letter. Use "Li Hua" instead. You do not need to write the address.

Part B

Below is a cartoon about a couple's talk over cable theft. Look at the cartoon and write an essay of about 120 words making reference to the following points:

1. describe the story;

2. point out why the couple are wrong and what they should do.

模拟试题（五）

Section Ⅰ   Listening Comprehension

Directions: *This section is designed to test your ability to understand spoken English. You will hear a selection of recorded materials and you must answer the questions that accompany them. There are two parts in this section, Part A and Part B.*

Remember, while you are doing the test, you should first put down your answers in your test booklet. At the end of the listening comprehension section, you will have 3 minutes to transfer your answers from your test booklet onto your ANSWER SHEET 1.

If you have any questions, you may raise your hand NOW as you will not be allowed to speak once the test has started.

Now look at Part A in your test booklet.

Part A

You will hear 10 short dialogues. For each dialogue, there is one question and four possible answers. Choose the correct answer A, B, C or D, and mark it in your test booklet. You will have 15 seconds to answer the question and you will hear each dialogue ONLY ONCE.

Example:

You will hear:

W: Could you please tell me if the Beijing flight will be arriving on time?

M: Yes, Madam. It should be arriving in about ten minutes.

You will read:

Who do you think the woman is talking to?

[A] A bus conductor.   [B] A clerk at the airport.

[C] A taxi driver.   [D] A clerk at the station.

From the dialogue, we know that only a clerk at the airport is most likely to know the arrival time of a flight, so you should choose answer   [B] and mark it in your test booklet.

Sample Answer: [A] ■■■ [C] [D]

Now look at question 1.

1. Where does the conversation take place?

   [A] At a restaurant.   [B] In the office.

   [C] At the cinema.   [D] At a department store.

2. What do they think of Tom?

   [A] He gets nervous very easily.   [B] He is an inexperienced speaker.

   [C] He is an awful speaker.   [D] He hasn't prepared his speech well.

3. What might the result be if the woman doesn't take the man's advice?

[A] She might put on weight. [B] She might be attacked by someone some day.

[C] She might go on a diet. [D] Something might go wrong with her heart.

4. What can be inferred from the woman's answer?

[A] She'd like to have the windows open.

[B] She likes to have the air conditioner on.

[C] The air is heavily polluted.

[D] The windows are already open.

5. What's the man trying to do?

[A] Call a friend. [B] Join the party.

[C] Write a check. [D] Provide a service.

6. When will they probably discuss the plan?

[A] Before dinner. [B] After lunch.

[C] Over dinner. [D] Before lunch.

7. How many people died in the accident?

[A] 2 men. [B] 3 women. [C] None. [D] One child.

8. What are they talking about?

[A] A driving test. [B] A police movie.

[C] A traffic accident. [D] The best way to make signals.

9. How much is the yellow coat?

[A] $20. [B] $45. [C] $70. [D] $90.

10. What is the woman doing?

[A] Complaining. [B] Apologizing. [C] Explaining. [D] Crying.

Part B

You are going to hear four passages or conversations. Before listening to each conversation, you will have 5 seconds to read each of the questions which accompany it. After listening, you will have time to answer each question by choosing A, B, C or D. You will hear each passage or conversation ONLY ONCE. Mark your answers in your test booklet.

Questions 11 — 14 are based on the following conversation. You now have 20 seconds to read the questions 11 — 14.

11. What is the main topic of this conversation?

[A] The man's graduation. [B] The couple's engagement.

[C] The man's smoking. [D] The man's stress.

12. How does the man feel about the woman's decision?

[A] Patient. [B] Worried. [C] Irritated. [D] Gloomy.

13. What can we infer about the woman?

[A] That she has stopped smoking.

[B] That she does not want to get married.

[C] That she has asked the man to quit smoking many times.

[D] That she is not in love with the man.

14. What does the woman advice the man to do?

    [A] To see a psychiatrist.   [B] To see a general practitioner.

    [C] To see a dentist.   [D] To get rid of it by himself.

You now have 40 seconds to check your answers to questions 11—14.

Questions 15—17 are based on the following conversation. You now have 15 seconds to read the questions 15—17.

15. What is the characteristic of current account?

    [A] Its interest rate is higher.   [B] Its interest rate is very low.

    [C] It's convenient.   [D] It's inconvenient.

16. What must you do if you want to open a current accout?

    [A] You have to deposit some money.

    [B] You have to pay some money.

    [C] You have to present your ID card.

    [D] You have to present your credit card.

17. How long will it take the man to get the bank card?

    [A] Two weeks after he opened the account.

    [B] At least one week after he opened the account.

    [C] Less than a week after he opened the account.

    [D] Immediately after he opened the account.

You now have 30 seconds to check your answers to questions 15—17.

Questions 18—21 are based on the following news report. You now have 20 seconds to read the questions 18—21.

18. Who are likely to treat their only children as "special jewels"?

    [A] Those who are themselves spoiled and self-centered.

    [B] Those who expected to have several children but could only have one.

    [C] Those who like to give expensive jewels to their children.

    [D] Those who give birth to their only children when they are below 30.

19. Why do some only children become "little adults"?

    [A] Because their parents want them to share the family burden.

    [B] Because their parents are too strict with them in their education.

    [C] Because they have nobody to play with.

    [D] Because their parents want them to grow up as fast as possible.

20. What does the passage mainly discuss?

    [A] Two types of only children.

    [B] Parents' responsibilities.

　　[C] The necessity of family planning.

　　[D] The relationship between parents and children.

21. Why do some only children feel unhappy?

　　[A] They have no sisters or brothers.

　　[B] They are overprotected by their parents.

　　[C] Their parents expect too much of them.

　　[D] Their parents often punish them for minor faults.

You now have 40 seconds to check your answers to questions 18—21.

Questions 22—25 are based on the following conversation. You now have 20 seconds to read the questions 22—25.

22. What are the man and woman talking about?

　　[A] About the building of the zoo. 　　[B] About the lay-out of the zoo.

　　[C] About the function of the zoo. 　　[D] About the attractiveness of the zoo.

23. Why does the man think we still need zoos?

　　[A] To display rare animals.

　　[B] To prevent rare animals from extinction.

　　[C] To provide weekend amusement for children.

　　[D] To improve the environment.

24. Where does the woman think is the right place for animal?

　　[A] At one's home. 　　[B] In the zoos.

　　[C] In cages. 　　[D] In their natural environment.

25. What kind of function does the man think that zoos and safari parks should serve?

　　[A] As recreational centers. 　　[B] As research centers.

　　[C] As family picnic centers. 　　[D] As educational centers.

You now have 40 seconds to check your answers to questions 22—25.

Now you have 3 minutes to transfer your answers from your test booklet to the ANSWER SHEET 1.

That is the end of the listening comprehension section.

Section II Use of English

Directions: *Read the following text. Choose the best word or phrase for each numbered blank and mark A, B, C, or D on ANSWER SHEET 1.*

　　Scientists find that hard-working people live longer than average men and women. Career women are ___26___ than housewives. Evidence （证据） shows that ___27___ are in poorer health than the job-holders. A study shows ___28___ the unemployment rate increases by 1%, the death rate increases correspondingly （相应地） by 2%. All this ___29___ one point:

Work is helpful to health.

Why is work good for health? It is because work keeps people busy, __30__ loneliness and solitude (孤独). Researches show that people feel __31__ and lonely when they have nothing to do. Instead, the happiest are those who are __32__. Many high achievers who love their careers feel that they are happiest when they are working hard. Work serves as __33__ between man and reality. By work, people __34__ each other. By collective (集体的) activity, they find friendship and warmth. This is helpful to health. The loss of work __35__ the loss of everything. It affects man spiritually and makes him liable to (易于) __36__.

__37__, work gives one a sense of fulfillment (充实感) and a sense of __38__. Work makes one feel his value and status in society. When __39__ finishes his writing or a doctor successfully __40__ a patient or a teacher sees his students __41__, they are happy __42__.

From the above we can come to the conclusion __43__ the more you work, __44__ you will be. Let us work hard, __45__ and live a happy and healthy life.

26. [A] more healthier   [B] healthier   [C] weaker   [D] worse
27. [A] career women   [B] the busy   [C] the jobless   [D] the hard-working
28. [A] that whenever   [B] whether   [C] that though   [D] since
29. [A] comes down to   [B] equals to   [C] adds up to   [D] amounts to
30. [A] /   [B] off   [C] in touch with [D] away from
31. [A] happy, interested   [B] glad, joyful
    [C] cheerful, concerned   [D] unhappy, worried
32. [A] busy   [B] free   [C] lazy   [D] empty
33. [A] a river   [B] a gap   [C] a channel   [D] a bridge
34. [A] come across   [B] come into contact with
    [C] look down upon   [D] watch over
35. [A] means   [B] stands   [C] equals   [D] matches
36. [A] success   [B] death   [C] victory   [D] illnesses
37. [A] Besides   [B] Nevertheless   [C] However   [D] Yet
38. [A] disappointment [B] achievement   [C] regret   [D] apology
39. [A] a worker   [B] a farmer   [C] a writer   [D] a manager
40. [A] manages   [B] controls   [C] operates on   [D] deals with
41. [A] raise   [B] grow   [C] rise   [D] increase
42. [A] in a word   [B] without a word
    [C] at a word   [D] beyond words
43. [A] that   [B] which   [C] what   [D] /

44. [A] the lonelier and weaker　　　　[B] lonelier and weaker

　　　[C] happier and healthier　　　　　[D] the happier and healthier

45. [A] study well　　　　　　　　　　[B] studying well

　　　[C] study good　　　　　　　　　　[D] studying good

Section Ⅲ　Reading Comprehension

Part A

Directions: *Read the following three texts. Answer the questions on each text by choosing A, B, C or D. Mark your answers on the ANSWER SHEET 1.*

Text 1

Health food is a general term applied to all kinds of foods that are considered more healthful than the types of foods widely sold in supermarkets. For example, whole grains, fried beans, and corn oil are health foods. A narrower classification of health food is natural food. This term is used to distinguish between types of the same food. Raw honey is a natural sweetener, whereas refined sugar is not. Fresh fruit is a natural food, but canned fruit, with sugars and other additives, is not. The most precise term of all and the narrowest classification within health foods is organic food, used to describe food that has been grown on a particular kind of farm. Fruit and vegetables that are grown in gardens, that are sprayed only with organic fertilizers, that are not sprayed with poisonous insecticides, and that are not refined after harvest, are organic foods. Meat, fish, dairy and poultry products from animals that are fed only organically grown feed and that are not injected with hormones are organic foods.

In choosing the type of food you eat, then, you have basically two choices: inorganic, processed foods, or organic, unprocessed foods. A wise decision should include investigation of the allegations that processed foods contain chemicals, some of which are proven to be toxic, and that vitamin content is greatly reduced in processed foods.

Bread is typically used by health food advocates as an example of a processed food. First, the seeds from which the grain is sprayed with a number of very toxic insecticides. After the grain has been made into flour, it is made white with another chemical which is also toxic. Next a dough conditioner is added, along with a softener. The conditioner and softener are poisons, and in fact the softener has sickened and killed experimental animals.

A very toxic anti-fungal compound, is added to keep the bread from getting moldy.

Other foods from the supermarket would show a similar pattern of processing and preserving. You see we buy our good on the basis of smell, color, and texture, instead of vitamin content, and manufacturers give us what we want, even if it is poisonous. The alternative? Eat health foods, preferable the organic variety.

46. Which term is used to distinguish between types of the same food?

　　　[A] Refined foods.　　　　　　　　[B] Natural foods.

　　　[C] Organic foods.　　　　　　　　[D] Unprocessed foods.

47. What do all of the addictives in bread have in common?

[A] They all used to keep the bread from getting moldy.

[B] They are all poisonous.

[C] They are all organic.

[D] They have all killed laboratory animals.

48. What happens to food when it is processed?

[A] The ultimate content remains the same.

[B] The vitamin information is not available after processing.

[C] The vitamin content is reduced altogether.

[D] The vitamin content is greatly reduced.

49. We normally buy foods on the basis of _____.

[A] organic variety   [B] beauty

[C] refined contents   [D] color and texture

50. What is the main idea of this passage?

[A] Health food.   [B] The processing of bread.

[C] Organic gardens.   [D] Poisons.

Text 2

Punctuation makes the written language intelligible. It does the job, on the page, of the changes of pitch, pace and rhythm which make it possible to understand speech. Unsurprisingly, therefore, a requirement for some knowledge of how to punctuate makes an early appearance in an English curriculum.

The trouble is, that necessary though punctuation is, the task of teaching it to children is considerably more challenging than it might appear. For example, it is possible that to instruct children about writing in sentences by telling them about full stops and capital letters is to court frustration and failure. The notion of the sentence as a statement—a free-standing chunk of information — is something that children come to gradually. As written work grows longer and more complicated, so the perception of sentence increases. Good teachers will, in their teaching of early writing, watch for the child's ability to compose in sentences, and then point out how the use of punctuation will define them more clearly.

So, where, in all this, comes the mechanical definition of a sentence—that it needs a verb, for example? The pragmatic answer is that it comes nowhere at all. Adult writers do not, on the whole, look back at their sentences to make sure they contain verbs. We all surely feel our sentences intuitively. Most of the time, to be sure, they will contain verbs. Occasionally, though, they may not—and where's the harm? What is certain is that you cannot possibly use the grammatical rule as a tool with which to teach a seven-year-old about sentence-writing. The child can be nudged and helped towards writing in sentences, but on the whole he will not do it until he is ready.

The point is that punctuation is an aid which the writer brings into play to illuminate an already formed idea. Before you can learn the punctuation, you have to know what you want to punctuate. Thus you teach capital letters, full stops, question marks and exclamation marks to a child who is already writing sentences, questions and exclamations. The development of a child's writing will always be a step ahead of the punctuation, and to reverse the process in response, say, to the short-term demands of a curriculum is to put later progress at risk.

51. Which statement can best sum up the main idea of the passage?

[A] it is necessary to require the knowledge of punctuation in an English curriculum.

[B] Punctuation is very important in written language.

[C] Punctuation can make sentences more clear.

[D] Punctuation should be taught after the development of children's writing.

52. The author believes that sentences which do not contain a verb are _____.

[A] carelessly written sentences   [B] useful in teaching punctuation

[C] not incorrect sentences   [D] based on grammar

53. What does the word "nudged"(the last sentence, Para. 3) probably mean?

[A] Hindered.   [B] Removed.

[C] Encouraged.   [D] Prevented.

54. According to the text, punctuation is naturally used when _____.

[A] a writer already knows what he/she means to say

[B] a writer needs an aid

[C] long or complex sentences are written

[D] writing sentences with question and exclamation marks

55. What, according to the passage, might make a teacher teach punctuation before children have the ability to write sentences?

[A] The demand of a curriculum.

[B] The demand of parents.

[C] The need of children.

[D] The intention to help children in their writing.

Text 3

The word conservation has a thrifty meaning. To conserve is to save and protect, to leave what we ourselves enjoy in such good condition that others may also share the enjoyment. Our forefathers had no idea that human population would increase faster than the supplies of raw materials; most of them, even until very recently, had the foolish idea that the treasures were "limitless" and "inexhaustible". Most of the citizens of earlier generations knew little or nothing about the complicated and delicate system that runs all through nature, and which means that, as in a living body, an unhealthy condition of one part will sooner or later be harmful to all the others.

Fifty years ago nature study was not part of the school work; scientific forestry was a new idea; timber was still cheap because it could be brought in any quantity from distant woodlands; soil destruction and river floods were not national problems; nobody had yet studied long-term climatic cycles in relation to proper land use; even the word "conservation" had nothing of the meaning that it has for us today.

For the sake of ourselves and those who will come after us, we must now set about repairing the mistakes of our forefathers. Conservation should, therefore, be made a part of everyone's daily life. To know about the water table in the ground is just as important to us as a knowledge of the basic arithmetic formulas. We need to know why all watersheds need the protection of plant life and why the running current of streams and rivers must be made to yield their full benefit to the soil before they finally escape to the sea. We need to be taught the duty of planting trees as well as of cutting them. We need to know the importance of big, mature trees, because living space for most of man's fellow creatures on this planet is figured not only in square measure of surface but also in cubic volume above the earth. In brief, it should be our goal to restore as much of the original beauty of nature as we can.

56. According to the author, the greatest mistake of our forefathers was that _____.

    [A] they had no idea about scientific forestry

    [B] they were not aware of the significance of nature study

    [C] they had little or no sense of environmental protection

    [D] they had no idea of how to make good use of raw materials

57. It can be inferred from the third paragraph that earlier generations didn't realize __

    _____.

    [A] the importance of the proper use of land

    [B] the value of the beauty of nature

    [C] the harmfulness of soil destruction and river floods

    [D] the interdependence of water, soil, and living things

58. To avoid the mistakes of our forefathers, the author suggests that _____.

    [A] we plant more trees

    [B] we return to nature

    [C] natural sciences be taught to everybody

    [D] environmental education be directed toward everyone

59. What does the author imply by saying "living space ... is figured ... also in cubic volume above the earth." (Para. 3)?

    [A] We need to take some measures to protect space.

    [B] Our living space should be measured in cubic volume.

    [C] Our living space on the earth is getting smaller and smaller.

    [D] We must preserve good living conditions for both birds and animals.

60. The author's attitude towards the current situation in the exploitation of natural resources is _____.

    [A] critical   [C] positive   [B] neutral   [D] suspicious

Part B

Directions: *Read the texts from an article in which five people talked about why they like or dislike salesmen. For questions 61 to 65, match the name of each person (61 to 65) to one of the statements (A to G) given below. Mark your answers on ANSWER SHEET 1.*

Mrs. White

I hate salesmen. I mean they are always pestering me to buy things I don't want. Why should I waste my time listening to their lies and looking at the junk they are trying to sell me? When I need something, I go out and buy it. Things are cheaper at the supermarket and there's a much better selection there.

Mrs. Lee

People prefer to buy from door-to-door salesmen because they are so friendly. A good salesman always brings things like candies for the children, sympathy for the tired housewife and a smile for the lonely old people. And the customers always have a chance to try things before they actually buy them. You don't get that kind of service at the supermarket.

Mrs. Ros

I just don't trust those salesmen. Once you let in a salesperson you can never get rid of him. They just keep talking and talking until you buy his goods. When you come to use the thing, you find out it's a piece of junk. But you can't get your money back. They use all kinds of dishonest tricks to get people to buy overpriced goods which they don't need and can't afford.

Mr. Wales

I have met salesmen who sell only quality products. Customers test everything in their own homes and at their own convenience. I've heard a few cases of salesman harassing customers or making false claims. I suppose there are a few bad salesmen. But there are also bad doctors, bad policemen and so on. They aren't typical of their profession.

Mr. Baker

Salesmen often came by for a coffee and a nice talk. I'm so glad they do so. I don't have many visitors and the salesmen are interesting people. They talk in vivid language, and they are usually polite people. I'm a little too old to go out to the stores and buy things. I don't mind paying a little extra when they are brought to my home.

Now match each of the people (61 to 65) to the appropriate statement.

Note: There are two extra statements.

Statements

61. Mrs. White   [A] Salesmen often come to ask for a lot of coffee.

62. Mrs. Lee   [B] Salesmen are usually adolecents.

63. Mrs. Ros   [C] I prefer to buy things in a supermarket because things there are cheaper.

64. Mr. Wales   [D] I never trust salesmen.

65. Mr. Baker   [E] Salesmen provide better service than supermarkets do.

[F] Most salesmen don't take in their customers.

[G] Salesmen are interesting and usually polite people.

Section IV   Writing

Directions: *You should write your responses to both Part A and Part B of this section on ANSWER SHEET 2.*

Part A

Suppose your foreign teacher Bill announced at your classroom that he's got four extra tickets for the coming Irish Tap Dance at the Science and Art Center, and that students who are interested in watching it should write to him and tell him the reasons. You are now writing to Bill to express your willingness to watch the dance.

You should write approximately 100 words. Do not sign your own name at the end of your letter. Use "Zhang Hua" instead. You do not need to write the address.

Part B

Below is a cartoon about the Internet and the police's measures to keep the online world clean. Look at the cartoon and write an essay of about 120 words making reference to the following points:

1. describe the cartoon;

2. your understanding on the police's measures.

第**3**章

专家预测试题

Section I   Listening Comprehension

Directions: *This section is designed to test your ability to understand spoken English. You will hear a selection of recorded materials and you must answer the questions that accompany them. There are two parts in this section, Part A and Part B.*

Remember, while you are doing the test, you should first put down your answers in your test booklet. At the end of the listening comprehension section, you will have 3 minutes to transfer your answers from your test booklet onto your ANSWER SHEET 1.

If you have any questions, you may raise your hand NOW as you will not be allowed to speak once the test has started.

Now look at Part A in your test booklet.

Part A

You will hear 10 short dialogues. For each dialogue, there is one question and four possible answers. Choose the correct answer A, B, C or D, and mark it in your test booklet. You will have 15 seconds to answer the question and you will hear each dialogue ONLY ONCE.

Example:

You will hear:

W: Could you please tell me if the Beijing flight will be arriving on time?

M: Yes, Madam. It should be arriving in about ten minutes.

You will read:

Who do you think the woman is talking to?

[A] A bus conductor.   [B] A clerk at the airport.

[C] A taxi driver.   [D] A clerk at the station.

From the dialogue, we know that only a clerk at the airport is most likely to know the arrival time of a flight, so you should choose answer and mark it in your test booklet.

Sample Answer: [A] ▆▆ [C] [D]

Now look at question 1.

1. How much does the woman have to pay?

   [A] 20 yuan.   [B] 20 dollars.   [C] 30 yuan.   [D] 30 dollars.

2. What do we learn from the conversation?

   [A] The man hates to lend his tools to other people.

   [B] The man hasn't finished working on the bookshelf.

   [C] The tools have already been returned to the woman.

   [D] The tools the man borrowed from the woman are missing.

3. What is the probable relationship between the two speakers?

   [A] Teacher and student.   [B] Doctor and patient.

   [C] Manager and office worker.   [D] Travel agent and customer.

4. What are the speakers doing?

   [A] Talking about sports.   [B] Reading newspapers.

   [C] Writing up local news.   [D] Putting up advertisements.

5. What color is the shirt?

   [A] Yellow.   [B] Blue.   [C] Green.   [D] White.

6. When is the train leaving?

   [A] At 10:30.   [B] At 10:40.   [C] At 10:25.   [D] At 10:45.

7. What does woman think Elien should do?

   [A] Move the washing machine to the basement.

   [B] Turn the basement into a workshop.

   [C] Repair the washing machine.

   [D] Finish his assignment.

8. What is Frank planning to do?

   [A] Move to a big city.   [B] Go back to school.

   [C] Become a teacher.   [D] Work in New York.

9. What do we learn about the man?

   [A] He is taking care of his twin brother.

   [B] He has been in his perfect condition.

   [C] He must be feeling ill in his health.

   [D] He is worried about Rod's health.

10. What do we learn from the conversation?

   [A] The woman is watching an exciting film with the man.

   [B] The woman can't take a photo of the man.

   [C] The woman is running toward the lake.

   [D] The woman is filming the lake.

Part B

You are going to hear four passages or conversations. Before listening to each conversation, you will have 5 seconds to read each of the questions which accompany it. After listening, you will have time to answer each question by choosing A, B, C or D. You will hear each passage or conversation ONLY ONCE. Mark your answers in your test booklet.

Questions 11—14 are based on the following passage. You now have 20 seconds to read the questions 11—14.

11. Why did Peter go to the Union Trust bank?

　　[A] To withdraw his deposit.　　　　[B] To cash a cheek.

　　[C] To get his prize.　　　　　　　　[D] To rob the bank.

12. What was Peter's job?

　　[A] A radio announcer.　　　　　　　[B] A bank employee.

　　[C] A car mechanic.　　　　　　　　[D] A movie actor.

13. What did the guards do when Peter started gathering the money?

　　[A] They let him do what he wanted to.　　[B] They called the police.

　　[C] They helped him find large bills.　　　　[D] They pressed the alarm.

14. Why didn't Peter take more money from the bank?

　　[A] He was afraid that be would be caught on the spot.

　　[B] The maximum sum allowed was $5,000.

　　[C] He was limited by time and the size of his pockets.

　　[D] Large bills were not within his reach.

You now have 40 seconds to check your answers to questions 11—14.

Questions 15—18 are based on the following passage. You now have 20 seconds to read the questions 15—18.

15. Why does the speaker say that picking somebody's pocket is an honorable job in southeast London?

　　[A] It takes skill.　　　　　　　　　[B] It's a full-time job.

　　[C] It's admired worldwide.　　　　　[D] It pays well.

16. According to the speaker, who is most likely to become a victim of pickpockets?

　　[A] A woman whose bag is hanging in front.

　　[B] A lone female with a handbag at her right side.

　　[C] An old lady carrying a handbag on the left.

　　[D] A mother with a baby in her arms.

17. In the speaker's opinion, what is the best place for a man to keep his wallets?

　　[A] A side pocket of his jacket.　　　　[B] The top pocket of his jacket.

　　[C] The back pocket of his tight trousers.　　[D] A side pocket of his trousers.

18. What is the perfect setting for picking pockets according to the speaker?

　　[A] Clothing stores where people are relaxed and off guard.

[B] Airports where people carry a lot of luggage.

[C] Hotels and restaurants in southeast London.

[D] Theater lobbies with uniformed security guards.

You now have 40 seconds to check your answers to questions 15—18.

Questions 19—20 are based on the following news report. You now have 10 seconds to read the questions 19—20.

19. Where did the storms first strike?

    [A] The eastern US.   [B] The Gulf of Mexico.

    [C] The Canadian border.   [D] Some areas in Cuba.

20. The storms have resulted in the following EXCEPT _____.

    [A] death and damage   [B] disruption of air services

    [C] destruction of crops   [D] relocation of people

You now have 20 seconds to check your answers to questions 19 — 20.

Questions 21 — 25 are based on the following passage. You now have 25 seconds to read the questions 21—25.

21. What do Tom's parents expect him to be in the future?

    [A] An artist.   [B] A teacher.   [C] A student.   [D] A doctor.

22. Where is Tom studying now?

    [A] In an art school.   [B] In a medical school.

    [C] In a university.   [D] In a high school.

23. What does Tom think of studying medicine?

    [A] It's interesting.   [B] It's too much hard work.

    [C] It's terrible.   [D] It's boring.

24. Which of the following is Tom's wish?

    [A] He can be a doctor.

    [B] He can please both his parents and himself.

    [C] He can study medicine better.

    [D] His parents can help him to be a doctor.

25. Why can't Tom make up his mind to be an artist?

    [A] Because he doesn't want to spend too much of his father's money.

    [B] Because he doesn't know what an art school is.

    [C] Because he isn't sure whether he can support himself.

    [D] Because he can not decide which career to choose.

You now have 50 seconds to check your answers to questions 21—25.

Now you have 3 minutes to transfer your answers from your test booklet to the ANSWER SHEET 1.

That is the end of the listening comprehension section.

Section Ⅱ Use of English

Directions: *Read the following text. Choose the best word or phrase for each numbered blank and mark A, B, C, or D on ANSWER SHEET 1.*

LG Electronics Inc, the world's No. 3 mobile phone handset maker, said on Tuesday that it had __26__ picked to __27__ third-generation (3G) mobile handsets to all three carriers in China. As Chinese operators roll out long-waited advanced mobile services this year, the __28__ for 3G handsets in China was __29__ to more than __30__ to 30 million units in 2010 from 14 million this year, LG said in a statement.

Analysts said South Korean mobile phone __31__ Samsung Electronics Co. Ltd and LG could benefit __32__ China's 3G service launches, as they had technological leads __33__ Chinese companies in making phones __34__ sophisticated 3G features.

The world's top handset maker Nokia is __35__ to focus on the WCDMA network in China, __36__ Korean makers have been selling phones for different standards __37__ home and __38__.

LG, which trails Nokia and Samsung, said it was named __39__ a supplier to China Mobile, the world's largest mobile carrier by subscribers, __40__ is set to offer 3G mobile service using the nation's homegrown TD-SCDMA technology. Few handsets for the TD-SCDMA network __41__ available from international brands.

"LG has so far had weak sales in China due __42__ its low coverage of distribution networks there. Direct __43__ to supply major operators mean that its business model is changing," said Harrison Cho, an analyst at Mirae Asset Securities, "but as for __44__ fast the Chinese 3G market will __45__, uncertainties remain."

26. [A] being   [B] been   [C] to be   [D] be
27. [A] supply   [B] offer   [C] support   [D] distribute
28. [A] order   [B] demand   [C] market   [D] need
29. [A] calculated   [B] added   [C] increased   [D] estimated
30. [A] double   [B] twice times   [C] triple   [D] three times
31. [A] leaders   [B] makers   [C] creators   [D] investors
32. [A] from   [B] to   [C] at   [D] over
33. [A] ahead   [B] towards   [C] over   [D] against
34. [A] with   [B] from   [C] of   [D] by
35. [A] hopeful   [B] likely   [C] possible   [D] perhaps
36. [A] though   [B] and   [C] when   [D] while
37. [A] at   [B] from   [C] in   [D] inside

38. [A] board   [B] board   [C] abroad   [D] away

39. [A] for   [B] as   [C] be   [D] being

40. [A] whom   [B] as   [C] who   [D] which

41. [A] are   [B] is   [C] were   [D] was

42. [A] towards   [B] for   [C] to   [D] of

43. [A] deals   [B] deal   [C] order   [D] demands

44. [A] whatever   [B] how many   [C] what   [D] how

45. [A] increase   [B] bring   [C] improve   [D] grow

Section Ⅲ   Reading Comprehension

Part A

Directions: *Read the following three texts. Answer the questions on each text by choosing A, B, C or D. Mark your answers on ANSWER SHEET 1.*

Text 1

Are you happy? Do you remember a time when you were happy? Are you seeking happiness today?

Many have sought a variety of sources for their feeling of happiness. Some have put their heart and efforts into their work. Too many turned to drugs and alcohol. Meanwhile, untold numbers have looked for it in the possession of expensive cars, exotic vacation homes and other popular "toys". Most of their efforts have a root in one common fact: people are looking for a lasting source of happiness.

Unfortunately, I believe that happiness escapes from many people because they misunderstand the journey of finding it. I have heard many people say that, "I'll be happy when I get my new promotion," or "I'll be happy when I get that extra 20 pounds." It is dangerous because it accepts that happiness is a "response" to having, being or doing something.

In life, we all experience stimulus and response. Today, some people think that an expensive car is stimulus. Happiness is a response. A great paying job is stimulus. Happiness is a response. This belief leaves us thinking and feeling: "I'll be happy when ..."

It has been my finding that actually the opposite is true. I believe that happiness is a stimulus and response is what life brings to those who are truly happy. When we are happy, we tend to have more success in our work. When we are happy, we more naturally take better care of our bodies and enjoy good health. Happiness is not a response but a stimulus.

Happiness is a conscious choice we make in daily life. For unknown reasons to me, many choose to be upset and angry most of the time. Happiness is not something that happens to us after we get something we want — we usually get things we want after we choose to be happy.

46. From the second paragraph, we know too many people _____.

[A] are not happy when they work hard

[B] are not happy when they drink or take drugs

[C] all desire exotic vacation homes

[D] are happy when they possess their own expensive cars

47. Generally speaking, most people feel happy because _____.

[A] they think happiness is rooted in their deep hearts

[B] they get what they want to have

[C] they get a long vacation

[D] they get a great paying job

48. In the author's opinion, which of the following is the most important if you want to be happy?

[A] Losing weight. [B] An expensive car.

[C] Success in work. [D] Feeling happy.

49. Which of the following is right according to the author?

[A] If you want to get what you want, you first choose to be happy.

[B] Most people today are happy.

[C] Work is a necessary part in our daily life.

[D] We should try to get more and then we'll be happy.

50. From the viewpoint of the author, happiness is _____.

[A] limited [B] out of reach

[C] unconditional [D] based on our needs

Text 2

Some futurologists have assumed that the vast upsurge of women in the workforce may portend a rejection of marriage. Many women, according to this hypothesis, would rather work than marry. The converse of this concern is that the prospects of becoming a multi-paycheck household could encourage marriage. In the past, only the earnings and financial prospects of the man counted in the marriage decision. Now, however, the earning ability of a woman can make her more attractive as a marriage partner. Data show that economic downturns tend to putting off marriage because the parties cannot afford to establish a family or are concerned about rainy days ahead. As the economy comes to life, the number of marriages also rises.

The increase in divorce rates follows to the increase in women working outside the home. Yet, it may be wrong to jump to any simple cause-and-effect conclusions. The impact of a wife's work on divorce is no less cloudy than its impact on marriage decisions. The realization that she can be a good provider may increase the chances that a working wife will choose divorce over an unsatisfactory marriage. But the reverse is equally plausible(似是而非

的). Tensions grounded in financial problems often play a key role in ending a marriage. By raising a family's standard of living, a working wife may strengthen her family's financial and emotional stability.

Psychological factors also should be considered. For example, a wife blocked from a career outside the home may feel caged in the house. She may view her only choice as seeking a divorce. On the other hand, if she can find fulfillment through work outside the home, work and marriage can go together to create a stronger and more stable union.

Also, a major part of women's inequality in marriage has been due to the fact that, in most cases, men have remained the main breadwinners. A working wife may rob a husband of being the master of the house. Depending upon how the couple reacts to these new conditions, it could create a stronger equal partnership or it could create new insecurities.

51. The word "portend" in the first sentence of the passage is closest in meaning to "_____".

    [A] signal   [B] defy   [C] suffer from   [D] result from

52. It is said in the passage that when the economy slides _____.

    [A] men would choose working women as their marriage partners

    [B] more women would get married to seek financial security

    [C] even working women would worry about their marriages

    [D] more people would prefer to remain single for the time being

53. If women find fulfillment through work outside the home, _____.

    [A] they are more likely to dominate their marriage partners

    [B] their husbands are expected to do more housework

    [C] their marriage ties can be strengthened

    [D] they tend to put their career before marriage

54. One reason why women with no career may seek a divorce is that _____.

    [A] they feel that they have been robbed of their freedom

    [B] they are afraid of being bossed around by their husbands

    [C] they feel that their partners fail to live up to their expectations

    [D] they tend to suspect their husbands' loyalty to their marriage

55. Which of the following statements can best summarize the author's view in the passage?

    [A] The stability of marriage and the divorce rate may reflect the economic situation of the country.

    [B] Even when economically independent, most women have to struggle for real equality in marriage.

    [C] In order to secure their marriage women should work outside the home and remain independent.

    [D] The impact of the growing female workforce on marriage varies from case to case.

Text 3

American society reports many negative messages about bicycling in traffic. Bicycling in traffic is considered by many to be reckless, foolhardy, and sometimes rude. The most common advice given to cyclists is to avoid busy roads that provide convenient access to important places; presumably cyclists should only go to unpopular destinations on undesirable and inconvenient roads. Another popular idea is that cyclists should stay as close to the edge of the road as possible in order to stay out of the way of cars. Getting in the way of cars is supposedly an invitation to certain death, because car drivers are often expected to run into anything that is slower or more vulnerable. The rules of the road that apply to bicyclists are considered to be of no use because they involve mixed with motor traffic, which is thought to be suicide. Roads are believed to be designed for cars and not for bicycles, which are tolerated at the pleasure of motorists, who really own the roads. Inferior bicyclists may have an obsolete legal right to use the road, but they had better stay out of the way of superior users or they will be "dead right".

As a result of these "common-sense" beliefs, American bike-safety programs developed by motoring organizations and "pedestrian-style" bicyclists during the twentieth century attempted to teach cyclists to provide a clear path to motorists at all times by hugging the edge of the road, riding on sidewalks where present, and even riding facing traffic so cyclists can see when to get out of the way. Some towns and states tried to prohibit bicyclists from operating on important roads or roads without shoulders. Engineering projects designed for "bicycle safety" have usually involved construction of mandatory side paths to get cyclists off of roads and mandatory bike lanes to keep cyclists out of the way of motorists. The publicized benefit of these efforts is to protect cyclists from collisions from behind, which are widely believed to be the greatest danger to cyclists and caused by cyclists' failure to keep up with the desired speed of motor traffic. This is the taboo that afflicts American bicycle transportation policy: that bicyclists must be kept out of the paths of motorists or they will surely be killed.

56. In many people's eyes, bicycling should be _____.

　[A] supported　　　[B] banned　　　[C] controlled　　　[D] cancelled

57. From the first paragraph, the person riding a bicycle in the city should take _____.

　[A] main roads　　[B] streets　　　[C] highways　　[D] sidewalks

58. Why do many people not agree that people should ride on roads?

　[A] Roads are for cars not for cyclists.

　[B] People riding bicycles are considered superior.

　[C] People's riding on the road is against the law.

　[D] People riding bicycles are not experienced.

59. The underlined phrase "cyclists' failure to keep up with the desired speed of motor traffic" in the second paragraph means _____.

　[A] cyclists' speed is beyond the limit

[B] cyclists' speed is much lower than that of motorists' and they easily get hurt

[C] cyclists often compete with motorists on the roads

[D] motorists usually look down upon cyclists.

60. The measures taken by government in some states in the second paragraph are for the purpose of _____.

[A] protecting people's convenience

[B] protecting the cars and motors

[C] protecting cyclists' safety

[D] protecting the flowing of the traffic

Part B

Directions: *Read the texts from an article in which five people talked about the Swine flu. For questions 61 to 65, match the name of each person (61 to 65) to one of the statements (A to G) given below. Mark your answers on ANSWER SHEET 1.*

Slater

Swine influenza (also called swine flu, hog flu, and pig flu) refers to influenza caused by those strains of influenza virus, called swine influenza virus (SIV), that usually infect pigs. Swine influenza is common in pigs in the Midwestern United States (and occasionally in other states), Mexico, Canada, South America, Europe (including the United Kingdom, Sweden, and Italy), Kenya, Mainland China, Taiwan, Japan and other parts of eastern Asia.

Mike Smith

Transmission of swine influenza virus from pigs to humans is not common and properly cooked pork poses no risk of infection. When transmission results in influenza in a human, it is called zoonotic swine flu. People who work with pigs, especially people with intense exposures, are at risk of catching swine flu. Rarely, these strains of swine flu can pass from human to human. In humans, the symptoms of swine flu are similar to those of influenza and of influenza-like illness in general, namely chills, fever, sore throat, muscle pains, severe headache, coughing, weakness and general discomfort.

Baker

The 2009 flu outbreak in humans, known as "swine flu", is due to a new strain of influenza A virus subtype H1N1 that contained genes most closely related to swine influenza. The origin of this new strain is unknown, however, and the World Organization for Animal Health (OIE) reports that this strain has not been isolated in pigs. This strain can be transmitted from human to human, and causes the normal symptoms of influenza.

Bob David

If a person becomes sick with swine flu, antiviral drugs can make the illness milder and make the patient feel better faster. They may also prevent serious flu complications. For treatment, antiviral drugs work best if started soon after getting sic (within 2 days of symptoms). Beside antivirals, palliative care, at home or in hospital, focuses on controlling fevers and maintaining fluid balance. However, the majority of people infected with the virus make a full recovery without requiring medical attention or antiviral drugs.

Tom Brown

In the US, on April 27, 2009, the FDA issued Emergency Use Authorizations to make available Relenza and Tamiflu antiviral drugs to treat the swine influenza virus in cases for which they are currently unapproved. The agency issued these EUAs to allow treatment of patients younger than the current approval allows and to allow the widespread distribution of the drugs, including by non-licensed volunteers.

Now match each of the persons to the appropriate statement.

Note: there are two extra statements.

Statements

61. Slater

[A] Swine influenza is common in pigs all over United States, Mexico, Canada, South Africa,, Europe, Kenya, Mainland China, Taiwan, Japan and other parts of eastern Asia.

62. Mike Smith

[B] It is risky for people intensively exposed to the work with pigs.

63. Baker

[C] The origin of the new strain of influenza A virus subtype H1N1 is unknown yet.

64. Bob David

[D] Transmission of swine influenza virus from pigs to humans is very common.

65. Tom Brown

[E] Some drugs are still unapproved to treat the swine influenza virus.

[F] Antiviral drugs work best to the patients within 2 days of symptoms.

[G] A brief introduction of Swine influenza.

Section IV   Writing

Directions: *You should write your responses to both Part A and Part B of this section on ANSWER SHEET 2.*

Part A

You are supposed to give a play with your partners tomorrow morning. But you haven't got time to prepare the scripts, not to mention to act in advance. You are writing to your teacher Professor Li to make an apology and ask if it can be postponed to next Wednesday.

You should write approximately 100 words. Do not sign your own name at the end of your letter. Use "James" instead. You do not need to write the address.

Part B

Below is a cartoon showing the difficulty to look for a job under the financial crisis. Look at the cartoon and write an essay of about 120 words making reference to the following

points:
1. describe the cartoon;
2. your comments.

专家预测试题（二）

Section Ⅰ　Listening Comprehension

Directions: *This section is designed to test your ability to understand spoken English. You will hear a selection of recorded materials and you must answer the questions that accompany them. There are two parts in this section, Part A and Part B.*

Remember, while you are doing the test, you should first put down your answers in your test booklet. At the end of the listening comprehension section, you will have 3 minutes to transfer your answers from your test booklet onto your ANSWER SHEET 1.

If you have any questions, you may raise your hand NOW as you will not be allowed to speak once the test has started.

Now look at Part A in your test booklet.

Part A

You will hear 10 short dialogues. For each dialogue, there is one question and four possible answers. Choose the correct answer A, B, C or D, and mark it in your test booklet. You will have 15 seconds to answer the question and you will hear each dialogue ONLY ONCE.

Example:

You will hear:

W: Could you please tell me if the Beijing flight will be arriving on time?

M: Yes, Madam. It should be arriving in about ten minutes.

You will read:

Who do you think the woman is talking to?

[A] A bus conductor. 　　　　[B] A clerk at the airport.

[C] A taxi driver. 　　　　　[D] A clerk at the station.

From the dialogue, we know that only a clerk at the airport is most likely to know the arrival time of a flight, so you should choose answer 　[B] and mark it in your test booklet.

Sample Answer: [A] ■ [C] [D]

Now look at question 1.

1. What did the man win in his dream?

[A] A holiday. 　　　　　[B] A new car.

[C] Some money. 　　　　[D] A desert.

2. Will the woman come to the party?

    [A] Maybe.   [B] Yes, she will.

    [C] Yes, certainly.   [D] No, she will not.

3. How long has the woman been an author?

    [A] About 30 years.   [B] About 40 years.

    [C] About 60 years.   [D] About 70 years.

4. What does the woman want?

    [A] A radio.   [B] Some pens.   [C] Some radios.   [D] Some batteries.

5. What is the woman doing?

    [A] Asking for information.   [B] Asking for an apology.

    [C] Asking for help.   [D] Asking for a taxi.

6. When does this conversation take place?

    [A] At 5:00.   [B] At 5:15.   [C] At 4:45.   [D] At 4:15.

7. What can we learn about the man's enperiment?

    [A] It is going on well.   [B] It has failed several times.

    [C] It will soon be finished.   [D] It may have to be stopped.

8. How long will the man stay in this hotel?

    [A] Just one month.   [B] 32 days.

    [C] 33 days.   [D] 34 days.

9. Where does this conversation take place?

    [A] In a post office.   [B] In a hotel.

    [C] In a bank   [D] In a school.

10. What do we know about Tom's secretary?

    [A] She's not efficient.   [B] She's often late.

    [C] She's capable.   [D] She's honest.

Part B

You are going to hear four passages or conversations. Before listening to each conversation, you will have 5 seconds to read each of the questions which accompany it. After listening, you will have time to answer each question by choosing A, B, C or D. You will hear each passage or conversation ONLY ONCE. Mark your answers in your test booklet.

Questions 11—14 are based on the following passage. You now have 20 seconds to read the questions 11—14.

11. What is the main topic of this talk?

    [A] Television's effects on the movie industry.

    [B] The relationships between different media.

    [C] Radio news as a substitute for newspapers.

    [D] The role of print media.

12. According to the speaker, what is the relationship between radio and the newspaper industry?

    [A] People who listen to the radio also buy newspapers.

    [B] Radio is a substitute for newspapers in the radio industry.

    [C] Newspapers discourage people from listening to the radio.

    [D] Many newspaper reporters also work in the radio industry.

13. According to the speaker, how did the introduction of television affect motion pictures?

    [A] Movie attendence increased due to advertising on television.

    [B] Old motion pictures were often broadcast on television.

    [C] Television had no effect on movie attendance.

    [D] Motion picture popularity declined.

14. Why does the speaker mention a football game?

    [A] To illustrate another effect of television.

    [B] To demonstrate the importance of televised sports.

    [C] To explain what television replaced radio broadcasting.

    [D] To provide an example of something motion pictures can't present.

You now have 40 seconds to check your answers to questions 11—14.

Questions 15—18 are based on the following conversation. You now have 20 seconds to read the questions 15—18.

15. What do we learn from the conversation about Miss Rowling's first book?

    [A] It was about a little animal.

    [B] It took her six years to write.

    [C] It was adapted from a fairy tale.

    [D] It was about a little girl and her pet.

16. Why does Miss Rowling consider her so very lucky?

    [A] She knows how to write best-selling novels.

    [B] She can earn a lot of money by writing for adults.

    [C] She is able to win enough support from publishers.

    [D] She can make a living by doing what she likes.

17. What dictates Miss Rowling's writing?

    [A] The characters.　　　　　　　　[B] Her ideas.

    [C] The readers.　　　　　　　　　[D] Her life experiences.

18. According to Miss Rowling where did she get the ideas for the *Harry Porter* books?

    [A] She doesn't really know where they originated.

    [B] She mainly drew on stories of ancient saints.

    [C] They popped out of her childhood dreams.

    [D] They grew out of her long hours of thinking.

You now have 40 seconds to check your answers to questions 15—18.

Questions 19—22 are based on the following news report. You now have 20 seconds to read the questions 19—22.

19. What does the passage say about the secondhand smoke?

    [A] It threatens public health.

    [B] It gets more serious in the United States.

    [C] It is more dangerous than AIDS.

    [D] It is a topic of public debate.

20. What can be inferred from the passage?

    [A] If the parents are somkers, infants may suffer from breathing problems.

    [B] If the parents are smokers, their children will die.

    [C] If the parents are smokers, their children may have a fast lung growth.

    [D] If the parents give up smoking, their children will recover from lung diseases.

21. What is the estimated number of adults killed by secondhand smoke each year in the United States?

    [A] 40,000.   [B] 50,000.   [C] 430.   [D] 15,000.

22. Which of the following is NOT a solution to preventing the harm of secondhand smoke?

    [A] We should stay away from smokers.

    [B] We should clean the air in buildings.

    [C] We should establish smoke-free area.

    [D] We should lay a ban on tobacco production.

You now have 40 seconds to check your answers to questions 19 — 22.

Questions 23 — 25 are based on the following passage. You now have 15 seconds to read the questions 23 — 25.

23. According to the passage, which of the following is uncommon in the US?

    [A] A policeman questions a person who is just taking a walk.

    [B] A dog pursues a person who walks past a house.

    [C] A road that does not have any sidewalk.

    [D] A person takes a walk just for pleasure.

24. Why do cars need to travel slowly along some suburban roads in the US?

    [A] Because children brought up in the suburbs are not accustomed to walking in busy streets.

    [B] Because there are no traffic lights in streets in the suburbs.

    [C] Because some suburban roads are so bad.

    [D] Because some suburban roads are very narrow.

25. Where is the passage most probably taken from?

    [A] A fiction book.   [B] A history book.

    [C] A book on American culture.   [D] A book on political science.

You now have 30 seconds to check your answers to questions 23 — 25.

Now you have 3 minutes to transfer your answers from your test booklet to the AN-SWER SHEET 1.

That is the end of the listening comprehension section.

Section II   Use of English

Directions: *Read the following text. Choose the best word or phrase for each numbered blank and mark A, B, C, or D on ANSWER SHEET 1.*

From childhood to old age, we all use language as a means of broadening our knowledge of ourselves and the world about us. When humans first ___26___, they were like newborn children, unable to use this ___27___ tool. Yet once language developed, the possibilities for mankind's future ___28___ and cultural growth increased.

Many linguists believe that evolution is ___29___ for our ability to produce and use language. They ___30___ that our highly evolved brain provides us ___31___ an innate language ability not found in lower ___32___. Proponents of this innateness theory say that our ___33___ for language is inborn, but that language itself develops gradually, ___34___ a function of the growth of the brain during childhood. Therefore there are critical ___35___ times for language development.

Current ___36___ of innateness theory are mixed; however, evidence supporting the existence of some innate abilities is undeniable. ___37___, more and more schools are discovering that foreign languages are best taught in ___38___ grades. Young children often can learn several languages by being ___39___ to them, while adults have a much harder time learning another language once the ___40___ of their first language have become firmly fixed.

___41___ some aspects of language are undeniably innate, language does not develop automatically in a vacuum. Children who have been ___42___ from other human beings do not possess language. This demonstrates that ___43___ with other human beings is necessary for proper language development. Some linguists believe that this is even more basic to human language ___44___ than any innate capacities. These theorists view language as imitative, learned behavior. ___45___, children learn language from their parents by imitating them. Parents gradually shape their child's language skills by positively reinforcing precise imitations and negatively reinforcing imprecise ones.

26. [A] generated   [B] evolved   [C] born   [D] originated

27. [A] valuable   [B] appropriate   [C] convenient   [D] favorite

28. [A] attainments   [B] feasibility   [C] entertainments   [D] evolution

29. [A] essential   [B] available   [C] reliable   [D] responsible

30. [A] confirm   [B] inform   [C] claim   [D] convince

31. [A] for   [B] from   [C] of   [D] with

32. [A] organizations [B] organisms   [C] humans   [D] children

33. [A] potential   [B] performance   [C] preference   [D] passion

34. [A] as   [B] just as   [C] like   [D] unlike

35. [A] ideological   [B] biological   [C] social   [D] psychological

36. [A] reviews   [B] references   [C] reactions   [D] recommendations

37. [A] In a word   [B] In a sense   [C] Indeed   [D] In other words

38. [A] various   [B] different   [C] the higher   [D] the lower

39. [A] revealed   [B] exposed   [C] engaged   [D] involved

40. [A] regulations   [B] formations   [C] rules   [D] constitutions

41. [A] Although   [B] Whether   [C] Since   [D] When

42. [A] distinguished   [B] different   [C] protected   [D] isolated

43. [A] exposition   [B] comparison   [C] contrast   [D] interaction

44. [A] acquisition   [B] appreciation   [C] requirement   [D] alternative

45. [A] As a result   [B] After all   [C] In other words [D] Above all

Section III   Reading Comprehension

Part A

Directions: *Read the following three texts. Answer the questions on each text by choosing A, B, C or D. Mark your answers on the ANSWER SHEET 1.*

Text 1

Americans are getting ready for the biggest soccer event in the world. For the first time the world cup soccer competition will be held in the United States. While millions play the game around the world, soccer or football has only recently become popular here. It is only in the last 30 years that large numbers of young Americans became interested in soccer. Now it is the fastest growing sport in the country. A recent study found that almost 8 million young boys and girls play soccer in the United States.

The study has also found that soccer is beginning to replace more traditional games like American football as the most popular sport among students. And so, when the world cup begins next week, more than one million Americans are expected to go and see the teams play. Organizers say this year's world cup will be the biggest ever. All the seats at most of the 52 games have already been sold.

Soccer has been played in the United States for a little more than one hundred years. But how did the sport come to this country? And how long has it existed in other parts of the world? No one knows exactly where the idea for soccer came from, or when people began playing the game. Some scientists say there is evidence that ball games using the feet were played thousands of years ago. There is evidence that ancient Greeks and Romans and native American Indians all played games similar to soccer.

Most experts agree that Britain is the birthplace of modern soccer. They also agree that the British spread the game around the world. Unlike the game today, which uses balls of man-made material or leather, early soccer balls were often made of animal stomachs. The rules of early soccer games also differed from those we have today.

46. Which of the following statements is NOT true according to the text?

[A] Americans were preparing for the world cup when the author wrote this article.

[B] More and younger Americans became interested in soccer in the last 30 years.

[C] Soccer is the fastest developing sport in the world.

[D] The article was written before the world cup held in the United States.

47. Which was the most popular sport as a traditional game among students?

[A] Basketball.   [B] American football.

[C] Soccer.   [D] Tennis.

48. For how long has soccer been played in the United States?

[A] About a hundred years.   [B] About fifty years.

[C] Only recently.   [D] About thirty years.

49. Who invented the modern soccer game?

[A] American Indians.   [B] The British.

[C] The Greeks.   [D] The Romans.

50. What is the author going to state in the next paragraph?

[A] There have been attempts to start a professional soccer organization in the US.

[B] In the 12th century soccer games in Britain often involved whole towns.

[C] Professional soccer grew quickly in Europe.

[D] Experts believed that the United States would win.

Text 2

The campaign is over. The celebrations have ended. And the work for US president-elect Barrack Obama has begun.

The 47-year-old politician rose to the highest post because of his stand against the war in Iraq and his plans to fix a weak economy. But what will the first 47-year-old African-American president do for race relations?

Obama's victory appears to have given blacks and other minorities a true national role model. For years, many looked to athletes and musicians for inspiration. As Darius Turner, an African-American high school student in Los Angeles, told *The Los Angeles Times*, "Kobe doesn't have to be everybody's role model any more."

Recent polls also suggest that Obama's victory has given Americans new optimism about race relations. For example, a *USA Today* poll found that two-thirds of Americans believe relations between blacks and whites "will finally be worked out". This is the most hopeful response since the question was first asked during the civil rights revolution in 1963.

However, it's still too early to tell whether Obama's presidency will begin to solve many of the social problems facing low-income black communities.

Although blacks make up only 13 percent of the US population, 55 percent of all prisoners are African-American. Such numbers can be blamed on any number of factors on America's racist past, a failure of government policy and the collapse of the family unit in black communities.

It is unlikely that Obama will be able to reverse such trends overnight. However, Bill Bank, an expert of African-American Studies, says that eventually young blacks need to find role models in their own communities. "That's not Martin Luther King, and not Barack Obama," he told *The Los Angeles Times*. "It's actually the people closest to them. Barack only has so much influence."

In the opinion of black British politician Trevor Phillips, Obama's rise will contribute more to multiculturalism than to race relations in the US.

"When the G8 meets, the four most important people in the room will be the president of China, the prime minister of India, the prime minister of Japan and Barrack Obama," he told London's *The Times* newspaper. "It will be the first time we've seen that on our television screens. That will be a huge psychological shift(心理转变) for both the white people and the colored ones in the world."

51. For years, before Obama was elected president of the US, _____.
[A] Kobe was the only role model for all the blacks
[B] blacks could only find role models on the basketball court
[C] minorities in America couldn't find role models in their real life
[D] American blacks had no role model who was successful in the political field

52. According to Bill Bank, _____.
[A] it's better for young blacks to find role models in those who are close to them
[B] young blacks should not be so much influenced by Obama
[C] blacks should find other role models because Obama is far from their reality
[D] Obama is not the proper role model for African-Americans

53. What does "work out" (in paragraph 4) probably mean?
[A] work outside the house   [B] help have a clear explanation
[C] solve the problem   [D] train their ability

54. What would be the best title for this passage?
[A] The First African-American President   [B] America's New Role Model
[C] Obama—A Successful Black   [D] Choosing a Right Role Model

55. What will be the huge psychological shift Trevor mentioned at the end of the passage?
[A] The other three leaders all support Obama.
[B] Obama is an African-American president.
[C] None of the four leaders is white.
[D] The other three leaders except Obama are from Asian countries.

Text 3

The research carried out by the University of Bari in Italy could help prove hospitals who are accused of wasting money on art and decoration as it suggests a pleasant environment helps patients ease discomfort and pain.

A team headed by Professor Marina de Tommaso at the Neurophysiopathology Pain Unit asked a group of men and women to pick the 20 paintings they considered most ugly and most beautiful from a selection of 300 works by artists such as Leonardo da Vinci and Sandro Botticelli. They were then asked to look at either the beautiful paintings, or the ugly painting, or a blank panel while the team zapped a short laser pulse at their hand, creating a sensation as if they had been stuck by a pin. The subjects rated the pain as being a third less intense while they were viewing the beautiful paintings, compared with when looking at the ugly paintings or the blank panel. Electrodes measuring the brain's electrical activity also confirmed a reduced response to the pain when the subject looked at beautiful paintings.

While distractions, such as music, are known to reduce pain in hospital patients, Prof de Tommaso says this is the first result to show that beauty plays a part.

The findings, reported in New Scientist, also go a long way to show that beautiful surroundings could aid the healing process.

"Hospitals have been designed to be functional, but we think that their artistic aspects should be taken into account too," said the neurologist. "Beauty obviously offers a distraction that ugly paintings do not. But at least there is no suggestion that ugly surroundings make the pain worse. " "I think these results show that more research is needed into the field how a beautiful environment can alleviate suffering."

Pictures they liked included Starry Night by Vincent Van Gogh and Botticellis Birth of Venus. Pictures they found ugly included works by Pablo Picasso, the Italian 20th century artist Anonio Bueno and Columbian Fernando Botero. "These people were not art experts so some of the pictures they found ugly would be considered masterpieces by the art world," said Prof de Tommaso.

56. The underlined word "alleviate" in the fifth paragraph probably means "_____".

　　[A] cure　　　[B] ease　　　[C] improve　　　[D] kill

57. How many artists have been mentioned in the passage?

　　[A] 4.　　　[B] 5.　　　[C] 6.　　　[D] 7.

58. Which of the following is TURE about the view of Prof de Tommaso's?

　　[A] Beautiful surroundings could help to heal sufferings completely.

　　[B] Hospitals must take their artistic aspects into consideration first.

　　[C] Ugly surroundings will surely make the pain worse.

　　[D] Both music and beauty can reduce pain in hospital patients.

59. From the last paragraph, we know that _____.

    [A] some artists' paintings were beautiful, so they were masterpieces

    [B] only art experts could judge they were masterpieces or not, though ugly

    [C] the artists mentioned above were not really art masters.

    [D] some of them were art masters, while others were not.

60. Which of the following is the suitable title for the passage?

    [A] Beautiful Surroundings Can Ease Pain.

    [B] Ugly Paintings Could Be Masterpieces.

    [C] More Research Should Be Done In the Field.

    [D] Latest Environmental Research.

Part B

Directions: *Read the texts from an article in which five people talked about their view of time allotment. For questions 61 to 65, match the name of each person (61 to 65) to one of the statements (A to G) given below. Mark your answers on ANSWER SHEET 1.*

Netasha

The recent university students among you may have had a culture shock: with no parents peering over your shoulder to check on homework and no teachers looming with threats of detention, independence reigns. As such, the temptation to give in to the power of procrastination when you should be working is suddenly very strong! Procrastination takes many forms. Things like checking if you have any unread emails. Perhaps seeing if you have any new text messages. Then, with mobile in hand, taking the time to change the ringtone, just before phoning a friend to tell them about your new ringtone. When they tell you that they haven't finished their essay either, it's time to go and make a cup of tea, do the washing up and make a sandwich.

Shaikh

Once you've put an essay, project, or revision stint off until the very last minute, you then have the strenuous task of completing it under pressure, which makes it seem deceptively difficult. As a result, the next time you have to knuckle down you remember it as being something horrendous, so you put it off again—and so it goes on.

Mark

Resist the temptation. Even if your chosen distraction isn't utterly pointless, remember that you would have much more fun doing it if you got the most pressing burden of what you're supposed to be doing out of the way first. So, be paradoxical and put off procrastination!

Thomas

The prospect of sitting down and doing nothing but write an essay for a few hours straight can be daunting enough to stop you doing it at all. So, make it more achievable by breaking it down. If it's a 2,000 word essay, reward yourself by taking a half-hour break after you've reached 500 words. Make sure your target is one of quantity rather than time, though: if you tell yourself you'll take a break after an hour of work, you could spend the entire hour producing three sentences then gleefully skip off. Also, keep said break to half an hour: if you use it to watch an episode of your favorite show, make sure you don't end up watching the entire box-set.

Peter

"Nothing is so fatiguing as the eternal hanging on of an uncompleted task"—so goes the quote from late American psychologist William James, and he has a point. Once you've triumphed over that elusive essay or properly prepared for your exam, you'll feel much better with yourself. You may even find that the prospect of rearranging your socks has suddenly lost its allure (strangely enough), giving you the opportunity to get out there and do something exciting with your time!

Now match each of the people (61 to 65) to the appropriate statement.

Note: There are two extra statements.

Statements

61. Netasha
62. Shaikh
63. Mark
64. Thomas
65. Peter

[A] While doing an essay, we should make it more achievable by breaking it down.

[B] We should only pay attention to the quality and forget about the time.

[C] If we get the most pressing burden of what we're supposed to be doing out of the way first, we can easily have fun.

[D] Nothing is so fatiguing as the eternal hanging on of an uncompleted task.

[E] Things like checking if you have any unread emails or perhaps seeing if you have any new text messages are the typical forms of "Procrastination".

[F] Once you've put an essay, project, or revision stint off, you will be likely to put it off again.

[G] If you tell yourself you'll take a break after an hour of work, you will definitely spend the entire hour working efficiently, then go to enjoy your free time.

Section Ⅳ   Writing

Directions: *You should write your responses to both Part A and Part B of this section on ANSWER SHEET 2.*

Part A

Suppose you are the monitor of the class and your oral English teacher Professor Yang asked you to borrow a digital card to turn on the computer in Room 201 next Monday so that your class could watch movie there. Unfortunately, Room 201 won't be available for you. You are writing to tell him about that and ask him whether Room 203 would be okay.

You should write approximately 100 words. Do not sign your own name at the end of your letter. Use "David" instead. You do not need to write the address.

Part B

Below are three pictures showing the changes taken place in writing letters between 1978 and 2008. Look at the pictures and write an essay of about 120 words making reference to the following points:

1. A description of the pictures.
2. Your feelings about it.

爷爷写信找人帮

爸爸写信自己忙

儿子写信最夸张

第4章 历年真题

2008年9月全国英语等级考试真题

Section I Listening Comprehension

1—25(略)

Section II Use of English

Directions: *Read the following text. Choose the best word or phrase for each numbered blank and mark A,B,C or D on ANSWER SHEET 1.*

A webcam is a digital camera that sends video images to other computer users. It's about the __26__ of a golf ball and typically __27__ on top of your computer monitor. Once the webcam is __28__ to the USB port of your computer with the necessary software, __29__ images of you can be sent to one or more users over the Internet __30__ an instant messaging(IM) service.

A webcam costs about $50. More expensive models come with added __31__, such as better picture resolution. Two leading makers, Logitech and Creative, offer a range of models, __32__ software is included. There is no extra Internet __33__ to send or receive video images, though you'll have to __34__ for a free instant messaging service. Everyone can see and hear one another in __35__ time. Grandparents can see their grandkids more __36__. Webcams can work with almost any computer bought in the past five years and can __37__ long distance phone bills.

__38__ you have broadband, that is, a high-speed cable-modem or DSL connection, images may __39__ a long time to download, __40__ a slide show rather than a movie. While webcams are easy to link to your computer, learning to __41__ the software can take time. You have to make some rearrangement with the configurations.

__42__ you have a 56k modem and the people you want to __43__ won't mind seeing live shots instead of perfect video, a webcam is still fun, __44__ before you buy, be sure everyone, __45__ for the same IM service.

26. [A] weight   [B] size   [C] volume   [D] space
27. [A] rests   [B] remains   [C] stays   [D] sits

28. [A] joined [B] attached [C] connected [D] fastened

29. [A] live [B] living [C] lively [D] lovely

30. [A] via [B] with [C] from [D] in

31. [A] devices [B] features [C] designs [D] attachments

32. [A] so [B] but [C] for [D] and

33. [A] limit [B] charge [C] registration [D] rate

34. [A] check in [B] log in [C] sign up [D] draw up

35. [A] true [B] actual [C] genuine [D] real

36. [A] recently [B] frequently [C] realistically [D] immediately

37. [A] reduce [B] reform [C] remove [D] retain

38. [A] Although [B] Because [C] Unless [D] Whereas

39. [A] waste [B] have [C] spend [D] take

40. [A] resembled [B] resembling [C] to resemble [D] resemble

41. [A] use [B] write [C] download [D] fix

42. [A] because [B] though [C] if [D] unless

43. [A] reach [B] touch [C] know [D] show

44. [A] nevertheless [B] so [C] besides [D] but

45. [A] register [B] pays [C] seeks [D] asks

Section Ⅲ   Reading Comprehension

Part A

Directions: *Read the following three texts. Answer the questions on each text by choosing A, B,C or D. Mark your answers on ANSWER SHEET 1.*

Text 1

A former town hall worker made legal history last week when she was awarded 67,000 pounds for stress brought on by her work. The ruling made Beverley Lancaster the first person to get their employer to accept legal responsibility for stress-related personal injury in a British court. It is likely to start a flood of other worker's claims; Mrs. Lancaster's union already has 7,000 stress-related cases on its books.

The 44-year-old mother of two started a legal case against Birmingham City Council after falling ill while working as a troubleshooter in a neighborhood housing office. Dealing with rude and abusive members of the public pushed her into periods of gloom and she suffered anxiety, Birmingham county court heard. Mrs. Lancaster joined the council at 16, working her way up from junior clerk to senior draughtswoman. Her problems began when she was promoted to housing officer in Sutton Oldfield. "With no continuity, a constant high workload and little clerical support, I found it difficult to switch from one problem or situation to another," she said. "My concentration swung and I suffered sleepless nights. It made me feel like I was in a hole with no key to open the door. I would break down in tears. I was being in paperwork and at times my mind would just go blank."

In awarding compensation of 67,491 pounds, assistant recorder Frances Kirkham said she understood the position of troubleshooter was very different from Mrs. Lancaster's precious job. She rejected claims from the council that Mrs. Lancaster would be able to go back to her former profession, saying she accepted that the possibility of future work would be less capacity.

After the hearing Mrs. Lancaster said she was relieved and pleased. She added, "I hope this will act as a warning to employers. Everything I did was right. The council made promises to me and they failed me. I felt isolated, let down, that I was not good enough, not wanted." The payout, the first of its kind to be decided in a county court, covers loss of wages and future loss of earnings.

A spokesman for Birmingham City Council said action had been taken by the authority to review its staff and management procedures.

46. Mrs. Beverley Lancaster was awarded 67,000 pounds for _____.

　　[A] illness caused by her job

　　[B] her successful and good luck

　　[C] the courage she showed in court

　　[D] the amount of work she did

47. Mrs. Beverley Lancaster took legal action against the city council because _____.

　　[A] it refused to award her for her job

　　[B] she had to deal with rude members of the council

　　[C] it was responsible for her problems

　　[D] it denied her any clerical support

48. The Lancaster case shows that employees have the right to get compensation if they _____.

　　[A] are given work that they are unable to do

　　[B] suffer mental injury caused by their work

　　[C] are forced to do work that they don't like

　　[D] feel isolated, let down and extremely anxious

49. It can be inferred that _____.

　　[A] Mrs. Lancaster will find a better paid job in the future

　　[B] the job of draughtswoman is very demanding

　　[C] the court may hear more stress-related cases

　　[D] the job of housing officer causes mental injuries

50. If Birmingham City Council plans to move an employee to a new job, it will definitely make sure that _____.

[A] there is continuity between the two jobs

[B] no complaints from the employee occur

[C] the amount of work is reduced for the new job

[D] the employee is prepared for any mental problems

Text 2

Life learning (sometimes called un-schooling or self-directed learning) is one of those concepts that are almost easier to explain by saying what it isn't, than what it is. And that's probably because our own schooled backgrounds have convinced us that learning happens only in a dedicated building on certain days, between certain hours, and managed by a specially trained professional.

Within that schooling framework, no matter how hard teachers try and no matter how good their textbooks, many bright students get bored, many slower students struggle and give up or lose their self-respect, and most of them reach the end of the process unprepared to enter into society. They have memorized a certain body of knowledge long enough to rush back the information on tests, but they haven't really learnt much, at least of the official curriculum.

Life learners, on the other hand, know that learning is not difficult, that people learn things quite easily if they're not compelled and forced, if they see a need to learn something, and if they are trusted and respected enough to learn it on their own timetable, at their own speed, in their own way. They know that learning cannot be produced in us and that we cannot produce it in others — no matter what age and no matter whether we're at school or at home.

Life learning is independent of time, location or the presence of teacher. It does not require mom or dad to teach, or kids to work in workbooks at the kitchen table from 9 to noon from September to June. Life learning is learner-driven. It involves living and learning — in and from the real world. It is about exploring, questioning, experimenting, making messes, taking risks without fear of making mistakes, being laughed at and trying again.

Furthermore, life learning is about trusting kids to learn what they need to know and about helping them to learn and grow in their own ways. It is about providing positive experiences that enable children to understand the world and their culture and to interact with it.

51. It is implied in the text that it is hard to _____.

[A] carry life learning though   [B] tell the nature of life learning

[C] learn without going to school   [D] find a specially trained teacher

52. According to the author, the schooling framework often _____.

[A] produces slow students with poor memories

[B] ignores some parts of the official curriculum

[C] fails to provide enough knowledge about life

[D] gives little care to the quality of teaching materials

53. Life learners recognize that learning will not be difficult if they are _____.

[A] clear about why to learn   [B] careful to make a time table

[C] able to respect other people   [D] cautious about any mistakes

54. According to the author, life learning _____.

[A] could prevent one from running risks

[B] could be a road full of trials and errors

[C] makes a kid independent of his parents

[D] teaches a kid how to avoid being scorned

55. Through life learning, children _____.

[A] will grow without the assistance from parents

[B] will learn to communicate with the real world

[C] will be driven to learn necessary life knowledge

[D] will be isolated from the negative side of society

Text 3

To find Kim Hyung Gyoon's office in Samsung's R&D complex, just follow the baskets of dirt clothes. No, Kim is not running the company laundry. As chief of Samsung's Washing & Cleaning Technology Group(WCTG), he's the man behind a new washing machine that deposits tiny silver particles(small pieces of things) — about 1/10,000 the thickness of a human hair — onto clothes to make them germ-and-odor-free without the need of hot water. The device represents the first mass-produced application of this tape of nanotechnology — the science of very small structures — to home appliances. "In summer of 2002, I asked everyone in the office to take off their socks," says Kim. "took one sock from each person and placed it in a regular washing machine; the others were washed in a machine with the Ag+ Nano System. The next day, I asked everyone to check the odor of their socks after a day's wear. One began produce a strong unpleasant smell, and the other was odorless."

Kim says he came up with the idea five years ago while on a business trip to Japan, where he learned of a brand of socks that retained their freshness even after many days of unwashed wear and tear. Tiny sticks of sliver with germ-killing chemicals were woven into the fabric. When he got back to Seoul, Kim applied the principle to washing machines.

According to the Korea Testing & Research Industry, Samsung's device kills 99.9% of germs. Kim says garments stay germ-free for up to a month after being laundered. The Ag+ Nano device went on sale in March 2003 and costs around $1,150; the revolutionary technology is also being used in Samsung's refrigerators and air conditioners.

No wonder: consumers seem to a little sliver in their spin cycles. Since Samsung's nano-armed products were first launched, they have brought in an estimated $779 million in revenue. Overall, nanotech has been one of science's fastest-growing fields in recent years, with potential applications in fields as diverse as energy production and toothpaste manufacture. The nanotech market is projected to be worth $1 trillion by 2015.

56. Which of the following best describes the nature of Kim Hyung Gyoon's work?

[A] Product development.　　　[B] Market investigation.

[C] Research designing.　　　[D] Sales promotion.

57. One advantage of nano-armed washing machines is that _____.

[A] one wash-load is much larger than before

[B] the clean-up is done with an additional benefit

[C] cleaning powder is no longer necessary

[D] a lot of water could be saved

58. In terms of nanotechnology, Kim was the first _____.

[A] to use it in washing machines　　　[B] to come up with the idea

[C] to introduce it to Korea　　　[D] to apply it to socks

59. The author believes that the future of nanotechnology will be _____.

[A] conspicuous　　　[B] distinctive

[C] foreseeable　　　[D] promising

60. This text centers on _____.

[A] the success of an enterprise

[B] the application of a technology

[C] the market share of Samsung's WCTG

[D] the mass-production of a home appliance

Part B

Directions: *Read the following texts in which 5 people expressed their opinions about the concept of "happiness". For questions 61 to 65, match the name of each person(61 to 65) to one of the statements (A to G) given below. Mark your answers on ANSWER SHEET 1.*

Heather McCoy

Entering a bookstore, one cannot help but notice entire shelves devoted to books boating knowledge of the true path to happiness.

Whether this wave of infomercials and books can actually make people happier is the question. Happiness cannot be found by adhering to a narrow set of steps or rules. Finding happiness is not as simple as following a how-to manual, it's something that every person must find in his or her own way.

Gary Russell

Does happiness grow proportionally with wealth? Hardly.

Experiences teaches us material satisfaction comes only when one finds himself wealthier than those around him; and, in a like manner, one feels of being lowered when confronting a billionaire, while a worker with a monthly salary of several hundred dollars becomes the envy of the villagers in remote mountainous regions.

David Niven

True happiness is not a result from human action. Results are temporary whereas happiness is everywhere and can neither be created nor destroyed. True happiness is realized by understanding one's own SELF. With true happiness there is no place for disappointments! True happiness may mean pain and restraint in the beginning but will lead to eternal joy and freedom. To achieve true happiness, we should isolate and remove the negatives.

Joshua Party

Happiness is a state of mind. You can be happy in almost any situation. Likewise, you can be unhappy in an equal number of situations. In the end, it's your decision.

If one can control one's unhappiness, then one must be able to control one's happiness. As far as I know, the Human Genome Project has not been able to identify a single part of any human chromosome which is responsible for happiness.

Laura Johnson

So what makes me a happy person? Studying to be a journalist because I loved to write, not because it pays a lot of money. Skiing in the winter snow and swimming in the summer sun. Spending time with my close friends from home that like the real me just as much as the old me. Being in a stable family. Reading romance novels and watching bizarre movies. Having a boyfriend who knows more about rock and roll history than I do.

Now match the name of each person(61 to 65) to the appropriate statements.

Note: there are two extra statements.

Statements

61. Heather McCoy　　[A] Happiness lies in persistent pursuit.

62. Gary Russell　　　[B] Happiness is in your own hand.

63. David Niven　　　[C] Freedom is positively related to happiness.

64. Joshua Party　　　[D] Happiness is based on comparison.

65. Laura Johnson　　[E] There does not exist a guide to happiness.

　　　　　　　　　　[F] Happiness is a balance between man and nature.

　　　　　　　　　　[G] Happiness is all about doing what you want to.

Section Ⅳ　Writing

Directions: *You should write your responses to both Part A and Part B of this section on ANSWER SHEET 2.*

Part A

Your TV broke down only one week after it was bought. Write a letter of complaint to the store where your TV set was bought,

1. to express what is wrong with your TV set;

2. to make your request (change for a new one, or return the broken one ...);

3. to urge the store to give an early reply.

You should write approximately 100 words. Do not sign your own name at the end of your letter. Use "Wang Lin" instead. You do not need to write your address and the date.

Part B

Bellow is a cartoon about Chinese domestic migration of human resources in recent years. Look at the cartoon and write an essay of about 120 words, make reference to the following points:

1. a description of the cartoon;

2. the cause and effect of this migration.

2009 年 3 月全国英语等级考试真题

Section I Listening Comprehension

1—25（略）

Section II Use of English

Directions: *Read the following text. Choose the best word or phrase for each numbered blank and mark A, B, C, or D on ANSWER SHEET 1.*

The United States is a confederation of states. Each state has the __26__ to make laws with regard to the state. __27__, based on public opinion, states can __28__ policies regarding education, and they may __29__ a state income tax; they also determine the speed __30__, housing codes, and the drinking age.

In most parts of the United States, you __31__ be 21 years old to buy alcohol in a liquor store, bar, __32__ restaurant. In some states you may buy beer in a grocery store. If a store sells alcohol to a minor, the __33__ of the store is usually __34__ a large sum of money. __35__, many areas have an open-container law, __36__ means that people may not drink alcohol on the street or in a car. Anyone __37__ with an open container of alcohol may be arrested.

__38__, with all of these laws, the __39__ of alcohol is a serious __40__ in the United States and Canada. Drinking on college campuses, __41__ there are many underage drinkers has __42__ greatly. In fact, alcohol sales have gone up __43__ the legal drinking age was __44__ from 18 to 21. Some people believe that if there were no legal drinking age, __45__ in some other countries, North American youth would drink less.

26. [A] privilege   [B] advantage   [C] right   [D] tradition

27. [A] As a result   [B] For example   [C] In other words   [D] In this case

28. [A] demand   [B] disagree   [C] discuss   [D] determine

29. [A] collect   [B] issue   [C] demand   [D] implement

30. [A] limit   [B] control   [C] rule   [D] regulation

31. [A] can   [B] shall   [C] may   [D] must

32. [A] and   [B] or   [C] also   [D] not

33. [A] clerk   [B] salesperson   [C] owner   [D] host

34. [A] fined   [B] charged   [C] punished   [D] suffered

35. [A] In addition   [B] In fact   [C] In reality   [D] In general

36. [A] that   [B] this   [C] it   [D] which

37. [A] exposed   [B] suspected   [C] caught   [D] detected

38. [A] Nevertheless [B] Anyway   [C] Moreover   [D] Therefore

39. [A] application [B] consumption   [C] expenditure [D] usage

40. [A] condition   [B] crisis   [C] question   [D] problem

41. [A] though   [B] as   [C] where   [D] which

42. [A] raised   [B] increased   [C] peaked   [D] climaxed

43. [A] when   [B] since   [C] before   [D] after

44. [A] shifted   [B] upgraded   [C] uplifted   [D] changed

45. [A] same   [B] for   [C] as   [D] similar

Section III   Reading Comprehension

Part A

Directions: *Read the following three texts. Answer the questions on each text by choosing A,B,C or D. Mark your answers on ANSWER SHEET 1.*

Text 1

A pioneering study by Donald Appleyard made the surprise sudden increase in the volume of traffic through an area affects a sudden increase in crime does. Appleyard observed this by fir house in San Francisco that looked much alike and had middle-class and working-class residents. The difference was that only 2,000 cars a day ran down Octavia in Appleyard's terminology while Gough Street （MEDIUM street） had 9,000 cars a day and Franklin Street (HEAVY street) had around 16,000 cars a day.

Franklin Street often had as many cars in an hour as Octavia Street had in a day. Heavy traffic brought with it danger, noise, fumes, and soot, directly, and trash secondarily. That is, the cars didn't bring in much trash, but when trash accumulated, residents seldom picked it up. The cars, Appleyard determined, reduced the amount of territory residents felt responsible for. Noise was a constant intrusion into their homes. Many Franklin Street residents covered their doors and windows and spent most of their time in the rear of their houses. Most families with children had already left.

Conditions on Octavia Street were much different. Residents picked up trash. They sat on their front steps and chatted with neighbors. They had three times as many friends and twice as many acquaintances as the people on Franklin.

On Gough Street, residents said that the old feeling of community was disappearing as traffic increased. People were becoming more and more preoccupied with their own lives. A number of families had recently moved. And more were considering it. Those who were staying expressed deep regret at the destruction of their community.

46. Appleyard's study focuses on the influence of _____.

    [A] traffic volume on the residents　　[B] rate of crime on the neighborhood

    [C] social classes on the transportation　[D] degree of pollution on the environment

47. Appleyard discovered that increase in the volume of traffic _____.

    [A] made people more violent

    [B] would lead to increase in crime

    [C] was accompanied by increase in crime

    [D] had the same effect on people as increase in crime

48. The author's main purpose in the second paragraph is to _____.

    [A] discuss the problem of handling trash

    [B] suggest ways to cope with traffic problems

    [C] point out the disadvantages of heavy traffic

    [D] propose an alternative system of transportation

49. People on Gough Street _____.

    [A] felt sorry that their block had been pulled down

    [B] felt indifferent about people moving out

    [C] thought their old community was gone

    [D] thought mostly of themselves

50. What can we learn about Franklin Street?

    [A] It is not a nice neighborhood for children.

    [B] People often throw trash out as they drive through.

    [C] People there have made friends with people on Octavia.

    [D] People there own twice as many cars as people on Gough Street.

Text 2

Imagine, if you will, the average games player. What do you see? A guy who never grew up? Or a nervous 18-year-old pushing buttons on his controller, lost and alone in a violent onscreen world? Sorry, you lose. The average gamer is starting to look pretty much like the average person. For the first time, according to a US poll commissioned by AOL Games, roughly half of those surveyed, ages 12 to 55, are tapping away at some kind of electronic game—whether on a PC, a cell phone or another handheld device—for an average of three hours every week.

The games people play say a lot about who they are. Machines like the Xbox and PlayStation 2 are largely the territory of twenty-something men, who prefer to picture themselves as sports stars and racing drivers. Men 50 and older prefer military games. Teenage girls are much more likely than boys to play games on their phone, while older women make up the majority of people playing card games such as Hearts on line.

Is it a good thing, all this time spent on games? Or is it as harmful as television, pulling people ever further from reality? The AOL survey suggests some players are in denial about the extent of their habit. One in 10 gamers find it impossible to resist games; 1 in 4 admits to losing a night's sleep to play games; and another quarter has been too absorbed to have meals.

But don't think we're all heading into a world with everyone plugged into, if not totally controlled by, his own game. Quite the contrary: gamers appear to be more engaged with reality than other kinds of couch potatoes. According to a comprehensive survey by the Entertainment Software Association (ESA-whose members, of course, want you to think video games are healthy), gamers spend an average of 23 hours a week volunteering and going to church, concerts, museums and other cultural events. More enthusiastic gamers who play 11 hours a week or more spend ever more time out in the cultural world (34 hours).

51. The AOL survey finds that electronic games _____.

[A] do not present a violent onscreen world

[B] no longer keep gamers from growing up

[C] are no longer exclusive to young people

[D] are not as popular with teenagers as before

52. Who does the author say tend to identify themselves with the characters in the game?

[A] Teenage girls.   [B] Older women.

[C] Men in their 20s.   [D] Men 50 and older.

53. When asked about the extent of their habit, some players _____.

[A] refused to provide an answer to this question

[B] denied they were affected by electronic games

[C] wondered why they were asked such a question

[D] stressed their interest in playing electronic games

54. It can be inferred from the text that _____.

[A] electronic games are less harmful than television

[B] television viewers are more realistic than gamers

[C] television is more popular than electronic games

[D] gamers have less self-control than TV viewers

55. According to the writer, the ESA members _____.

[A] have sufficient knowledge of games

[B] think their games are healthy products

[C] serve as the role models for game players

[D] are concerned about gamers' cultural activities

Text 3

The ostrich, the largest bird in the world at present, lives in the drier regions of Africa outside the actual deserts. Because of its very long, powerful legs and the floating effect of its extended wings, it is able to run at great speed over considerable distances.

The female ostrich normally produces about twenty eggs every rainy season. When the female ostrich begins to lay her eggs, however, she does not begin in her own nest. Instead she goes off in search of the nests of neighboring females and lays two or three eggs in each of them.

By the time she has laid eight or nine eggs, she returns and lays the rest in her own nest.

Because of the size of the eggs, the female ostrich cannot lay more than one every two days, so it takes her three weeks to finish laying in her own nest. During that period, she spends a lot of time away from her nest looking for food. And while she is off her nest, other females visit it to lay their eggs amongst hers. By the time she is ready to sit on the eggs to hatch them, there could be up to thirty eggs in her nest, over half of which are not her own.

The female ostrich can comfortably cover only about twenty eggs when she is sitting on the nest so before settling down she pushes the surplus ten or so eggs out of the nest. The rejected eggs, however, never include any of her own. Each female is remarkably consistent in the size and shape of the eggs she produces, so it is not difficult for her to distinguish her own from those of strangers.

Of all the eggs laid by a colony of ostriches, only a very small number hatch into young birds. There are times when nests are left unprotected, for there are too few males to sit on all the nests at night. Thus there are ample opportunities for their natural enemies to raid the nests and eat the eggs. In fact, nearly 80% of the nests are destroyed. But even if a particular female's nest suffers this fate, there is a good chance that one or two of her eggs will be hatched in the nest of one of her neighbors.

56. We learn from the text that an ostrich can go a long distance at high speed as _____.

    [A] it is a special kind of bird   [B] it lives in large desert areas

    [C] it has special wings and legs   [D] it is the largest bird in the world

57. Normally, in every rainy season, the female ostrich produces about _____.

    [A] 12 eggs in her nest   [B] 18 eggs in her nest

    [C] 20 eggs in her nest   [D] 30 eggs in her nest

58. The female ostrich would push some of the eggs out of her nest because _____.

    [A] she can only hatch her own eggs

    [B] those eggs are unlikely to be hatched

    [C] those eggs are to be hatched by others

    [D] she can only hatch a limited number of eggs

59. The female ostrich identifies her own eggs by their size and _____.

    [A] color   [B] number   [C] shape   [D] weight

60. The female ostrich lays her eggs in her neighbors' nests most probably because _____.

    [A] her nest is not big enough   [B] she cannot protect all her eggs

    [C] she cannot tolerate all her eggs   [D] her nest is not comfortable enough

Part B

Directions: *Read the opinions given by five scholars on challenges facing today's single women. For questions 61 to 65, match the name of each scholar (61 to 65) to one of the statements (A to G) given below. Mark your answers on ANSWER SHEET 1.*

Timothy Constance

What the women I spoke with said was that they want a husband who is independent and dedicated to his career, but that he doesn't have to make a lot of money. The emphasis was always on finding a best friend—a soul mate—someone you could tell all your troubles to and who would be supportive. So it doesn't seem to be the case that these women were looking for super high-achieving men.

Grise Levison

I think that for women, as well as for men, the standard for someone who you'd want to spend your life with depends much more today on emotional intimacy. It takes some trial and error and a pretty long and dedicated search to identify the kind of person who is emotionally matching you and who is able to communicate and listen to trouble talk.

Marry Brown

In recent decades girls have been raised to be more competitive and stronger than they were in the past. Several women I talked to mentioned that in their life they felt that their intelligence or intellectual achievement seemed to work against them in their romantic relationships with men. However, most of the women I interviewed felt that there were some men "out there" who would be attracted to smart women. The problem was finding them.

Donna Smith

I think, for the women I talked to, their ultimate sense of what they want in life includes family and children, but they aren't willing to think about the fact that they therefore will probably have to give up some of their own individual pursuits and career goals. I think the definition of success includes both love and work, and that the challenge is how to arrange that in a particular order.

Elizabeth Budy

I think that people who have done at least some of the things that are essential for a wise judgment about a partner are more likely to eventually end up in a stable marriage. It's also true that they're likely to marry someone who is similar to them in education and earning power, which means that those marriages are likely to have more money in them.

Now match the name of each scholar (61 to 65) to the appropriate statement.

Note: there are two extra statements.

Statements

61. Timothy Constance   [A] Career success is in fact not a disadvantage.

62. Grise Levison   [B] The ability to choose a right partner ensures a stable marriage.

63. Marry Brown   [C] How to balance career with family is key to success.

64. Donna Smith   [D] The essential part of marriage is the union of soul.

65. Elizabeth Budy   [E] Finding an emotionally intimate mate isn't a piece of cake.

                 [F] Career success ensures a solid marriage.

                 [G] Social assistance is needed for today's single women.

Section Ⅳ   Writing

Directions: *You should write your responses to both Part A and Part B of this section on ANSWER SHEET 2.*

Part A

Your friend Li Ming has written to invite you to go to his hometown together with him and you are willing to accept his invitation. Write a reply to Li Ming,

1. to express your appreciation and acceptance of his invitation;

2. to ask about his schedule for the trip;

3. to ask about what necessary preparations you need to make.

You should write approximately 100 words. Do not sign your name at the end of your letter. Use "Wang Lin" instead. You do not need to write the address.

Part B

Below is a picture showing rubbish left in a park. Look at the picture and write an essay of about 120 words making reference to the following points:

1. a description of the picture;

2. your comment on this picture and suggested solutions to the problem.

第5章 参考答案与解析

模拟试题（一）

Section I Listening Comprehension

Part A

1. A 【解析】女士说她正在控制体重，便让男士自己点自己的就好了，因此不会尝试任何甜食。

2. A 【解析】原文中提到的是 getting and sending e-mails, searching for information, booking tickets, and making friends 这四点，而没有提到 playing games。

3. B 【解析】说到 The sun is out. There is no cloud in the sky. 因此今天是晴天。

4. C 【解析】女士说应该下周二还书，男士说书可以多保留三天，因此应当是下周五还书。

5. B 【解析】男士说到 ... go to his office after class. 因此他课后应当是先去见教授。答案为 B。

6. B 【解析】根据 I've got a hospital appointment at 2:30. 说明女士的医院的预约是在 2:30。

7. A 【解析】根据 Why don't you stop and ask a policeman? 可知男士可能马上会去寻求警察的帮助。

8. A 【解析】由整篇对话可以得出，男士在咨询寄信的相关信息，因此该对话应当发生在邮局。

9. B 【解析】That's the last thing in the world I ever want to do. 的意思就是不会去 go climbing。

10. C 【解析】由 My classmates already asked for them. 可知拿走邮票的是他的同班同学。

Part B

11. A 【解析】由对话的第一句可知该男士是一位导游。

12. A 【解析】原文中，女士特别提到了长城和颐和园。

13. C 【解析】原文中，男士说到 Just an hour and a half's trip by car. 因此选 C。

14. C 【解析】仔细听原文的列举信息，并没有涉及到 C。

15. D 【解析】根据 ... so badly damaged that it had to be pulled away to a garage. 故选 D。

16. A 【解析】原文中最后一句提到了司机在超市里面。

17. D 【解析】根据后面一句 He was so busy chasing his car that he didn't get the name of the driver of the sports car ... 可以得出跑车的司机应当为事故负责人。

18. A 【解析】原文中并没有提及两个女孩或者 Paul 或者其他的人受伤。

19. C 【解析】根据 ... have a clear idea about what they want to learn. 因此选 C。

20. A 【解析】根据 This type of course ... every area of professional and working life. 可知答案为 A。

21. D 【解析】根据最后一句 ... most popular ESP courses are for business English. 可知答案为 D。

22. D 【解析】对全文进行把握，结合人们清楚了解他们的学习情况，得知 D 为正确答案。

23. B 【解析】女生说 ... review one more time before the test ... 因此她的目的是为了参加考试。

24. C 【解析】原文中女生自己也说了 But I'm still worried about it. 因此选 C。

25. B 【解析】B 选项在原文中没有提到，可用排除法。

附：听力原文

Section I Listening Comprehension

Part A

1. **M:** What would you like for dessert? I hear that this cafe is special for its apple pie and ice cream.

I will order them.

W: The chocolate cake looks so great, but I have to watch my weight. You go ahead and get yours.

2. **M:** Do you often visit the Internet?

W: Certainly. It's really helpful in our life these days. Getting and sending emails, searching for information, booking tickets, and making friends. It seems that nothing will be kept outside the Internet.

3. **M:** The newspaper says it'll be cloudy and rainy today. What do you think?

W: I don't believe it. Look! The sun is out. There is no cloud in the sky.

4. **W:** Today is Saturday. I will return the book next Tuesday.

M: Take your time. You can keep it for three more days.

5. **M:** Professor Smith asked me to go to his office after class. So it is impossible for me to make it for the bar at ten.

W: Then it seems that we'll have to meet an hour later at the library.

6. **M:** We are going to the movies tomorrow afternoon at two. I wonder if you like to come with us.

W: I'd love to, but I can't. I've got a hospital appointment at 2:30.

7. **M:** What did I do wrong? Did I take a wrong turn?

W: I'm not sure. Maybe you turned left when you should have turned right.

M: Well, now the problem is how to get back onto the main highway.

W: Why don't you stop and ask a policeman?

8. **W:** Can I help the next person in line?

M: I just need to send this letter the fastest way possible.

W: Let me see. We have overnight business service. That takes just two days.

9. **W:** Would you like to go mountain climbing with us this Sunday?

M: That's the last thing in the world I ever want to do.

10. **W:** I've noticed that you got some letters from Canada. Would you mind saving the stamps for me? My sister collects them.

M: I am sorry. My classmates have already asked for them.

Part B

11—14

M: Before making out a plan for sightseeing trips for you, I'll be glad to know if you have anything special in mind that you would like to see.

W: Well, as a matter of fact, we were discussing this question last night. We all spoke of the Great Wall, one of the Seven Wonders in the World. We wouldn't leave China without seeing that if it was possible. How far is it from here?

M: Only about 80 kilometers. Just an hour and a half's trip by car. We'll put down the Great Wall then.

W: Good. And we talked a lot about the Summer Palace. We would like to see that, too.

M: All right, the Summer Palace. Well, and there are a number of places that I think you will find interesting; the Temple of Heaven, the Former Imperial Palaces and Ming Tombs.

15—18

Paul, a salesman from London, was driving past a sports car parked outside a supermarket, when he saw it start to roll slowly down the hill. Inside the car were two young girls on the passenger seat — but no driver. Paul stopped quickly, jumped in front of the sports car and tried to stop it, pushing against the front of the car. Another man who was standing nearby got into the car and put on the handbrake, saving the girls from injury.

It was at this point that Paul noticed his own car rolling slowly down the hill and going too fast for him to stop it. It crashed into a bus at the bottom of the hill and was so badly damaged that it had to be pulled away to a garage.

As if this was not bad enough, Paul now found he had no one to blame. He was so busy chasing his car that he didn't get the name of the driver of the sports car, who just came out of the supermarket and drove away without realizing what had happened.

19—22

There are three groups of English learners: beginners, intermediate learners, and learners of special English. Beginners need to learn the basics of English. Students who have reached an intermediate level benefit from learning general English skills. But what about students who want to learn special English for their work or professional life? Most students, who fit into this third group have a clear idea about what they want to learn. A bank clerk, for example, wants to use this special vocabulary and technical terms of finance. But for teachers, deciding how to teach special English is not always so easy. For a start, the variety is enormous. Every field from airline pilots to secretaries has its own vocabulary and technical terms. Teachers also need to have an up-to-date knowledge of that specialized language, and not many teachers are exposed to working environments outside the classroom. These issues have influenced the way special English is taught in schools. This type of course is usually known as English for Specific Purposes, or ESP and there is an ESP course in almost every area of professional and working life. In Britain, for example, there are courses which teach English for doctors, lawyers, reporters, travel agents and people working in the hotel industry. By far, the most popular ESP courses are for business English.

23—25

M: Hi, Jeanny. Why have you come to school an hour early?

W: I want to get a front row seat and review one more time before the test because I failed a course last term. Why are you here so early, Jack?

M: I get out of my car here at this time every day. You seem to be nervous about your lessons. Have you finished your review?

W: I've only been studying night and day for the last week. If I don't get an A in this class, I won't get the support of my country. Why do you seem so calm?

M: This class is really just a review for me. I've been learning it for two years.

W: That's lucky for me.

M: Jeanny, can you guess what the test will be like? Will it be difficult?

W: I hope not. But I'm still worried about it.

M: Well, cheer up. Hope for good luck.

W: Thanks for wishing me luck. I'm going to need it.

Section II   Use of English

[参考译文]　2009年5月30日,一辆轿车飞速冲向载有荷兰女王的敞篷巴士,接着冲入正在观看王室游行的人群后,造成4人死亡。

开车者为一名驾驶一辆黑色掀背车的38岁荷兰人,此人因涉嫌袭击王室已经被捕。

观众有13人受伤,其中5人伤势严重,不过荷兰女王及随行王室成员无人受伤。那辆黑色铃木冲入人群时,阿珀尔多伦市的人们正在游行庆祝举行"女王日"。那辆黑色铃木飞速擦过王室人员所乘的车辆几米开外,目睹这一袭击场面的亚历山大王储王妃马克西玛惊恐万分地用手捂住嘴巴。事件录像镜头显示,这辆车撞入人群之后继续高速行驶。车辆横冲直撞地冲破了安全线,将人们撞得飞入空中。当时,数百名观众正在期待着观看女王。直到小车撞上阿珀尔多伦市中心的一块纪念碑,才停下来。阿珀尔多伦市离阿姆斯特丹约 50 英里。

当天中午,贝娅特丽克丝女王在一次全国性广播节目中对此做出了回应。她说:"今天的开始原本非常美好,却以这样糟糕的悲剧而结束。这起事件让我们感到震惊。"

荷兰检查署发言人称,人们认为那个嫌疑犯是蓄意袭击王室的。"我们有理由相信这是蓄意行为。"检察官古森斯称。古森斯还称,此次事件与恐怖组织并无关联,也没有任何存在爆炸物的迹象。

26. A 【解析】本题考查现在分词的用法。an open top bus 与 carry 的关系是主动关系,因此用 carrying,答案为 A。【知识拓展】carry 可表示"载有,刊载,携带"等。

27. B 【解析】本题考查连词的用法。从文章中可以看出 hurtle 与 smash 两个动作发生的先后顺序为先猛冲后撞击,所以应该是"在撞击之前",答案为 B。

28. C 【解析】本题是对几个关于看的动词的辨析。see 不用于进行时态,意为"看见,察觉";view 意为"仔细观察和注视";look 仅仅是"瞧,看"的意思,没有 watch 所要表示的观看节目、赛事等意思,根据本题目是指看皇家游行,可知答案为 C。

29. C 【解析】本题考查动词的过去分词。从文中 has been 可以看出应该填一个动词的过去分词来构成一个现在完成时的被动语态,故答案为 C。

30. D 【解析】本题考查短语的固定搭配。on/under suspicion of 意为"有嫌疑,涉嫌",故答案为 D。【知识拓展】suspect 用于肯定式时,其意思接近于 think,而非 doubt。

31. B 【解析】本题考查的是受伤动词的用法。首先排除 D,与题意不符合。wound 是用于在战争方面的受伤,如刀伤,枪伤;hurt 是指心灵或者是肉体上受的创伤,但是相比较 injure 而言,injure 一般比 hurt 更为正式,常用于交通事故的受伤,故答案为 B。

32. C 【解析】本题考查动词的搭配。remain 接副词或介词,remain in a serious condition"还处于严重状态";maintain, stay"保持,维持",不符合文意。十三人受伤,其中五人还伤势严重,表达的是一个客观事实,没有必要用过去时,因此不选 D,故答案为 C。

33. C 【解析】本题考查固定搭配。fellow members "随行人员,同伴",故答案为 C。the other 表"其余所有的",不合逻辑。

34. B 【解析】本题考查动词的搭配。plough through sth. 指"车辆猛冲过,失控地冲过"。rush 有"冲过"的意思,但未能突出"失控"的含义;crush 是指"压或挤坏,压或挤伤某人",也不符合;head 仅能体现一个前进的动作,不能表示"冲撞"的意思。故答案为 B。

35. A 【解析】本题考查介词短语作方式状语的用法。in horror 相当于一个副词 horrifiedly"震惊地,恐惧地";honor 为"荣誉",是迷惑项;文章交代了王室人员并未出现危险,in danger(处于危险之中)与文意不符;fear 可以和 in 搭配,但表示惊恐的强烈程度不及 in horror。故答案为 A。

36. B 【解析】本题考查介词的使用。此处 with her hands over her mouth(不由自主的用手盖住自己的嘴巴)作伴随状语,意为"惊恐地用手捂住嘴",也可以说 put one's hand over one's mouth;in front of 表示"在……前面",没有"覆盖在……上面"的意思;cover 的范围更广,有掩盖住脸面的意思,文章只是表示捂住嘴避免发出尖叫声,cover 略显过头,与文意不符。故答案为 B。

37. C 【解析】本题考查介词的用法。根据常识可知汽车撞人会把人撞得飞起来,即 throw up into air,into 有"到里面,进入"的意思。还有"撞上,碰上"的意思。故答案为 C。

38. D 【解析】本题考查定语从句中关系副词的使用。police railings 是警方交通管制设置的栏杆,人们正是在栏杆外面观看他们的女王,police railings 是先行词,where 引导一个非限制性定语从句并在从句中作地点状语。故答案为 D。

39. C 【解析】本题考查动词的使用。halt 是及物动词,同 make sb. / sth. stop,文章中 only 一词以及下文给出暗示:肇事车辆仅是由于撞到一座纪念碑才被停下的,意思是说司机并没有让车停下,而恰恰是纪念碑的阻力使得车子强行停住的,因此文章用的是被动语态。故答案为 C。

40. B 【解析】本题考查动词的使用。slam into=to crash into sth. with a lot of force 表示"(使)重重地撞上",体现速度之快,同时强调撞车的力量,had 接词过去分词,所以用 had slammed;smash"打碎";crunch"嘎吱嘎吱地响(或碾踩)",不符合题意;crash 是指交通工具的相互撞击,未体现撞车的力量。

41. A 【解析】本题考查方位名词的用法。方位名词+of+地点时，不需要加冠词。答案为 A。

42. D 【解析】本题考查的是常识性问题。事情发生在国内，女王发表广播应该面向的是全国的民众，所以答案为 D。

43. B 【解析】本题考查动词搭配。end in 或 end up with，意思为"以……收场，结束"。答案为 B。

44. C 【解析】本题考查副词修饰动词的用法。shock us deeply"使我们深受震惊"。答案为 C。

45. B 【解析】本题考查名词的用法。suspect 意为"嫌疑犯，嫌疑分子，可疑对象"；suspicion 是名词，意为"嫌疑"；suspicious 是形容词，意为"令人怀疑的"；suspected 是动词，suspect 的过去分词。所以答案为 B。

Section Ⅲ Reading Comprehension

Part A

Text 1

[文章概述] 本文讲述了贝克汉姆的妻子维多利亚对于小贝各个方面的影响。

46. A 【解析】推理判断题。根据第五段可知贝克汉姆在家里面是言听计从的，从而 B、C 都不正确。但这不等于说小贝没有主见，因此 D 过于片面。所以答案为 A。

47. D 【解析】细节题。根据第三段和第四段第一句可知，在遇见维多利亚之前，贝克汉姆仅仅是一位受欢迎的足球运动员。而遇见辣妹之后，贝克汉姆则是名利双收。他之前并不能被称为普通或者不出名，而是一名受到欢迎并被人看好的运动员。通过比较，答案为 D。

48. C 【解析】大意理解题。由第四段第一句可知，自从二人结婚以后，维多利亚把小贝成功带入名人圈，使他成为最具影响力的英国人之一。所以，很大程度上贝克汉姆的成功归功于维多利亚。

49. B 【解析】细节题。根据第六段第一句可知 2000 年，贝克汉姆被停训，是因为他不遵守球队规定，擅自回家照看孩子，而不是因为他到美国度假。

50. A 【解析】主旨大意题。通过全文的阅读，可以发现，维多利亚对贝克汉姆的影响，从形象包装到球队转会，再到生活细节等等，无处不在。

Text 2

[文章概述] 本文是一篇关于新西兰黑色知更鸟的文章。作者认为，黑色知更鸟的濒危也是适者生存的大自然法则的结果，这与一般提倡爱护动物，保护自然的观点立场不同。

51. B 【解析】细节题。根据第二段第四句可知食物短缺问题导致黑色知更鸟减少。

52. A 【解析】细节题。根据第二段最后一句可知有笔钱是用于保护地球上濒临灭绝的动物。

53. D 【解析】细节题。根据第四段第三句可知适者生存，答案为 D。

54. C 【解析】细节题。根据第五段第一句可以得出适者生存的道理。C 更加切合这句话。

55. A 【解析】句义理解题。由第五段最后一句可知当人类灭亡的时候，没有其他生物会来援助。所以答案为 A。

Text 3

[文章概述] 文章介绍的是日本的终身就业体系的基本情况，同时还将其与美国的就业体系进行比较。

56. C 【解析】细节题。第一段就指出终身就业体系。

57. D 【解析】句意理解题。根据第二段第二句 In the first place not every Japanese worker has the guaran tee of a lifetime job. 可知答案为 D。

58. C　【解析】细节题。在第三段中 In the United States, corporations lay off those workers with the least seniority(资历). 即是 junior workers 的意思。故选 C。．

59. A　【解析】句意理解题。第二段中 Additionally, Japanese firms maintain some flexibility through the extensive of subcontractors. This practice is much more common in Japan than in the United States, 这与 Japanese use subcontractors more extensively 的意思一致。

60. D　【解析】是非判断题。Moving to a new firm means lower pay 即为 A 的意思；changing jobs means losing these benefits 即为 B 选项的意思；teamwork is an essential part of Japanese production 则为 C 的内容；D 选项没有被提到，是不属于事实的。

Part B

61. D　【解析】细节题。讲自己在得不到朋友的理解时寻求专业咨询人士的帮助。

62. E　【解析】细节题。一个电话使我获得了专业的帮助。

63. G　【解析】细节题。自己在重重困难当中通过自己的努力改变现状，自己更加了解自己并掌握了保持健康的知识。

64. C　【解析】细节题。一开始自己并不知道压抑从何而来，且从心理上拒绝向专业人士寻求帮助。

65. B　【解析】推理题。接受专业的帮助可以使我摆脱抑郁症。

Section Ⅳ　Writing

Part A

本例要求考生写一则抱怨信：因为饭店提供的饭菜质量差而且服务员态度极其恶劣而向饭店经理表达不满。

解题步骤：

　　第一步：确定题材——投诉信，注意书信格式(一般需要写信的时间)；

　　第二步：列出要点——事情发生地时间、原因、证明等；

　　第三步：列出关键词——make / lodge a complaint; turned out to be; have no appetite; do justice to, etc.

　　第四步：落笔成文

May 10th, 2009

Dear Sir or Madam,

　　I am writing to make a complaint about the lunch I had in your distinguished restaurant last Sunday.

　　It was a terrible experience. My classmates had intended to have a happy get-together and we had especially chosen your restaurant as the best place for our lunch. But it turned out to be irritating. The food was cold and the soup was too salty. The table was wet and the waiter was away to fetch us a new tablecloth for ten minutes. We had no appetite to eat anything and made our complaint to the waiter but he tore the tablecloth into pieces and went away. I don't think your service does justice to your claims.

　　I would appreciate it if you could give us a reply. I'm looking forward to a reasonable explanation to this matter.

Sincerely yours,
Michael

Part B

解题步骤：

第一步：审题

　　1. 题型：图表作文

　　2. 文体：论述说明文

第二步:框架分析

1. 说明图表内容,点出每个要点;

2. 从图表现象发生得出一个结论。

第三步:列出写作思路

1. 根据题干提示,在过去的十年里,你所在城市的家庭消费情况的变化,可以看出人们在吃喝等生活水平上提高了,更为明显的就是买房的投入也大幅提高;

2. 得出结论:尽管生活水平提高了,但是人们仍然要花一大部分钱来满足基本的生活设施。

第四步:列出关键词和词组

increase from to;structure of the average family consumption;as a result;a conclusion can be drawn that ... ; improve one's living step, etc.

第五步:落笔成文

The average family income in our city increased from 6,000 yuan per year in 1998 to 18,000 yuan in 2008. In the meantime, the structure of the average family consumption has changed, too. These graphs show the change clearly.

The biggest part of the average family expenses is housing. In 1998, the average family spent 25 percent of its income on housing. In 2008, expenses on housing rose to 42 percent. Food and drink are the second biggest part of the average family expenses. In 1998, about 18% of the average income was spent on this item. In 2008, the figure grew to 30%. As a result of such increase in the expenses on housing and food, expenses on other items have been reduced from 57% in 1998 to 28% in 2008.

Thus, a conclusion can be drawn that as income increases, people can improve their living standards. But still the average family has to spend a large part of its income on the basic life necessities.

模拟试题(二)

Section I Listening Comprehension

Part A

1. B 【解析】男士说会在半个小时内,也就是八点半的时候到女士那里接她,因此现在是八点。

2. D 【解析】女士说 I'd just drink the tea I have right here. 因此选 D。

3. B 【解析】女士向售货员要的是十二号的毛衣。

4. A 【解析】男士热情地说 I'll show you how easy it is to work the copies of this paper for you. 这就意味着他可以帮女士。

5. A 【解析】男士说 ... but it's important to do your best. 也就意味着努力去做才是最重要的,换句话说没有人能做到绝对的好。

6. A 【解析】两人是在讨论关于艺术展览的票价的问题,由此推断两人所在的地点为艺术博物馆的外面。

7. D 【解析】男士说 Up till now I have been an official for three years. 因此他到现在还应当是official。

8. B 【解析】原文中男士说 I guess we'll have to change our sailing plans. 而题目中问的是两人原来打算做什么,因此选 B。

9. A 【解析】原文中女士说 ... my office number has changed since I began to work at Morrison. 而之前男士也在问女士要地址,因此选择 A。

10. A 【解析】从两人对话的内容可判断出两人为师生关系。

Part B

11. B 【解析】男士说 Maybe we should buy a bigger one. 所以答案为 B。

12. D 【解析】女士说的第一点理由是 ... your sitting room isn't big enough.

13. C 【解析】根据原文第一句话,可以得出两人为同学。

14. C 【解析】根据原文判断出两人为医生和病人的关系,因此 Tom 现在在医院。

15. C 【解析】男士说 I'll miss my birthday party on Saturday.可知生日应在周六。

16. A 【解析】女士说到 Give a chance to think about it, and I'll get a new idea. 故答案为 A。

17. B 【解析】根据原文的后半段可以得出答案为 B。

18. D 【解析】根据第一段最后一句 Yet their cause and control remain a serious problem that is difficult to solve. 可知答案为 D。

19. B 【解析】根据 Improved design has helped to make highways much safer. 可知答案为 B。

20. D 【解析】根据 ... the total of accidents continues to rise because of human failure ... 可知答案为 D。

21. A 【解析】根据最后一句 they want to know how cars can be built better to protect the drivers.可知答案为 A。

22. D 【解析】根据排除法以及文中的 a load of details,得出选项 D 为正确答案。

23. C 【解析】根据 ... the way he dealt with the Western developments, that wasn't bad ... 可知答案为 C。

24. B 【解析】根据男士说的最后一段话得出 Potter 适合对研究生的教学。

25. C 【解析】原文中男士抱怨 I think he tends to forget where he is.由此得到对话中两人均为 undergraduate。

附:听力原文

Section Ⅰ Listening Comprehension

Part A

1. **M:** I can come to your house and pick you up in half an hour. Is it all right?

   W: Good. That means you will be here at 8:30.

2. **M:** I'm going out to get some coffee. Would you like something?

   W: Well, I've been drinking too much coffee recently. Thanks for asking. I'd just drink the tea I have right here.

3. **M:** Hello, can I help you?

   W: Yes, please! I like this sweater very much. But it's too small for me. Do you have it in size 12?

   M: I am afraid not. Size 10 is the largest we have.

4. **W:** I'm still waiting for the clerk to come back and make some copies of this paper for me.

   M: Why trouble him? I'll show you how easy it is to work the copies of this paper for you.

5. **W:** I don't think the job has to be done perfectly.

   M: Maybe, but it's important to do your best.

6. **W:** The admission price of the gallery is ten dollars per person. I think that's too expensive for a single exhibit.

   M: But if we have student cards, we can get in for two.

   W: Really? Let's have a try.

7. **W:** What jobs have you done in the last ten years?

   M: Many kinds of jobs. I was once an engineer and later a teacher. Up till now I have been an official for three years.

8. **W:** There was a storm warning on the radio this morning. Did you happen to be listening?

   M: No, but what a pity! I guess we'll have to change our sailing plans. Would you rather play tennis or go bicycle-riding?

9. **W:** Don't forget to write to me, Jason.

   M: I won't. But let me make sure I have the right address. Is it 42 East Drive Birmingham?

W: That's right. By the way, my office number has changed since I began to work at Morrison.

M: Oh, has it? Tell me what it is, then.

10. **W:** Could you please explain the homework for Monday again, Mr. Tang?

M: Certainly. Read the next chapter and prepare to discuss what you've read.

Part B

11—13

M: Hi, Mary. We haven't seen each other since we graduated. Where have you been?

W: I have been to Australia. Do you still live there?

M: Oh, no. We have just moved into the new house.

W: Really? Congratulations.

M: Thank you, and we want to buy a new television.

W: What kind of television do you want to buy?

M: A color TV, of course, but I'm not sure about the size. Maybe we should buy a bigger one. If we buy a smaller one, we might have to change it in a few years' time for a bigger one. That would be a waste of money. What is your opinion?

W: In my opinion, I don't think it's necessary to buy a very big one.

M: Any reason?

W: Yes. As I know, your sitting room isn't big enough. If you put in a very big television, that will be bad for your eyes, and a smaller size TV can also pick up good programs.

M: Mmm, that's quite true. I'll think about it.

W: You'd better make a quick decision because the price may go up soon.

14—17

W: Tom, does your throat hurt?

M: Yes.

W: OK. Do you want to get better?

M: Yes.

W: OK. We want you to get better, too. You'll have your tonsils(扁桃腺) out tomorrow, and you won't get so many colds any more.

M: But if I have my tonsils out tomorrow, I'll miss my birthday party on Saturday.

W: I know. It's a problem, isn't it? Let me try to work something out.

M: What?

W: I have to think about it.

M: You're joking with me.

W: Oh, I'm not, Tom. Give a chance to think about it, and I'll get a new idea.

M: A surprise?

W: Maybe. But you just put on your clothes, and I'll think of a surprise.

M: Will it hurt?

W: No. There are other boys and girls, and they are having tonsils out.

M: I don't want to.

W: Change your clothes, Tom. Everything will just be fine.

18—21

As the car industry develops, traffic accidents have become as familiar as the common cold. Yet their cause and control remain a serious problem that is difficult to solve.

Experts have long recognized that this discouraging problem has multiple causes. At the very least it is a problem that involves three factors: the driver, the vehicle and the roadway. If all drivers exercised good judgment at all times, there would be few accidents. But this is rather like saying that if all people were honest, there would be no crime. Improved design has helped to make highways much safer. But the total of accidents continues to rise because of human failure and an enormous increase in the number of automobiles on the road. Attention is now turning increasingly to the third factor of the accident, that is, the car itself. Since people assume that the accidents are bound to occur, they want to know how cars can be built better to protect the drivers.

22—25

M: What do you think of Professor Potter's course, Jane?

W: Not much.

M: Why, what's wrong with it?

W: Oh, I don't know. It's just that he overloads it with details. The course he gave on town planning last year, it was just the same—a load of details, which you could have got from a book anyway. There was no overall ...

M: No general overview you mean?

W: Yes. I suppose you could call it that. I couldn't see the town for the buildings.

M: But you've got to have the details in this kind of subject. Anyway I think he's good. You take his first lecture for instance. I thought that was very interesting, and not at all over-detailed.

W: Well, he starts off all right, but then he just piles on the details.

M: Now you're exaggerating.

W: Well, the way he dealt with the Western developments, that wasn't bad, I suppose.

M: You seem to have got something. Perhaps Potter is a little disorganized, but I think he's good.

W: Do you really think so?

M: He does do most of his teaching to the postgraduates. He only does the one undergraduate course each year. After all, I think he tends to forget where he is. He starts off being nice and general and then tries to cram in a bit too much specialized information.

W: The main thing I object to is the lack of direction.

Section Ⅱ　Use of English

[**参考译文**]　每周五晚,当朋友们还在为看哪场电影而举棋不定的时候,卡琳娜·伍德已在前往娱乐俱乐部的路上了。在那儿,她照顾着有学习困难的成年人。她已在斯通黑文的俱乐部志愿工作两年了。她负责为一个30人的小组组织社会活动,这个小组成员的年龄老少不等。

如今,因自己的志愿者工作卡琳娜·伍德已成为70名被授予戴安娜奖的年轻人中的一员。戴安娜奖是为了表彰那些在自己的社区中做出杰出贡献或无私奉献的青少年和儿童而设立的奖项。

明天,这个为纪念威尔士王妃戴安娜而设立的奖项的颁奖典礼将在苏格兰议会召开。这是其在北部地区的第一次颁奖礼。麦琪学校一名六年级学生卡琳娜将与为自己提名的导师伊文·里奇一同前往参加颁奖仪式。卡琳娜现在正在学习高等化学、数学和生物。她希望将来自己能成为医生,她坚持认为自己做志愿者的目的并不是为了得到认可。

"志愿工作是一种绝好的经历。"她说,"在工作过程中,我可以结识许多人,学到许多技能。"她并不在意自己是伙伴中惟一一个从事志愿者工作的人。她说,她并不在乎周五晚上的同学聚会。

"我不知道他们是怎么想的,我只知道我喜欢志愿者工作。这太有意思了。"虽然威尔士王妃去世时卡琳娜只有7岁,她说道:"我知道威尔士王妃非常喜欢慈善工作。她是人民的王妃,人民可以亲近她。我很高兴这个奖项是以她的名字命名的。"

26. C　【解析】本文讲述的是卡琳娜·伍德因参加志愿者工作而获得认可和表彰的事迹。本题考查了从句中动词时态的用法,在 when 引导的时间状语从句中,主句谓语动词的时态应与从句中动词的时态保持一致。在本题中,when 从句中的谓语动词为 are,是一般现在时,所以从句谓语动词应该是一般现在时"heads",答案为 C。

27. A 【解析】本题考查了动词的搭配。look after后的宾语是adults,为人,因此应为"照顾,照料"; take after意为"以……为榜样,学……的样子;追赶,追捕",用在此处与文章意思不符;attend 后不跟after,一般用to表示"处理,照顾";D选项的care后也不跟after。故答案为A。

28. D 【解析】本题考查了动词的时态。根据上下文可以知道,卡琳娜还在做志愿者,所以这里用 现在完成进行时最恰当,答案为D。

29. A 【解析】本题考查了动词搭配和非谓语动词的用法。首先,根据搭配可以用排除法,arrange 意思为"安排,筹备",与题意不符;vary"变化",也不符合题意。只有range是表示 "从……到……"的意思。故答案为A。

30. B 【解析】本题考查了形容词表示名词的用法。根据题意可知"年轻的成人和年老的成人都 有"。A选项"elders":当elder用复数时表示(相比之下)年纪较大的人往往有所指,因为此处没 有比较所以elders不太合适,与elderly相比,就不如B更符合题意;elderly是形容词,"the+形 容词"表示一类人,所以the+elderly可表示老年人(泛指);C选项olders是一种错误表达形式, older为形容词的比较级,一般不可直接加"s"表复数;D选项olderly也是一种错误的形式。故 答案为B。【知识拓展】指两者之间较大的则通常可以用the older表达。比较年龄大小时不用 elder,而用older。

31. B 【解析】本题考查了动词辨析。encourage"鼓励";recognize"认可";admit"录取,承认(接句 子,表示做了什么)";compliment"恭维"。

32. A 【解析】本题考查了动词的固定搭配。bestow sth. on/upon sb."把……赠与;把……给于", 在 这里意为"给孩子和青少年的一项荣誉",B项give用法为give sth. to sb. 故答案为A。

33. C 【解析】本题考查了名词短语。因为effort和endeavor同样都是"努力"的意思,而且努力与 前面的定语outstanding or selfish不搭配,而应该是杰出和无私的贡献,故答案为C。

34. A 【解析】本题考查了动词的固定搭配。dedicate的用法是be dedicated to,意为"奉献,献给"; design的用法是be designed for;aim的用法是be aimed at;intend的用法是be intended for。故 答案为A。

35. B 【解析】本题考查了动词及动词词组的意思。give out"发表,公布";present"颁发";deliver "发表(演讲);递送,传递";hand out"分发"。根据题意,应是颁发这个奖项的意思,故答案为B。

36. C 【解析】本题考查了专有名词。根据题意,这里应该是"导师"的意思,而导师的翻译应为 guidance teacher,其他选项均不符。故答案为C。

37. B 【解析】本题考查了动词的搭配和对应意思。联系上下文,导师应该是提名她去参加该奖项 评选的,所以此处为nominate sb. for the award,答案为B。

38. D 【解析】本题考查了对全文的整体理解和意思相近词的辨析。根据全文的主要思想可知此 处说的是卡琳娜·伍德不寻求别人对她志愿者工作的认可。acknowledge是动词,可排除;ad- mission"承认,贡认(罪行等)";recognition"认可",与题意相符。故答案为D。

39. B 【解析】本题考查了动词的意思。根据上下文可知这里要说的是卡琳娜·伍德不在乎在自己 的朋友中她是否是惟一一个做志愿者工作的。这里应该只是强调"没去想,不在乎"而不是"担 心,害怕或抱歉",而"在乎"对应的词为concerned。故答案为B。

40. C 【解析】本题考查了动词的时态。根据前面的the only one和一般现在时可知从句中谓语动 词应为第三人称单数的形式,再根据主句的is可知从句也应为一般现在时。故答案为C。【知识 拓展】如指的是众中之一,则用复数。

41. A 【解析】本题考查了对上下文信息的把握。根据上文说到在她的朋友中她是惟一一个做志愿 者的,所以这里应该是说她因为太喜欢这份工作而不会想念她们在星期五晚上的聚会。根据 各选项的意思可判断出只有miss符合题意。故答案为A。

42. D 【解析】本题考查了动词的用法。前面她说不在乎他们怎么想,联系上下文可知是相对于去 参加聚会来说,卡琳娜更加喜欢做志愿者工作。prefer相对于其他三项来说能反映出对比的 含义,故答案为D。

43. A　【解析】本题考查了常识。根据文章提示知道是 princess。

44. B　【解析】本题考查了动词短语。A 项用到的短语是 be exhausted "筋疲力尽",与文意不符;B 项用到的短语是 be involved in"卷入某事,参与某事";C 项用到的短语是 be devoted to 但此处是 in,故可排除;D 项用到的短语是 be busy with sth.而此处是 in,故也可排除。故答案为 B。

45. C　【解析】本题考查了介词的用法。根据题意这里的意思是"这项奖沿用了她的名字"。在这些介词中只有 in 有这种用法。故答案为 C。

Section Ⅲ　Reading Comprehension

Text 1

[文章概述]　本文主要叙述了人们对女性平均比男性长寿原因的探究。研究发现,随着年龄的增长,男性心脏要比女性心脏功能衰竭得快。

46. B　【解析】词义推测题。根据第一段第一句 Why do men die earlier than women? 及全文内容可猜出,longevity 为"长寿"的意思。

47. D　【解析】主旨题。根据第一段第二句 ... the reason could be that men's hearts go into rapid decline when they reach middle age. 和第二段中的 ... women's longevity may be linked to the fact that their hearts do not lose their pumping power with age.及全文内容可知答案为 D。

48. C　【解析】细节题。根据第五段第一句 What surprises scientists is that the female heart sees very little loss of these cells. 可知答案为 C。

49. C　【解析】推理判断题。根据最后一段第一句 The good news is that men can improve the health of their heart with regular exercise. 及文章主题可知答案为 C。

50. B　【解析】推理判断题。根据文章倒数第二段 The team has yet to find why aging takes a greater loss on the male heart. 可知答案为 B。

Text 2

[文章概述]　本文介绍了 Harry Houdini 的特技,成功的经历和方法。

51. B　【解析】细节题。根据第四段第二句:Harry 把手、脚都训练得很灵活来摆脱手链脚铐,以及第四段第四句后半部分:妻子通过接吻传给他万能钥匙,可知答案为 B。

52. A　【解析】细节题。根据语境,this 指上文所表演的事情:第一次越狱成功。所以答案为 A。

53. C　【解析】细节题。从第三段最后一句和第四段第一句可知 Houdini 进监狱只是为了宣传他的特技而不是因为犯罪,故 C 对 A 错;由第三段倒数第三句可知 Houdini 并没有一开始就出名,故 B 错;由第一段第一句可知 Houdini 没有特异功能故 D 错。

54. D　【解析】推理判断题。根据第三段第一句可知他步入娱乐圈时是 1891 年,17 岁;根据第三段倒数第二句可知第一次成功是 1898 年,时隔 7 年,应是 24 岁,可推知答案为 D。

55. D　【解析】主旨题。由第一段第二句可知 Harry 因逃狱出名,后面列举的例子谈的是他从监狱成功地逃出,所以答案为 D。

Text 3

[文章概述]　如今,求职人员在求职过程中对自己的学历弄虚作假已成为普遍问题,文章论述了人们如何作假以及存在这一社会现象的原因。

56. B　【解析】主旨题。文章第一段简要概述了求职人员在求职过程中对自己的学历弄虚作假这一社会现象,然后在第二、三段分别给出一些具体的例子进行说明,故选 B。

57. B　【解析】推理判断题。由第二段第三、四句可知,imposter 和 special cases 指的都是编造虚假学历,所以答案为 B。

58. B 【解析】推理判断题。根据文意:人事部的人员发现,一些简历上所写的"与某个大学有过联系"可能只是指那个应聘人员曾到过他弟弟的学校参加过足球周,所以选 B。

59. D 【解析】推理判断题。由文章第一段倒数第二句可知,名牌大学的毕业生在求职过程中比其他人有优势,故选 D。

60. B 【解析】词义猜测题。该词所在句意为"如果你不想撒谎又不愿和盘托出,会有公司愿意卖给你_____文凭。"再结合下文提到的售卖假文凭的公司情况可知,B(假的)正确。thorough 意为"彻底的";ultimate 意为"最终的";decisive 意为"决定性的",均排除。

Part B

61. E 【解析】主旨题。讲经济危机的背景,主题在原文第一段的一、二两行。

62. B 【解析】主旨题。讲经济危机的程度加深及其表现。

63. G 【解析】细节题。讲引发经济危机的原始的因素可以追溯到美国经济的极端负债。

64. D 【解析】细节题。讲危机蔓延到全球范围,以及对欧洲银行造成的影响。

65. A 【解析】推理题。当前的金融股票有所回升。

Section Ⅳ Writing

Part A

本例要求考生写一则应征求职信:在杂志上看到招聘启示,启示上的要求与自身条件相符,于是写一封求职信。

解题步骤:

第一步:确定题材——求职信,注意格式;

第二步:列出要点——写信的目的、自身的工作经历、年限、水平、能力、资质、工作方法等;

第三步:列出关键词——apply for the position advertised in … ; I can type … ; fluent English; looking forward to receiving your notice, etc.

第四步:落笔成文

June 24th, 2009

Dear Sir or Madam,

I'm writing to apply for the position you advertised in the fifth issue of *Modern Times* of this year.

For the past six years, I've been working as secretary to the manager of a hotel. I can type about 150 words per minute. I can speak fluent English and am good at writing commercial articles. I am also good at communicating with others, which enables me to be an excellent teamworker.

I'd very much appreciate it if you could give me a chance for an interview. I'm looking forward to receiving your reply at your earliest convenience.

Enclosed are my resume and a photo.

Sincerely yours,

Xiao Tao

Part B

解题步骤:

第一步:审题

1. 题型:看图作文

2. 文体:论述说明文

第二步:框架分析

1. 说明图表内容,点出要点;

2. 图表现象发生的原因以及影响。

第三步:列出写作思路

1. 自1998年以来,城市里出国旅游的人数不断上升,特别是2004年来,数目急剧提高;

2. 根据图表内容分析原因:经济发展了,人们生活水平提高,国内景点多已经去过等;

3. 分析影响:刺激国内外经济发展,知识拓展人们视野等。

第四步:列出关键词和词组

policy; prefer to; living standards; the deepening of the reform and opening-up policy; when it comes to, etc.

第五步:落笔成文

The above table clearly mirrors an upward trend in the number of people who prefer to travel abroad over the last decade. In 1998, there are only two thousand tourists going overseas to take a trip. In 2004, the figure climbs to more than eight thousand, and peaks at 15 thousand in 2008.

There are a number of reasons for this phenomenon, of which the most important one is perhaps China's booming economy. Thanks to the deepening of the reform and opening-up policy, the citizens of the Central Kingdom enjoy a great improvement in their living standards. They have an enormous consuming power to pursue an increasingly higher level of living quality. Perhaps having already traveled to most of the scenic spots at home, an increasing number of them now choose foreign countries as their tourist destinations.

When it comes to what impacts it will bring, in my eyes, it will give a huge boost to the tourist industry both at home and abroad. Besides, it will give us the chance to open our eyes and give the world a chance to know more about China, which will surely make the world multiculturalized.

模拟试题(三)

Section Ⅰ　Listening Comprehension

Part A

1. A 【解析】根据原文的语气,男士对考试的结果并不满意。

2. C 【解析】根据两人对话的内容可知,两人是医生与病人的关系。

3. D 【解析】由原文判断出男士是在酒店的前台进行 check in,但是遇到了一些问题。

4. B 【解析】原文中男士为女士搬运行李,这应当是在旅店里面。

5. B 【解析】根据女士所说的 Now you know why I never missed a lecture. 可知答案为 B。

6. A 【解析】根据 ... ankle injuries heal quickly if you stop regular activity ... 可知答案为 A。

7. C 【解析】根据 ... it's something I haven't acquired a taste ... 可知他不喜欢抽象派的画。

8. C 【解析】原文中女士的办公室离那里很近,因此周四就可以收到电脑。

9. D 【解析】根据两人的对话内容,可知女士正对着一位木匠说话。

10. D 【解析】根据女士的 I probably buy her a new music record ... 可知答案为 D。

Part B

11. C 【解析】根据第一句 Halloween is celebrated every year. 可知答案为 C。

12. D 【解析】根据 It comes from ... November 1, is a Catholic day. 可知答案为 D。

13. A 【解析】根据 ... in order to frighten away spirits looking for living bodies. 可知答案为 A。

14. C 【解析】根据 ... being as wild as possible in order to frighten ... 可知答案为 C。

15. A 【解析】根据 It's time for my flight. 得知对话发生在机场。

16. B 【解析】根据No other city ... good restaurants or ... good music. 可知答案为 B。

17. A 【解析】根据文中女士所说的 I'm from a very small town in Pennsylvania. 可知答案为 A。

18. C 【解析】根据 But you speak English like a native speaker. 可知男士的英文应当很棒。

19. B 【解析】根据 ... the two-ton re-entry vehicle will hit the ocean ... 可知答案为 B。

20. C 【解析】根据 ... another six months, 可知答案为 C。

21. C 【解析】根据 ... is likely to splash down into the Pacific Ocean on Thursday. 可知答案为 C。

22. B 【解析】根据第三句可知伦敦的出租车司机接受一个特殊的培训。

23. C 【解析】根据第四句可知培训要持续两年到四年的时间。

24. A 【解析】从主考官的表现可以看处,主考官很严厉,不管你做得多么好,都不会有什么笑脸,不会有什么称赞,故答案为 A。

25. B 【解析】由文章最后一句可知在训的司机是不能像正式上岗的司机一样赚钱的。

附:听力原文

Section Ⅰ Listening Comprehension

Part A

1. **W:** Are you happy now that the exam is over?

    M: Happy? You've got to see my grade before you say that.

2. **W:** Do I need to take some medicine?

    M: Yes. And I strongly advise you to go on a low-fat diet.

    W: Do you really think that's important?

    M: Definitely. If you don't, you might have a heart attack some day.

    W: Well. I think I should take your advice. You have been very helpful. Thanks.

3. **W:** We don't think to have a reservation for you, sir. I'm sorry.

    M: But my secretary said that she had reserved a room for me here. I phoned her from the airport this morning just before I got on board the plane.

4. **M:** Your room number is 633 on the sixth floor. We'll take the lift.

    W: Here is my luggage.

5. **M:** I'm really surprised you got an "A" on the test. You didn't seem to have done a lot of reading.

    W: Now you know why I never missed a lecture.

6. **M:** Today is a bad day for me. I fell off a step and twisted my ankle.

    W: Don't worry. Usually ankle injuries heal quickly if you stop regular activity for a while.

7. **W:** I really like those abstract paintings we saw yesterday. What do you think?

    M: I guess it's something I haven't acquired a taste for yet.

8. **W:** Now, can we get the computers before Wednesday?

    M: Well, it depends. If it is less than 10 kilometers, we can deliver them on Thursday. But if it's farther away, it'll be on Friday. Where is your office?

    W: Just around the corner.

9. **M:** Now I have finished the furniture. If you can make up your mind about the color, I can start on the outside of your house early next week.

    W: Well, right now I think I want white for the window frames and yellow for the walls, but I'll let you know tomorrow.

10. **W:** Have you got any idea what you'll buy for Mary's birthday?

    M: Well, I'll get her a very new school bag. And I promised to take her to a film. What about you?

    W: Oh, I haven't decided yet. I will probably buy her a new music record as she likes it so much.

Part B

11—14

Halloween is celebrated every year. But just how and when did this custom happen? Is it just a harmless celebration? The word "Halloween" actually has its origins in the Catholic Church. It comes from a change of All Hallows Eve. All Hallows' Day, or All Saint's Day, November 1, is a Catholic day. But in the 5th century BC, summer officially ended on October 31. It was believed that, on that day, the spirits of all those who had died throughout the year would come back in search of living bodies for the next year. It was believed to be their only hope for the after life. Naturally, the living did not want to be taken away. So on the night of October 31, villagers would put out the fires in their homes, to make them cold and unwanted. They would then dress up in all manners of strange customs and noisily walked around the neighborhood, being as wild as possible in order to frighten away spirits looking for living bodies. Some accounts tell of how they would burn someone as sort of a lesson to the spirits.

15—18

M: Excuse me, do you mind if I sit here?

W: Not at all, go ahead.

M: Thank you.

W: Are you going somewhere or are you meeting someone?

M: I'm on my way to Washington, and you?

W: I'm on my way to San Francisco.

M: Really? I think San Francisco is probably the most exciting city in the US.

W: So do I. No other city has as many good restaurants or as much good music.

M: Is San Francisco your hometown?

W: No, I'm from a very small town in Pennsylvania. I wouldn't want to live there again either. I don't like small town living very much.

M: En, neither do I. But small towns have their advantages, less traffic.

W: And friendlier people. You know I'm beginning to feel homesick. By the way, where are you from?

M: China.

W: China? But you speak English like a native speaker. I didn't have any idea.

M: Oh, excuse me. It's time for my flight. Well, nice talking with you.

W: Me too. Bye.

19—21

US space authorities say part of an-out-of-control Chinese satellite is likely to splash down into the Pacific Ocean on Thursday.

The US space command says the two-ton re-entry vehicle will hit the ocean between Central America and Hawaii after blazing a fiery path through the earth's atmosphere. China disputes the US space command's claims. The Chinese Aerospace Corporation says that the satellite will not re-enter the earth's atmosphere for another six months. Chinese scientists recently lost control of the satellite when they were radioing re-entry commands.

22—25

London taxi drivers know the capital like the back of their hands. No matter how small or indistinct the street is, the driver will be able to get you there without any trouble. The reason London taxi drivers are so efficient is that they all have gone through a very tough training period to get a special taxi driving license. During this period, which can take two to four years, the would-be taxi driver has to learn the most direct route to every single road and to every important building in London. To achieve this, most learners go around the city on small motorbikes practicing how to move to and from different points of the city. Learner taxi drivers are tested several times during the training period by government officers. The exams are terrible experience. The officers ask you "How do you get from Birmingham palace to the Tower of London?" and you have to take them there in the direct line. When you get to the tower, they won't say "well done". They will quickly move on to the next question. After five or six questions, they will just say "See you in two months' time." And then you know the exam is over. Learner drivers are not allowed to work and earn money as drivers. Therefore, many of them keep their previous jobs until they have obtained the license. The training can cost quite a lot, because learners have to pay for their own expenses on the tests and the medical exam.

Section II   Use of English

[参考译文] 一位老木匠准备退休了。他把自己要离开房屋建造行业,与妻子过休闲生活,享受大家庭的天伦之乐的计划告诉了雇主。尽管他会怀念自己的周工资,但是他想要退休。他们还是可以维持基本生计的。看到自己这样一位出色的雇员即将离职,雇主感到非常遗憾,他询问老木工能否看自己的面子上再建造一所房屋。木匠答应了,但是,过了一段时间,明显可以看出老木工的心思不在自己的工作上。他所采用的工艺非常的糟糕,用的材料也很劣质。用这样的方式来为自己的事业画上句点是非常不幸的。

木匠完成了自己的工作后,他的雇主来考查他建造的房屋。接着,他就把大门的钥匙交给了木匠,说道,"这是你的房子,是我送给你的礼物。"木匠非常地震惊。多可惜!当初他要是知道他是在给自己建造房子的话,他会用截然不同的工作态度来对待的。

这对于我们来说何尝不是如此。我们每天都在打造自己的生活,经常不竭尽全力。接着,我们都会惊讶地意识到我们不得不在自己"建造的房子"中生活。如果可以从头开始再来一次,我们会用截然不同的态度来完成。

但是,你不可能退到过去。你就是那位木匠,每天钉一颗钉子、搭一块木板或者砌一面墙。有人曾经这么说过,"生活是一项自己独立完成的工程。"你的态度和你每天所做的选择都帮助你搭建你明天所居住的"房屋"。因此,还是在建造过程中明智点吧!

26. C 【解析】本题考查动词。由 retire 可知,他想离开自己的工作,答案为C。

27. A 【解析】本题考查副词。leisurely"悠闲的,慢悠悠的"; lonely"孤独的"; orderly"有秩序的,有条理的"; friendly"友好的"。人们退休了以后,生活常是悠闲的,故答案为A。

28. C 【解析】本题考查形容词。退休后,老人可以享受天伦之乐,这里的 extended family 指的是包括老人的配偶、子女和孙子、孙女等在内的家庭,故答案为C。

29. B 【解析】本题考查动词短语辨析。go off"开火,爆炸"; get by"维持生计";pass on"转交,递给"; work away"连续不停地工作"。根据前面的 extended family 和 miss the paycheck 可知,老人生活上悠闲,没有了工资,生活可能不如以前宽裕,但他们还是能设法维持,故答案为B。【知识拓展】extended family 指 "大家庭(即指三代及三代以上成员组成的家庭)";nuclear family 指 "核心家庭(即仅由父母及子女组成的家庭)"。

30. D 【解析】本题考查形容词。根据上文 retire 和下文的 his good worker 可知作为老板,自己的好员工要走了,自然会感到惋惜,故答案为D。

31. A 【解析】本题考查连词。从下文得知,老木匠的最后一座房子造得很不好,是因为他心不在焉。所以此处表示转折,应用 but,注意 while 是并列连词,表示前后对比,而非转折。故答案为A。

32. B 【解析】本题考查形容词。根据前文的 bad workmanship 和下文可知,老木匠用的建筑材料是劣质的,选 inferior,故答案为B。

33. D 【解析】本题考查动词。根据前文的 retire,go 和 asked if he could build just one more house 可知,这是老木匠为老板建造的最后一座房子,作为事业的结束,答案为D。

34. C 【解析】本题考查动词。作为老板,自己让人建设的房子完工了,自然来查看一下。下文也提到他并非来购买、出售或修理房子,而是把房子送给了老木匠。故答案为C。

35. C 【解析】本题考查名词。老板把刚刚建设的房子作为礼物(gift)送给了老木匠,应该给他房门钥匙,故答案为A。

36. A 【解析】本题考查名词。房子是老板给老木匠的礼物,故答案为A。

37. B 【解析】本题考查名词。老木匠为自己做的蠢事感到羞耻、后悔,故答案为B。

38. A 【解析】本题考查连词。So it is with ... 是一常见句型,相当于 It is the same with ... 意为"……也如此",是一种省略、替代。as 可以引导定语从句,但本句末是句号,因此缺少先行词,无法构成定语从句。其他两选项意思、结构均不正确。故答案为A。

39. D 【解析】本题考查比较级。根据文意,作者在向我们阐述一个道理,我们的生活也像老木匠建房子一样,没有投入全身心,即用的努力少(less),所以答案为D。

40. A 【解析】本题考查动词。根据上下文,开始我们没有觉察,但后来当我们认识到自己的愚蠢行为时,为时已晚。所以,此处选择 realize,答案为A。

41. B 【解析】本题考查固定搭配。do it over 意为"重做一次",故答案为B。

42. C 【解析】本题考查副词。根据下文可知,作者在引用某人(曾经说过)的话,所以用副词 once 最合适。其他选项与文意不符。故答案为C。

43. A 【解析】本题考查名词。根据上文,老木匠既有经验,技艺也高超,但因态度不端正而自食其果。因此,一个人做事的态度决定结果,答案为A。

44. D 【解析】本题考查动词搭配。make a choice/choices 是固定搭配,"做出选择"。故答案为D。

45. B 【解析】本题考查副词。根据最后一段和上文中的 therefore 可知,作者是在告戒读者:我们既然明白了这个道理,"建造自己的房子时"就明智些吧!故答案为B。

Section Ⅲ Reading Comprehension

Text 1

[文章概述] 本文是以提出观点—举例论证的结构,阐述了 malnutrition(营养不良)的问题:营养不良对人类健康所起的破坏作用。

46. B 【解析】细节题。由文章的第一句即可知营养不良的问题一直都很严重,答案为B。

47. D 【解析】句意理解题。根据第三段最后一句可知(孩子)营养不良比大人严重的原因是他们需要更多的蛋白质。

48. A 【解析】细节题。根据第二段 account for the plumpness of hands, feet, belly, and face 得出"浮肿"的问题,而由 Lean shoulders reveal striking thinness. 得出"特殊的肩膀"。故答案为A。

49. D 【解析】句意理解题。根据第三段第一句即可得到D是正确的答案。

50. D 【解析】数字细节题。根据最后一句 of the 74 million people ... four out of five will be born in a country unable to supply its people's nutritional needss 可知答案为D。

Text 2

[文章概述] 本文是一篇关于人工智能的议论文。作者对真正的人工智能表示怀疑,认为人工智能不可能超越人脑。

51. C 【解析】句意理解题。根据第一段第二句可知"人工智能可能快要实现了,但是人们还不确定具体的时间。"因此科学家还尚未发现人工智能。

52. A 【解析】细节题。由第二段第三句可知作者认为科学家的抱怨是有原因的。故答案为A。

53. B 【解析】推理判断题。由第二段的后半部分,得出"计算机在下棋时会计算接下来好多种走法,并且每种可能性都算几步棋"以及"而人不会这样",可以得出计算机在下棋时的优势。

54. D 【解析】句意理解题。第三段的首句"呆板的思维是机器智能的弱点"可知答案为D。

55. C 【解析】细节题。根据最后一段倒数第二句可知电脑经过训练是可以听懂人们说的一些话的,答案为C。

Text 3

[文章概述] 本文介绍了法国著名足球运动员蒂埃里·丹尼尔·亨利。

56. B 【解析】句意理解题。根据第二段 ... his professional debut in 1994 ... 可知答案为B。

57. B 【解析】细节题。striker "前锋,射手"; goalkeeper "门将"; wing "边锋",文中提到亨利在这个位置表现不佳; captain "队长",不是足球比赛的位置。所以答案为B。

58. D 【解析】词义理解题。根据第三段第四句可以得出 the gunners 是和他并肩作战的队友。大写的 Gunners 是 Arsenal 的绰号。

59. D 【解析】细节题。该题定位于文中第三、四段。the France Cup 在文中没有被提及。

60. C 【解析】是非判断题。根据第三段的 Under long-time mentor and coach Arsène Wenger, Henry became a prolific striker ... 得出 Arsene Wenger 是亨利的良师益友。

Part B

61. A 【解析】细节题。讲我们每个人掌握着自己的未来。

62. E 【解析】细节题。讲老板可以通过脑电波判断你工作的表现。

63. G 【解析】主旨题。讲化学明胶一旦受到刺激,可以增强人们对高脂肪的食物的食欲。

64. C 【解析】主旨题。讲电脑在人们日常生活中不可替代的作用。

65. B 【解析】推理题。讲保持健康的好方法应该是变换饮食和积极锻炼。

Section IV   Writing

Part A

本例要求考生写一则请假条:因为母亲生病住院,向老师请两天假,必须注意措辞,阐明请假的原因,恳请老师批准。

解题步骤:

第一步:确定题材——便条,注意格式;

第二步:列出要点——请假时间、原因、证明等;

第三步:列出关键词——ask for two days' leave; take care of; make up the missed class, etc.

第四步:落笔成文

June 21st, 2009

Dear Professor Zhang,

I'm writing to ask for two days' leave. My father just informed me that my mother's ill in hospital and needs surgery tomorrow. So I have to go to the hospital and take care of her, which means I can't attend your class this afternoon. I've asked my classmates to record your class for me. I'll be back the day after tomorrow and will make up the missed class by listening to the tape and take down the notes.

Sincerely yours,

Li Hua

Part B

解题步骤:

第一步:审题

1. 题型:图表作文

2. 文体:论述说明文

第二步：框架分析

　　1. 说明图示内容，点出每个要点；

　　2. 图示现象发生的原因和影响。

第三步：列出写作思路

　　1. 简明扼要的描述图示的主要内容：总体而言，城市的空气质量提高了；

　　2. 重点描述图示内容：对每一年的好天气、重度污染天气天数进行描述、比较；

　　3. 分析原因：人们越来越关注环境，政府采取措施等；

　　4. 表示自己的愿望或者发出倡议：只要人们不断努力，加大保护力度，环境会越来越好。

第四步：列出关键词和词组

　　with the efforts of; gradually improve; climb to; reduce to; exception; due to the fact that; be aware of, etc.

第五步：落笔成文

　　Our city started the Blue Sky Project in 1998, when it saw only 100 days of blue skies but 141 heavily polluted days. With the efforts of the government and citizens over these years, the air condition of the city has gradually improved.

　　The number of blue skies climbed to 229 in 2004 while the heavily polluted days were greatly reduced to 17. The progress continued each year with an increase of 5－7 good days and decrease of 8－12 bad air days until the end of 2007, though there was an exception in 2006 with 24 days heavily polluted.

　　The changing numbers are due to the fact that people become more and more aware of the environment around them. In addition, the government has continued with its measures. Air quality monitoring, traffic control and tree planting are just some of the ways to improve the conditions.

　　We believe that the city will see more blue skies and fewer air-polluted days in the future and the people will be able to enjoy their life better.

模拟试题（四）

Section Ⅰ　Listening Comprehension

Part A

1. D　【解析】男士说："是啊，但我们想知道的是怎样去公园。"由此可知，他想找到公园在哪里。

2. B　【解析】男士说现在是 3：00，你可以乘到 Leeds 的火车，这班火车 15 分钟后就要开了。

3. A　【解析】女士说："你知道吗？Michael Owen 得了法国足球进球奖。"男士说："这有什么好稀奇，他本赛季得了 20 分。"由此可知，他们在谈论 Michael Owen 这个球员，所以答案为 A。

4. A　【解析】女士问字典在哪里，男士答，原价的字典在这儿，打折的在那儿。可知，对话发生在书店。

5. D　【解析】女士一上来就说："你出意外真是太遗憾了。"男士说："运气太差了，以后我要小心些。"可知在谈论男士的事故。所以答案为 D。

6. C　【解析】男士邀请女士去聚会，女士婉拒，说她周末要在饭店工作。所以答案为 C。

7. B　【解析】女士说她要给 Browning 寄张明信片，但她不知道写什么。所以答案为 B。

8. D　【解析】女士问修这只表要多少时间，男士答："修好了我会打电话给你。"可知女士在修表店修表，故他们是顾客和修理工的关系。

9. A　【解析】考虑虚拟语气。女士说："我多么希望我的头发长一点。"男士说："就是，可惜你把它剪了，如果你听了我的就好了。"可知男士不想女士剪头发。

10. B　【解析】Tom 迟到了，女士说："Tom 说这次他尽量不迟到，为什么他老是这样，这次我受够了。"从语气上可知她很生气。

Part B

11. C 【解析】女士说:"看在厨房里有些热水。"可知在家里。

12. B 【解析】男士头疼还在吸烟,说明他不会照顾自己。

13. D 【解析】女士说:"看在厨房里有些热水。给你,照我说的做。我放了些东西在水里,可以缓解你的症状。"可知女士给了他一些热水。

14. B 【解析】当男士说他头疼得厉害,女士建议他把烟灭了。当女士把水递给男士时,女士让男士用热毛巾包住头,把鼻子放在水上方,深呼吸。A、C、D都被提及。只有B没有被提到,所以答案为B。

15. C 【解析】男士答:"我家离公司很近(a stone's throw)",可知,他不开车是因为公司离他家不远。

16. B 【解析】男士说:"真不敢相信,在过去3年中,我浪费了这么多呼吸新鲜空气的机会。"可知他开车上班有三年了。

17. B 【解析】女士不理解男士的做法,可看出,她自己也是开车上班的,缺乏这种切身体会。答案为B。

18. D 【解析】由女士的话 ... 25 minutes to get to our company from here.可知他们是同事。

19. B 【解析】从文章第一句,旅游书大致可以分为3类,可知答案为B。

20. A 【解析】文章说第二种旅游书完全客观地描述了你该在旅游中看什么做什么。可知答案为A。

21. D 【解析】根据第二段第二句可知你也要注意书的出版日期,因为旅游是很实际的事,现在许多东西都变得太快了。所以答案为D。

22. D 【解析】由文章第二段第一句可知不要买只说好话的旅游书。

23. D 【解析】从文章第二段最后一句可知士兵的人数和音量影响着信息传播的速度,故答案为D。

24. D 【解析】罗马人靠士兵喊叫传递信息,非洲人靠打鼓传递信息,可知,他们都用声音传递信息,所以答案为D。

25. B 【解析】法国人可以用旗子传递字母,所以可以推测它可以传递复杂信息。A错,因为法国的信息是靠光传播的;B错,any太绝对,不是所有法国人都识字;D错,法国人的信息必须在眼力所及范围内,有局限,所以答案为B。

附:听力原文

Section I   Listening Comprehension

Part A

1. **W:** The map shows that this street goes downtown.

   M: Yes, but what we want to know is how to get to the park.

2. **W:** Excuse me. Could you tell me when the next train to Manchester leaves?

   M: Sure. Well, it's three now. The next train to Manchester leaves in two hours. But you can take the train to Leeds, which leaves in fifteen minutes and then get off at Manchester, because it stops at Manchester on the way.

3. **W:** Do you know that Michael Owen has won France Footballs Golden Ball Prize?

   M: Not a surprise. He has 20 goals this season.

4. **W:** Excuse me, where can I find dictionaries?

   M: The regular-priced ones are here. Plus, we have some on sale over on that table.

5. **W:** What a shame about your accident! What a way to end your holiday!

   M: Yes, it was bad luck. I suppose I should have been more careful.

6. **M:** The Students' English Club is having party on Saturday night. Would you like to come?

   W: I would like to, but I have to work at a restaurant on the weekend.

7. **M:** What's the matter? You've been sitting there for ages, just staring into space.

   W: I told the Browning I'd send them a postcard. Now I don't know what to say.

8. **W:** How long will it take you to fix my watch?

   M: I'll call you when it's ready. But it shouldn't take longer than a week.

9. **W:** I wish my hair were longer.

   M: Yes, pity you had it cut. If only you'd listened to me.

10. **W:** Look, it's already 8. Tom said he'd be here by 7.

   M: Yes, but you know what the traffic is like at this time of the evening.

   W: He said he'd try not to be late. Why does he always do this? I've had enough this time.

Part B

11—14

W: Shall I phone and tell your secretary you're not coming today?

M: Yes, please, dear. Tell her I've got a cold and have a headache, but hope to be back in a day or two. You'd better say I'm staying in bed.

W: But you are not in bed. Do you want me to tell a lie?

M: Oh, it's only a little one, dear. I'm not making a false excuse. I really have a bad headache.

W: Then put the cigarette out. It's very foolish of you to smoke when you've got a cold.

M: Very well, dear. You're quite right.

W: You never listen to me.

M: Don't I?

W: Look, There's some boiling water in the kitchen. Here you are. Do as I tell you now. I've put something in the water. That'll do you a lot of good. Wrap this cloth around your neck and put your nose over the water. That's right. Breathe in deeply.

M: It smells nice.

W: Now, another deep breath. Now breathe out. Slowly! Now, breathe in again. Go on doing that for five minutes. I will go and make that phone call to the office.

15—18

W: Peter, where is the car? I haven't seen you drive to work for a long time! Is it broken or stolen?

M: Hi, Susan! Oh, no! Of course not! I give up driving to work. Instead, I ride to my working place.

W: Why is that?

M: You see. There is only a stone's throw from my home to my working place. I think riding a bike to work is more convenient.

W: I don't think so. It will take you at least 25 minutes to get to our company from here.

M: Yes, sometimes, 30 minutes. But I love riding to work now. It is a totally different picture on my way to work.

W: Why do you think so?

M: You see, every morning, after I set off for work, I can breathe the new fresh air along the way. By the time I reach my office, I feel rather revived. I even don't rely on coffee to spend my morning hours.

W: Is it so magical?

M: At least, that's how I feel about riding to work. I can't believe I have wasted so much fresh morning air in the past 3 years!

W: Will you continue riding to work in the future?

M: I think so.

19—22

    It would seem that there are 3 kinds of travel books. The first are those that give a personal description of travels which the author has actually made himself. If they are informative and have a good index then they can be useful to you when you are planning your travels. The second kind are those books whose purpose is to give a purely objective description of things to be done and seen. If a well-read, cultured person has written such a book then it is even more useful. The third kind are those books which are called "a guide" to some place or another. If they are good, they will, in addition to their factual information, give an analysis or an interpretation.

Whatever kind of travel book you choose you must make sure that it does not describe everything as "marvelous", "fabulous" or "magical". You must also note its date of publication because travel is a very practical affair and many things change quickly in this century. Finally, you should make sure that the contents are well presented and easy to find.

23—25

In this high-tech digital world, it is very convenient for us to send messages. But in ancient times, people had to think hard to find ways to get the message sent.

Roman soldiers in some places built long rows of signal towers. When they had a message to send, the soldiers shouted it from tower to tower. If there were enough towers and enough soldiers with loud voices, important news could be sent quickly over distance.

In Africa, people learned to send messages by beating on a series of large drums. Each drum was kept within hearing distance of the next one. The drum beats were sent out in a special way that all the drummers understood. Though the messages were simple, they could be sent at great speed for hundreds of miles.

In the eighteenth century, a French engineer found a new way to send short messages. In this way, a person held a flag in each hand and the arms were moved to various positions representing different letters of the alphabet. It was like spelling out words with flags and arms.

Over a long period of time, people sent messages by all these different ways. However, not until the telephone was invented in America in the nineteenth century could people send speech sounds over a great distance in just a few seconds.

Section Ⅱ　Use of English

[参考译文]　我将车停在步行街商场前面,开始擦拭。一人从停车场对面朝我走来,就是社会上所谓的流浪汉。从外表看,他没车、没家、没干净衣服,也没钱。他在公交车站的前面坐了下来,但是看上去甚至连乘公车的钱也没有。他说:"这辆车子挺不错。"他看上去衣衫褴褛,但一副有尊严的样子。我说了声"谢谢",然后继续擦车。我干活的时候他静静地坐在那里。他一直没如我所料的那样来讨钱,沉默在我们之间蔓延,我心想:"问问他是不是需要帮助吧。"虽然确信他肯定说"是的"。"你需要帮助吗?"我问道。他回答了我的话,虽然只用了三个字,但意义深刻,让我永生难忘。"难道我们都不这样吗?"他说道。

此前我一直认为自己地位高、很成功,是个人物,可是这三个字像子弹一样击中了我。"难道我们都不这样吗?"我需要过帮助。也许不是车费或是一个容身之处,但是我需要过别人的帮助。我取出钱夹,给他的钱不仅足够他乘车,也够他那天晚上吃上一顿热饭,住进一个温暖的地方。这三个字现在似乎依然萦绕在我的耳际。不管你拥有多少,不管你取得多大的成就,你还是需要别人的帮助。不管你多么微不足道,不管你背负着多少困难,哪怕一文不名、无家可归,你仍然可以帮助别人。

26. B　**【解析】**本题考查关系连词。what 引导表语从句,作 consider 的宾语,有双重作用,what 相当于 a person that,所以答案为 B。

27. C　**【解析】**本题考查名词。此人衣衫破旧,因而"我"认为他一无所有。looks"外表",符合文意;expressions"面部表情"。所以答案为 C。

28. A　**【解析】**本题考查名词。下文提到我给了他足够的钱甚至可以买车票,所以答案为 A。

29. D　**【解析】**本题考查形容词。既然对方为无业游民,他应该是衣衫褴褛,所以答案为 D。

30. A　**【解析】**本题考查名词。由 dignity 可知,对方虽然贫穷,但有尊严。注意此处 air 表示"神态、感觉"。其他选项不符合文意,所以答案为 A。ragged 与 an air of dignity 形成鲜明的对比。

31. C 【解析】本题考查动词。文章开头提到我在擦车,而下文提到"as I worked",说明仍在擦车。所以答案为 C。

32. A 【解析】本题考查副词。由下文 silence 可知,他在旁边静静地看着我干活,答案为A。

33. B 【解析】本题考查动词。由上下文可推知,他一无所有,必然会开口向我要钱,故选 B 项,意为"所预料的"。

34. D 【解析】本题考查形容词。由上句 ... something inside said, "ask him if he needs any help." 可知,我相信像他这样的人,一定需要帮助,答案为 D。

35. A 【解析】本题考查形容词。由 but profound 和下文他说的话可知,他说的话是简单的 Don't we all 三个词,答案为 A。

36. B 【解析】本题考查动词。他的话直到现在我还记得,故答案为 B。

37. C 【解析】本题考查连词。通过 I had been feeling high, successful and important 可知,我在此之前一直认为自己地位高、很成功,是个重要人物,答案为 C。

38. D 【解析】本题考查动词。通过下文 like a shotgun,可知他的话对我震动很大,答案为D。

39. A 【解析】本题考查动词短语。reach in my wallet"伸手到钱包里拿(钱)";search for"搜寻……"；look up"在……里查找"; expose ... to"把……暴露于……"。根据文意,答案为 A。

40. A 【解析】本题考查名词。shelter 在此意为"居所,住处"。从下文的 for the day 和 sleep 可以推知,"我"给他的钱足够买车票、吃饭和寻找住处,答案为 A。【知识拓展】中文中"衣食住行"的对应表达为"food, clothing, shelter and travel"。

41. C 【解析】本题考查形容词。从上下文理解可知,他的话是对的,我至今没忘。ring true 意为"听起来是对的,真实的",所以答案为 C。

42. D 【解析】本题考查现在完成时。从上下文理解可知,无论你拥有多少,无论你取得了多大成功,都需要别人的帮助,答案为 D。

43. C 【解析】本题考查形容词。上文 how much 对比,应该是 how little。所以答案为 C。

44. A 【解析】本题考查形容词。从下文 even without money or a place to sleep 可知,我们的生活充满问题,甚至可能没钱或睡觉的地方。load with 意为"给……装上",其他选项不符文意。所以答案为 A。

45. B 【解析】本题考查动词。通过上文可知,即使我们生活很贫穷,仍然可以给予别人帮助,答案为 B。

Section Ⅲ　Reading Comprehension

Text 1

[文章概述]　文章介绍了诺贝尔奖得主 John Maxwell Coetzee 的个性、成名历程、作品以及其对文学的贡献。

46. B 【解析】细节题。根据第三段第二、三句可知他得知获奖后很惊讶。

47. B 【解析】细节题。根据第四段可知他对隐私的热爱让人们怀疑他参加颁奖典礼的可能性,所以答案为 B。

48. A 【解析】细节题。由倒数第二段可知 Coetzee 是一个素食主义者,比起骑摩托车,他更喜欢自行车,他不喜欢喝酒。由此选 A 排除 B、C。倒数第三段 he said in a rare interview, 从 rare 可以看出他不喜欢接受访问,所以 D 也排除。

49. C 【解析】细节题。由文章第八段第一、二句可知因为小说他获得英国最高的荣誉。所以答案为 C。

50. B 【解析】细节题。由文章最后一段可看出作者对 John Maxwell Coetzee 的肯定,所以答案为B。

Text 2

[文章概述]　作者对于许多年轻人想成为作家这一现象给予鼓励,但同时指出作家和写作

之间的巨大差异,成为作家不容易,要成为作家就一定要热爱写作,并且坚持不懈。

51. C 【解析】主旨题。作者在第一段便点明写作和成为作家是不同的,指出很多年轻人的想法是不成熟的。接下来又以亲身经历说明成为作家的艰辛。故答案为C。

52. B 【解析】细节题。根据最后一段可知几年后,作者还是没有突破,渐渐开始怀疑自己,可知答案为B。

53. A 【解析】细节题。根据第二段第二句可知在成千上万想成为作家的人中,可能只有一人有运气如愿。成为作家的几率很小,故答案为A。

54. C 【解析】推理判断题。因为这些人总去问 what if,说明他们总是犹豫不决,对自己的未来举棋不定,做不出最终决定,跟自己总是付诸实践形成对比。

55. C 【解析】词义推测题。根据最后一段倒数第二句可知我会以实践来完成我的梦想,即使那意味着我要生活在不决定和担心失败的状态中。由后一句 This is the shadowland ... 可知 shandowland 指代的就是不确定的这种状态。其他三个选项都是 shadowland 的字面意思。

Text 3

[文章概述] 本文主要讨论了现代城市处理垃圾的问题,首先介绍了18世纪如何处理垃圾,然后指出导致城市垃圾难处理的一些因素。

56. D 【解析】主旨题。由第一段第一句可知文章主要讨论垃圾处理的问题(A项),至于处理垃圾的地点(B项)、垃圾污染的危害(C项)和处理垃圾的方式(D项)都是垃圾处理问题的一个方面,不能以偏概全。

57. B 【解析】细节题。recycle"循环利用"。根据最后一段第一句对于垃圾的循环利用是最近才开始的一项技术,18世纪的时候是没有的,故答案为B。其他选项文中都被提及。

58. D 【解析】逻辑推断题。循环利用垃圾并没有导致城市垃圾处理问题,只是没能解决这个问题。

59. D 【解析】推理判断题。文章第四段提到 landfills(垃圾掩埋法)和 long-distance trash hauling (垃圾长途拖运),可见现代社会人们所使用的垃圾处理方法还和以前一样。

60. B 【解析】意图推断题。文章主要讨论了垃圾处理问题,为了引起读者的注意,而没有具体指明应该如何更好地处理垃圾,故排除C;由 Even the most efficient ... a city's reusable waste. 可知 D 错;A 项没有涉及垃圾处理的问题,偏离文章的主题,所以答案为B。

Part B

61. G 【解析】推理题。讲教育标准的提升是无形的,抽象的,不易察觉的。

62. E 【解析】推理题。讲学生自己愿意学习在教育过程中很重要。

63. A 【解析】细节题。讲所谓的现代教学技术应该为许多学校振聋发聩的噪音承担责任。

64. C 【解析】细节题。讲我们应该树立正确的教育评价体系,应从学生在学习过程中真正有多享受学习这方面进行考察。

65. B 【解析】细节题。讲现在有这么好的条件,人们不学习是可耻的。

Section Ⅳ Writing

Part A

本例要求考生写一则书信:因为朋友在大学里不知道如何准备大学英语四级考试,自己恰好经过努力已经通过了考试,于是给他提供一些学习备考的经验,鼓励朋友树立自信并通过考试。

解题步骤:

第一步:确定题材——书信,注意格式;

第二步:列出要点——自己的喜讯,总结考试通过的原因、分享经验,鼓励对方等;

第三步:列出关键词—— passed the CET-4; share with; in preparation for; be confident, etc.

第四步:落笔成文

June 26th, 2009

Dear Liu Yang,

I'm glad to tell you that I've successfully passed the CET-4. Now I'd like to share with you my tips in preparation for the test. Firstly, I spent one hour every day listening to VOA downloaded from the Internet. Secondly, I read a number of articles every day, which strengthened my reading comprehension and enlarged my vocabulary. Thirdly, I did a lot of practice on writing and talking about various topics with my partners. Be confident and work hard, then you can also pass the exam without much difficulty.

I hope you will find my experience of some use to you.

Sincerely yours,

Li Hua

Part B

解题步骤:

第一步:审题

1. 题型:看图作文

2. 文体:论述说明文

第二步:框架分析

1. 说明漫画内容,点出要点;

2. 漫画中人物的不良行为以及他们所应该做的事情。

第三步:列出写作思路

1. 在漫画中,女子让男子不要在她家附近偷电线,断电影响孩子学习;

2. 孩子由于断电不得不在屋子里点着蜡烛学习;

3. 评论漫画内容:很显然,这对夫妻很自私,只顾自己孩子,而不顾公共设施,况且盗窃本身就是违法行为;

4. 事实上,他们给孩子也树立了一个不好的榜样,影响孩子的健康成长,所以应该立即停止这种行为,而不是到别处去偷。

第四步:列出关键词和词组

power failure; selfish and stupid; care about; follows one's advice; commit a crime; set an example for; instead of, etc.

第五步:落笔成文

The cartoon tells us a ridiculous story. In front of a house, a woman said to her man with electric wires around his shoulder, "next time don't steal the electric wires in our neighborhood, or power failure will affect our son's studies." Behind them in the house their boy is doing his homework in the dim candlelight.

What selfish and stupid parents they are! They seem to care about their son, but how about the public interest? Even if the man follows his wife's advice and steals the electric wires somewhere else, he is still disturbing other people's everyday life and committing a crime. What's more, they are setting a very bad example for their son indeed! So what they should do is to stop their wrong doing immediately instead of repeating it somewhere else.

模拟试题（五）

Section Ⅰ Listening Comprehension

Part A

1. **D** 【解析】女士说："我们有那种颜色，但是我们只有中号了。"男士说："那样的话，我就买这件蓝色的吧。"由此可知，男士在买衣服，因而只有 D 项与此相符。

2. **B** 【解析】女士说："Tom 今天看起来特紧张，对吧？"男士说："是啊，我猜他还不太适应做演讲。"由此可知，Tom 演讲的次数不多，经验不老道。

3. **D** 【解析】医生建议女士减肥。女士问："你真的认为有那么严重吗？"医生答："是啊，如果不减肥的话，某天你可能会发生心脏病。"由此可知，如果不接受医生建议，女士就可能突发心脏病，答案为 D。

4. **A** 【解析】男士问："想开窗还是开空调。"女士答："如果你不介意的话，我想呼吸新鲜空气。"所以是开窗，答案为 A。

5. **A** 【解析】女士说："你所拨打的号码不在服务区内。"男士说："不可能，我早晨还和他在打电话，请确认一下。"由此可知他在打电话，故答案为 A。

6. **A** 【解析】女士说："你介不介意我们在晚饭前谈一下这个计划？"男士答："不介意，我可不想在吃饭的时候谈。"由此可知，他们会在晚饭前谈，故答案为 A。

7. **C** 【解析】从女士说的 Fortunately, no one was badly hurt. "幸运的是，无人受伤。"可知无人死亡。

8. **C** 【解析】女士说："如果你提早一点打闪光灯示意要转弯，这就不会发生了。"男士说："但是，我及时打了，看看你把我的车子弄得一团糟！你太莽撞了，而且超速！你才是罪魁祸首。"由此可见，男士与女士的车相撞了，发生了纠纷，据此推断这是一场交通事故。

9. **C** 【解析】女士说："红色的外套是 45 美金，黑的是 35 美金，你想要哪件？"男士说："都不要，我要这件黄色大号的，多少钱？"女士说："这件是黑色的两倍。"所以 35×2=70，可知黄色的要 $70。

10. **B** 【解析】女士把男士的书弄丢了，男士说："不要紧。"女士说："我觉得过意不去，让我买本新的给你吧。"男士说："不要傻了，我可没想着要你赔。"可知女士在道歉。

Part B

11. **C** 【解析】本对话内容是女士在劝男士戒烟。由此可知主题是关于男士抽烟的问题。故答案为C。

12. **C** 【解析】女士对男士说，如果男士还是不能戒烟，她就要重新考虑与他订婚的问题。男士听了说："你为了这个要取消我们的订婚？我简直不敢相信！"由此可知，男士很恼怒。

13. **C** 【解析】根据 We seem to be having this converstion over and over again. 可知女士劝男士戒烟已经很多次了。故答案为 C。

14. **B** 【解析】女士对男士说："你需要一些帮助，为何不去看看医生呢？"男士说："你指心理医生？"女士说："不是啊，我指全科医生。"由此可知，女士想让男士去看看全科医生，故选 B，排除 A，文中没有提及 C，D 是男士自己提出来的。

15. **C** 【解析】根据女士的回答："你只要出示你的银行卡、填写一张取钱单就可以随时取回你的钱。"由此可以看出，这种存款方式很便利。

16. **A** 【解析】根据女士的话可以知道如果要开一个活期存款的账户，就要填申请表、存款、出示护照、签名。由此可知应选 A，排除 B、C、D。

17. **B** 【解析】由女士的话 I'll mail you the bank card in a week. 可知他要一周后才能拿到银行卡。故答案 B。

18. **B** 【解析】由文章中"如果你的父母想要许多个孩子，但是只能生你一个，那么，他们非常可能把本来要分给几个孩子的精力和注意力都投注到你身上。我称之为'掌上明珠'现象。"可知应选 B。

19. B 【解析】根据第二段第一、二句"在另一方面，你成为一个独生子女也可能因为你的父母只计划生育一个小孩，并且把他们的生育的计划执行到底。你的父母可能给你非常严格、体系完备的教育，使你成为一个'小大人'。"可知答案为B。

20. A 【解析】文章开头"对于任何一个独生子女的关键问题在于：为什么你是一个独生子女？这个问题至少有两个答案。"说明本文要讨论的也就是两方面的原因。文章第二段开头 On the other hand 也提示了这一点，故答案为A。

21. C 【解析】由第二段最后一句"很多独生子女在不愉快中长大，因为他们不能不成为这样的'小大人'。"而造成这个'小大人'主要的原因还是前面讲的父母给他们严格的教育。说到底还是父母期望值比较高，故答案为C。

22. C 【解析】女士认为应该把动物放回大自然，通过改善环境来保护他们。而男士认为动物园可以用来保护濒危动物，又可以作为教育基地。由此可知他们在讨论动物园的功用。

23. B 【解析】男士说："对呀，但是如果没有动物园的话，动物会灭绝的。"由此可见男士认为动物园可以防止濒危物种灭绝。故答案为B。

24. D 【解析】女士说："动物远离了它们自然的生活环境来供人们参观。这一点也不自然。""我们所要做的是改善自然环境，保证他们在野外还有生存之地。"可见女士认为大自然才是它们真正的生存之地。

25. D 【解析】男士说："我认为现在有一种趋势，就是把动物园建设成为教育中心。"故答案为D。

附：听力原文

Section I Listening Comprehension

Part A

1. **W:** Yes, we do have that color. But unfortunately we don't have the medium size now.
   M: In that case, I'll have to take the blue one.

2. **W:** Tom looks awfully nervous, doesn't he?
   M: Yes. I'm afraid he is not used to making speeches.

3. **M:** As your doctor, I strongly advise you to go on a diet.
   W: Do you really think that's important?
   M: Definitely. If you don't, you might have a heart attack someday.

4. **M:** Do you want to turn on the air conditioner or open the window?
   W: I love fresh air if you don't mind.

5. **W:** I'm sorry, but the number you dialed is not in service.
   M: But that's impossible! I just spoke to him this morning. Please check for me.

6. **W:** Would you mind if we discuss our plan before dinner?
   M: Not at all. I certainly don't want to talk about it over dinner.

7. **W:** I think several people must have been killed in that road accident.
   M: There were 2 men in the truck and 3 women and a child in the car. Fortunately, no one was badly hurt.

8. **W:** If you had signaled your intention to return a little sooner, this wouldn't have happened.
   M: But I signaled in time! Just look at the mess you've made of my car! You were driving carelessly and your speed was above the limit! You're the one who's to blame!

9. **W:** The red coat is $45 and the black one is $35. Which one do you want?
   M: Neither. I want that large yellow one. How much is it?
   W: It's twice as much as the black one.

10. **W:** I am sorry, but I can't find the book you lent me.
    M: That's OK.

W: I really feel bad about it. Let me buy you a new one.

M: No. Don't be silly. I wouldn't dream of letting you do that.

Part B

11—14

M: We seem to be having this conversation over and over again.

W: You're right.

M: Look, I know how you feel about my smoking. You don't have to tell me every day.

W: I'm sorry. I worry about you.

M: Let's be honest. There's always going to be a reason. After you graduate, it's going to be hard to find a job, then there will be the stress from just starting a job.

M: OK, I get your point. It's just so hard. You don't really understand because you have never smoked.

W: You need some help. Why don't you go to a doctor?

M: You mean a psychiatrist?

W: No, I don't. I mean a general practitioner. Maybe you can get a patch, or some pills, well, I don't know, something to help you with the withdrawal.

M: Really, I believe I can quit on my own. But I'll think about it. I will.

W: All right. I won't mention it for a week. Then I want to know your decision. Because if you don't get some help, I need to rethink our plans.

M: You mean you'd break our engagement over this? I can't believe it!

W: I don't know.

15—17

W: May I help you?

M: Yes, please. I'd like to open a new account.

W: Yes, I'd be happy to help you. What kind of accounts would you like to open?

M: Well, I am not sure. What kind of accounts can I open here?

W: Usually we offer current account and fixed account for individuals.

M: Could you tell me the differences between them?

W: Of course I will. If you open a fixed account, the interest rate is higher.

M: Then how about the current account?

W: You may withdraw the money at any time and you just need to present your bank card and a withdraw slip.

M: I would rather open a current account.

W: OK, please fill in this application form.

M: Here is the filled out application form. Is everything all right?

W: Yes, quite all right. But you have to deposit some money at the same time you open the account.

M: Fine. Here are one hundred pounds.

W: Please show your passport.

M: Here you are.

W: Good. Please sign here. OK, everything is done. Here is your receipt and passport. I'll mail you the bank card in a week.

M: Thank you very much.

W: It's my pleasure.

18—21

The key question for any only child is this: why were you an only child? It's a key question for at least two reasons. If your parents had wanted several children but could have you only, they are most likely to pour into you all the energy and attention that had been intended for several children. I call this the "special jewel" phenomenon. Only children who are special jewels often arrive when their parents are older —usually in their thirties. These special jewels can become very spoiled and self-centered.

On the other hand, you may be an only child because your parents planned for only one and stuck to their plan. Your parents may give you a very strict and well-structured education to make you "a little adult". Many only children grow up feeling unhappy because they always had to be such "little adults".

22—25

W: Well, it's sort of attractive, but in the end I still find it a pretty depressing place.

M: Do you? Why?

W: The animals are out of their natural environment. They're just here for humans to look at. There's nothing natural about it.

M: Yeah, but if we didn't have any zoos, a lot of species would just, well, they'd face extinction.

W: Do you really believe that?

M: Well, don't you? I mean they have good breeding projects for some species that are dying out. Um, anyway, I think, there's a trend towards developing zoos to become education centers, stimulating information for kids and displays, and that kind of thing.

W: What we need to do is to take care of the natural environment, make sure that they've still got a place where they can live in the wild.

M: Well, yeah, OK. But it's just not happening, is it? I think in reality you've got to have zoos.

W: Well, I just can't agree with that. I mean, what is the pleasure in watching animals pacing up and down in cages?

M: Look, zoos are changing. Some older zoos put animals in cages, but what about safari parks? The animals are fine there. They've got a lot of space and people see them in a much more natural setting.

W: Well, maybe you're right.

Section II　Use of English

[参考译文] 科学家们发现,勤劳的人寿命比一般人要长。职业妇女比家庭主妇更健康。证据表明,没有工作的人身体素质比那些有工作的人要差。一项研究表明,失业率每增加1%,死亡率就相应地增加2%。所有这一切都可以归结为一点,那就是:工作有益于健康。

为什么工作有益于健康?这是因为工作让人处于忙碌中,使人们远离孤独和寂寞。研究表明,人们无所事事时,会感到不满、担忧和寂寞。相反,最快乐的是那些忙碌的人。许多热爱自己事业的人成就辉煌,他们觉得努力工作时最幸福。工作是人和现实之间的桥梁。通过工作,人们接触到他人。通过集体活动,人们发现友谊和温暖。这都有利于健康。丢掉工作就意味着丢掉一切。失业影响一个人的心理,并容易让人生病。

此外,工作能够给人充实感和成就感。工作使人感觉到自己的价值以及在社会中的地位。当一个作家完成自己的作品或医生给一个病人成功地动完手术或教师看到自己的学生在成长,他们的喜悦之情无以言表。

综上所述,我们可以得出这样的结论:工作越多,你将会越快乐和越健康。让我们努力工作,好好学习,并过着一种幸福而健康的生活吧。

本文作者首先提出观点:努力工作的人比一般人活得时间更长,并运用实例给予了科学的解释。

26. B 【解析】从文章的主题句 Scientists find that hard-working people live longer than average men and women.可得出"职业妇女比家庭主妇更健康"的结论。A 项为语法错误。

27. C 【解析】该选项与下文的 the job-holders 构成对比,"没有工作的人比有工作的人身体差"。

28. A 【解析】that 引导宾语从句,从句中又有一个 whenever 引导的时间状语从句。句意为"研究表明当失业率上升1%,死亡率相应上升2%。"

29. A 【解析】该题句意为"所有这些归结为一点。"come down to"归结为";equal to"等于"; add

up to "合计为"; amount to "总共到；相当于"。

30. D 【解析】该句句意为"这是因为工作使人忙碌，使人们远离孤独和寂寞。"keep sb. away from 是固定搭配，意为"使……远离/避开……"。

31. D 【解析】从下文 ... and lonely when they have nothing to do 进行逻辑推理，可知"没事做的人会感到不开心、焦虑和孤独"。

32. A 【解析】从上文内容可知，最快乐的人是那些大忙人。

33. D 【解析】该句句意为"工作充当了人与现实生活联系的桥梁。"

34. B 【解析】该句句意为"通过工作人们开始相互联系/接触。"

35. A 【解析】失去了工作就意味着失去了这一切。mean "意味着"。

36. D 【解析】从意义上分析，A、C 项不符合上下文的逻辑关系；B 项过于严重，失去工作还达不到死亡的程度。

37. A 【解析】从文章的篇章结构上分析，上文讲述的是工作给人们带来的益处，下文还是讲述这方面的内容，属递进关系，不是转折关系。

38. B 【解析】从意义上判断，此题必须同前面的 a sense of fulfillment(充实感)意义相类似，所以答案为 B "成就感"。【知识拓展】sense 常可以译作"观念、感、觉、感觉和意义"。如：a sense of time(时间观念)；a sense of duty(责任感)；a sense of humor(幽默感)；the sense of touch(触觉)；make sense(有意义)。

39. C 【解析】从下文的 his writing 可判断出答案为 C。

40. C 【解析】根据医生从事的工作性质可断定是"成功地为病人动手术"。

41. B 【解析】"学生成长"主要表现在知识、阅历上的长进。

42. D 【解析】beyond words（相当于 beyond description）"无法用语言表达"；in a word "简言之"；without a word "二话没说"；at a word"反应迅速地，立即"。

43. A 【解析】从语法结构上分析，conclusion 之后为同位语从句，that 引导同位语从句时，不作成分但不能省略。【知识拓展】与 conclusion 相关的短语有 in conclusion(总之)；arrive at a conclusion/reach a conclusion/draw a conclusion(得出结论)等。

44. D 【解析】这是一个"the +比较级，the +比较级"句型，句意为"工作越多，人就会越幸福、越健康"。【知识拓展】"the +比较级，the +比较级"是一个常考句型，如：The more we discuss with each other, the more we will get to know each other. The more I know him, the less I like him.

45. A 【解析】从句子结构上判断，此句有三个并列的谓语动词；同时注意修饰动词要用副词不能用形容词。

Section III Reading Comprehension

Text 1

[文章概述] 本文主要讨论的是健康食品，以及关于健康产品的分类。

46. B 【解析】细节题。在第一段第四句中提到 This term is used to distinguish between types of the same food. 而 this term 所指代的正是第三句中的 natural food。

47. B 【解析】推理判断题。第三、四段是对面包的制作加工过程的一个描述，但是我们发现从种粮食到面包的制成有添加剂的作用，而这些添加剂都是 toxic 或者 poisonous，即有毒的，故答案为 B。

48. D 【解析】细节题。根据第二段最后一句 ... vitamin content is greatly reduced in processed foods. 可知答案为 D。

49. D 【解析】细节题。根据第五段 ... we buy our good on the basis of smell, color, and texture ... 与选项 D 中的内容相吻合，所以答案为 D。

50. A 【解析】主旨推断题。纵观全文，作者在开头提出"绿色食品"的定义并且对定义进行解释说明，将人们日常生活中的食品进行了对比。作者在叙述全文时始终围绕"健康食品"展开。故答案为 A。

Text 2

[**文章概述**] 本文是一篇总分结构的议论文,主要探讨了写作教学过程中关于标点的一个误区。第一段指出了标点的作用,第二、三、四段则是讨论了教学过程中先教标点的做法。

51. D 【解析】主旨大意题。第二段到第四段一再提到标点的学习应当优先。

52. C 【解析】细节题。根据第三段的第五、六句可知此处用反问语气表明作者认为即使人们写出的句子没有动词,也不能算错。这与 C 项吻合。

53. C 【解析】猜测词义题。由 The child can be nudged and helped towards writing in sentences ... 可知,nudge 与 help 的意思相接近。这与 C 的“鼓励”最贴切。

54. A 【解析】推理判断题。第四段第二句 Before you can learn the punctuation, you have to know what you want to punctuate. 在学习实用标点之前,你必须首先知道你所要加的标点的内容。这与 A 选项相符合。

55. A 【解析】推理判断题。由文章最后一句话可以得知,为了适应课程要求而颠倒句子写作和标点学习的先后顺序的危害非常大。所以教师提前教授标点是为了“课程的需要”。

Text 3

[**文章概述**] 本文是一篇关于环境保护的议论文。文章首先驳斥了过去人们缺乏环保意识,然后提出了自己的观点,即为了自己和子孙后代,环境保护应当成为我们每个人生活的不可缺少的部分。

56. C 【解析】细节题。由第一段第三句得知,过去人们缺少或者缺乏环保意识,认为自然资源取之不尽、用之不竭,这与 C 选项相符合。其余 A、B、D 选项虽然在文章中都被提到,但却不具有概括性。

57. B 【解析】推理判断题。从第三段第四句到段末可得知,我们所需要知道的是水、土壤和生物之间是相互依赖的。A、D 选项都是由第二段得知的,而 C 则是无中生有。

58. D 【解析】推理判断题。由第三段句首可得知,我们必须改正祖先的错误,所以下文即提出了解决方案:Conservation should be made a part of everyone's daily life. 该段紧接着就介绍了一些具体的环保知识,由此可以推断出我们每个人都应当接受环保教育,这与 D 项符合。A 选项太过片面;B 在文中没有被提及;C 中的 natural science 与环保的概念不能等同。

59. D 【解析】猜测句意题。由此句得知,我们不仅要保护平面的空间(square measure of surface),还要保护立体的空间(cubic volume above the earth),二者分别指生活在陆地的动物和生活在空中的动物,即鸟类,因此这与 D 选项吻合。

60. A 【解析】主旨题。由作者论述前人对环保的无知和对环境保护的急切呼吁可以得知,作者所持的态度不是 positive(积极的)或者 suspicious(怀疑的)。而文中在论述时有很多代表作者观点的话,因而选择 neutral 也是片面的。作者对于目前的资源的利用持的是批评态度,所以答案为 A。

Part B

61. C 【解析】细节题。讲偏爱到超市购物是因为那里的商品价格便宜。

62. E 【解析】推理题。讲推销员上门服务,服务质量要比超市好。

63. D 【解析】细节题。讲自己不信任推销员。

64. F 【解析】推理题。讲大多数推销员还是好的,不会去欺骗顾客。

65. G 【解析】细节题。讲推销员很有趣且讲礼貌。

Section IV Writing

Part A

本例要求考生写一则书信:因为外教仅有额外的四张看爱尔兰踢踏舞的票,希望想去的学生自己主动申请并阐述理由。

解题步骤：

第一步：确定题材——书信,注意格式；

第二步：列出要点——观看踢踏舞的意愿,自己的兴趣,感激等；

第三步：列出关键词——would like to; learn to dance, be interested in the Irish Tap Dance; very much appreciate, etc.

第四步：落笔成文

June 11th, 2009

Dear Bill,

I'm writing to tell you that I would like to watch the Irish Tap Dance with you very much. I've been learning to dance for almost a year, yet so far I have never had a chance to watch a group of professional people dancing on the stage. If I should be granted such a good opportunity, I would very much appreciate it as it will surely boost my interest in learning Irish culture and make much more progress in dancing.

Please let me know if you could spare a ticket for me. Looking forward to your favorable reply.

Sincerely yours,

Zhang Hua

Part B

解题步骤：

第一步：审题

　　1. 题型：看图作文

　　2. 文体：论述说明文

第二步：框架分析

　　1. 说明漫画内容,点出要点；

　　2. 针对漫画人物所做的事情给予简要评价,谈谈自己的看法。

第三步：列出写作思路

　　1. 首先要肯定互联网给人们带来的方便；

　　2. 委婉指出互联网产生的不良影响：暴力、假象等影响青少年的健康发展,甚至让他们对学习失去兴趣；

　　3. 政府采取措施整顿网络环境,表达自己的看法：网络环境一定能变好,更好地为人们服务。

第四步：列出关键词和词组

　　benefit from; keep in touch with; have effect on; lose interest in; take measures, etc.

第五步：落笔成文

Keep the Online World Clean

There is no doubt that we have benefited a lot from the Internet in our everyday life. We can read news, watch films, keep in touch with our relatives, make friends, or play games to relax ourselves on the Internet.

But every coin has two sides. The Internet also has a bad effect on citizens, especially on the teenagers. Once they open a page on the Internet, things such as violence, sex, and cheating, will appear unexpectedly from nowhere in front of their eyes. On the one hand, they seriously pollute their hearts and souls. On the other hand, children will gradually lose interest in their studies.

Now, the government has realized the serious problems and is taking some drastic measures to purify the Internet environment. Some websites that disobey the rules are made public and even closed up. I'm sure we will have a better online environment quite soon so that the Internet can serve us better!

专家预测试题(一)

Section Ⅰ Listening Comprehension

Part A

1. C 【解析】该答案可从一个简单的计算得出。每本 10 元,3 本则 30 元。
2. D 【解析】根据男士的态度可以推断出女士借给他的工具已经遗失。
3. C 【解析】根据两人的对话内容得出两人是上下属的关系。
4. B 【解析】根据sports section 以及 the classified ads and local-news section 可以得出两人是在读报纸,所以答案为 B。
5. B 【解析】根据转折词 but 后面的内容得出答案为 B。
6. B 【解析】根据原文,火车将于 10 分钟以后发车,而现在是 10:30,所以答案为 B。
7. D 【解析】根据女士的反问 He isn't going to work on his term paper? 得出答案。
8. C 【解析】根据男士所说的 I am back in school taking courses for a teacher's certificate.得出他计划要做名教师。
9. B 【解析】根据原文 I've never found better in my life. 得出答案。
10. B 【解析】文中说到胶卷已经用完了,因此无法拍摄照片。所以答案为 B。

Part B

11. C 【解析】根据第三段第三句可知他进入银行的原因是为了获取他的奖励。
12. C 【解析】根据第二段第一句 Peter was an auto mechanic. 得出答案为 C。
13. A 【解析】根据 No one tripped an alarm. No one pulled a gun. No one called the police. Why did they allow him to get away with it?可知答案为 A。
14. C 【解析】根据原文,可以得出他不仅受到五分钟的时间限制,还受到了他的口袋大小的限制。
15. A 【解析】根据 ... picking somebody's pocket takes skill 可知答案为 A。
16. B 【解析】根据 My preferred target was the lone female, handbag at her side, the right side to be exact. 可知答案为 B。
17. C 【解析】根据 one of the best places to keep a wallet is in the back pocket of tight trousers. 可知答案为 C。
18. A 【解析】根据 The perfect setting is clothing store.可知答案为 A。
19. B 【解析】根据第二句可知暴风雨最先侵袭的是 The Gulf of Mexico,所以答案为 B。
20. D 【解析】文中提到暴风雨造成了人员伤亡,航空中断,农作物被毁等灾难。用排除法得出答案为 D。
21. D 【解析】根据第一句 ... he wants Tom to become a doctor,too. 可知答案为 D。
22. B 【解析】根据 Tom is now in a medical school ... 可知答案为 B。
23. D 【解析】根据 ... he finds studying medicine very boring. 可知答案为 D。
24. B 【解析】根据 He wishes he could please himself and make his parents happy, too.可知答案为B。
25. C 【解析】在最后一段 He wishes he didn't have to worry about money.可知答案为 C。

附:听力原文

Section Ⅰ Listening Comprehension

Part A

1. **W:** How much is the book?
   M: Ten yuan each.
   W: I'd like to buy three of them.

2. **W:** Simon, oh, well, could you return the tools I lend you for building the bookshelf last month?

   M: Oh, I hate to tell you this, but I can't seem to find them.

3. **W:** Mr. Watson, I wonder whether it's possible for me to take a vacation early next month?

   M: Did you fill out a request form?

4. **M:** Would you pass me the sports section please?

   W: Sure, if you give me the classified ads and local-news section.

5. **W:** In the shop, I thought this shirt was green, but out here in the sunlight I see it's really blue.

   M: Yes, the bright yellow display lights in the shop make things look a little different, don't they?

6. **M:** So, when are the other guys going to get here? The train is leaving in 10 minutes. We can't wait here forever!

   W: It's 10:30 already? They are supposed to be here by now! I told everybody to meet here by 10:15.

7. **M:** Elien is in the basement trying to repair the washing machine.

   W: He isn't going to work on his term paper?

8. **W:** Frank, I thought you were working in New York.

   M: I was, but I've moved back. I just couldn't get used to living in a big city, so here I am back in school taking courses for a teacher's certificate.

9. **W:** Hello, John, how are you feeling now? I hear you've been ill.

   M: They must have confused me with my twin brother Rod. He's been sick a week, but I've never found better in my life.

10. **M:** Look, the view is fantastic, could you take a picture for me with the lake in the background?

    W: I am afraid I just ran out of film.

Part B

11—14

Some people dream of being President of the United States. Some dream of becoming stars in a Hollywood movie, and others of making millions of dollars overnight. But, could a dream like that come true in real life? Well, it did happen to Peter Johnson.

Peter was an auto mechanic. One day, he walked into the Union Trust Bank in Baltimore and took 5,000 dollars that did not belong to him. The guards and other employees stood back and let him stuff the bills in his shirt and pants without trying to prevent him from taking the money. No one tripped an alarm. No one pulled a gun. No one called the police. Why did they allow him to get away with it?

Well, everything was legal. Peter had won a contest promoted by a Baltimore radio station. The first prize entitled him to enter the Union Trust Bank and gather up as much money as he could lay his hands within five minutes. Because he could not bring any large bags or boxes into the bank, all the money had to be placed in his pockets.

As the time went by, Peter ran about wildly, trying to pick up as many large bills as he could find. When his time was up, he was out of breath, but was $5,000 richer.

15—18

For 25 years I was a full-time thief, specializing in picking pockets. Where I come from in southeast London, that's an honorable profession. Anyone can break into a house and steal things. But picking somebody's pocket takes skill. My sister and I were among the most successful pickpocket teams in London. We worked in hotel and theatre lobbies, airports, shopping centers, and restaurants. Now we don't steal anymore, but this crime is worldwide. Here is how to protect yourself:

Professional pickpockets do not see victims, only handbags, jewels and money. Mothers with babies, the elderly, the disabled are all fair game. My preferred target was the lone female, handbag at her side, the right side to be exact. So if I'm next to her I can reach it cautiously with my right hand across my body. Only about one woman in a thousand carries her bag on the left, and I tended to steer clear of them. Women whose bags are hanging in front of them are tricky for the pickpocket, as there isn't a blind side. If you want to make it even harder, use a bag with handles rather than a strap. For men, one of the best places to keep a wallet is in the back pocket of tight trousers. You'll feel any attempts to move it. Another good place is in the buttoned-up inside pocket of a jacket. There's just no way in. Even better, keep wallets attached to a cord or chain that is fasten to a belt.

A pickpocket needs targets who are relaxed and off guard. The perfect setting is a clothing store. When customers wander among the racks, they are completely absorbed in the items they hold up. The presence of a uniformed security guard is even better. A false sense of security makes a pickpocket's job much simpler.

19—20

About 100 people are now known to have died in what have been described as the worst storms ever to hit the eastern US this century. The hurricane-force winds first struck the Gulf of Mexico, and have now spread across the Canadian border, continuing to bring record snowfalls, and severe flooding, causing millions of dollars of damage. All major airports have now reopened and airlines are beginning to cope with the backlog of thousands of stranded passengers. The storms also paralyzed areas of Cuba, where several people were killed and property and crops destroyed.

21—25

Tom's father is a doctor, and he wants Tom to become a doctor, too. However, Tom would rather be an artist. He loves to draw and paint. People say that he is very talented. Tom's parents say it would be foolish for Tom to become an artist, because artists don't make enough money to support themselves. Tom is now in a medical school, but he is not very happy. He doesn't mind the hard work, but he finds studying medicine very boring. Moreover, he doesn't like hospitals, either. Tom is still thinking of becoming an artist, but he isn't sure that he can do it. He doesn't know how he will support himself if his parents don't help him. He wishes he didn't have to worry about money. He wishes he could please himself and make his parents happy, too.

Section Ⅱ　Use of English

[参考译文]　世界第三大手机生产商 LG 电子周二表示,其已获选成为中国三家移动通信运营商的 3G 手机供应商。LG 在一份声明中称,随着今年中国运营商推出人们翘首期待的高端 3G 服务,预计 2010 年中国的 3G 手机市场的增长将超过一倍,即由今年的 1,400 万部增至 3,000 万部。

分析家称韩国手机制造商三星电子有限公司和 LG 公司可能从中国启动的 3G 业务中受益,因为这两家公司在生产精密 3G 手机方面的技术都领先于中国其他公司。

世界顶级手机生产商诺基亚可能关注中国的 WCDMA 网络,而韩国制造商则一直在国内外销售自己生产的各种手机。

紧随诺基亚和三星公司之后的 LG 公司称,自己之所以被命名为拥有世界上最多用户的移动手机供应商——中国移动的供应商,是因为中国移动旨在提供国内自主研发 TD-SCDMA 技术提供的 3G 手机服务。国际市场上的品牌手机很少能够利用这种服务。

"到目前为止,由于网络占有量低,LG 公司在中国销售还比较弱。直接为主要手机市场运营商提供手机的业务意味着其业务服务模式在变化。"Mirae 资产证券公司分析师 Harrison Cho 称,"不过,至于中国 3G 市场发展的速度究竟有多快,还存在着不确定因素。"

26. B 【解析】本题考查被动语态。根据题意"LG 被选为中国 3G 手机的供应商",LG 与 pick 之间是动宾关系,应用被动语态,所以答案为 B。

27. A 【解析】本题考查动词的用法。根据题意"LG 将给中国供应 3G 手机",supply"供应,供给,提供(尤指大量)"与题目中"供应 3G 手机"相符合;offer 一般是指主动的奉献,提供机会或是需求,所以不能用于本题,support"支持,拥护,帮助,援助",不能用于此处。所以答案为 A。

28. C 【解析】句意为"2010 年中国手机的市场据估算会比今年(14 million)的两倍还要多。"达到

30 million 符合题意,所以答案为 C。

29. D 【解析】本题考查动词的用法。据估算应用 estimate，calculate"计算";add"增加",be added to 是指"被附加"的意思,如果是 add to sth.则是指增加,用于主动态,所以不选 add,A、B、C 均不符合题意,答案为 D。

30. A 【解析】本题考查数据的分析。根据文章中的两个数据 14 和 30 可以分析得出 30 是 14 的两倍还多, triple 是指三倍; twice 本身即是"两倍、两次"的意思; three times 是"三次"的意思,所以答案为 A。【知识拓展】"一两次"的英语表达方式为"once or twice",两三倍则为"two or three times"或"twice or thrice"。一般而言,三倍以上用"three / four ... +times"。

31. B 【解析】本题考查名词辨析。手机制造商应是 mobile phone maker(固定搭配),根据下文三星和 LG 可以知道 maker 应用复数,所以答案为 B。

32. A 【解析】本题考查动词搭配。"从……中受益"应该是 benefit from,所以答案为 A。

33. C 【解析】本题考查介词的用法。句意为"三星和 LG 等手机制造商在手机制造方面比中国有优势",应该用 lead over,所以答案为 C。

34. A 【解析】本题考查介词短语作后置定语的用法。介词短语 with ... features 意为"带有……特色的",作后置定语修饰 phones,所以答案为 A。

35. B 【解析】本题考查固定搭配。be likely to ... 意为"有可能……",而且 be likely to 可以用 sb. 作主语; possible 主语不可以是人,此处诺基亚公司作为一个法人作主语符合题意。答案为 B。
【知识拓展】英语中有几对词汉语意义差不多,但用法却不一样,前者的主语只能为物或人,而后者的主语可以是人也可以是物,如:possible(物)和 likely(物或人),sure(人)和 certain(物或人),able(人)和 capable(物或人)等。

36. D 【解析】本题考查连词的用法,这里是起转折语气的作用,while 表示"与……作对比,然而"的意思,所以答案为 D。

37. A 【解析】本题考查固定搭配。从下题可以得知应该表达"国内外"的意思,即 at home and abroad,所以答案为 A。

38. C 【解析】本题考查固定搭配。这里要表达"国内外"的意思,即 at home and abroad,所以答案为 C。

39. B 【解析】本题考查介词用法。be named as 是指"任命为",符合题意,as"作为",和 a supplier 一起作 be named 的宾语补足语。所以答案为 B。

40. D 【解析】本题考查非限制性定语从句的关系代词的用法。which 指代 China Mobile,所以答案为 D。

41. A 【解析】本题考查主谓一致。few handsets 为复数,故谓语动词应相应地用复数,且时态为现在时,所以答案为 A。

42. C 【解析】本题考查固定搭配。due to ... "由于……",所以答案为 C。

43. A 【解析】本题考查名词的用法。直接交易应该用 deal,交易量不会是一个,而且谓语动词为 mean,所以 deal 要用复数 deals,答案为 A。

44. D 【解析】本题考查副词的用法。副词 how 修饰程度副词 fast, as for how fast 意为"至于有多快"。所以答案为 D。

45. D 【解析】本题考查动词的用法。grow 有"扩展,扩张"的意思,用在这里指中国 3G 手机市场的成长,符合题意,所以答案为 D。

Section Ⅲ Reading Comprehension

Text 1

[文章概述] 生活中,我们经常会有不快乐的时候,事实上,我们只有先快乐,才能得到自己想要的。幸福的源泉其实有很多,我们要学会选择幸福。

46. D 【解析】细节题。第二段告诉我们:很多人喜欢致力于工作,许多人喜欢吸食毒品或者酗酒,因为他们觉得快乐,所以 A、B 两项错误;第二段还告诉我们:许许多多的人只要拥有了自己昂贵的汽车后,他们就找到了快乐,所以 D 项正确。而 C 项与原文叙述不符,太绝对化。

47. B 【解析】推理判断题。根据第四段可知,如今,人们都认为昂贵的轿车、高薪的工作都是一种刺激,而后才有了快乐,也就是说,他们得到了自己想要的东西,所以他们觉得快乐。A 项说反了,C、D 是 B 的具体表现形式。

48. D 【解析】推理判断题。文章最后两段说:幸福才是刺激,而非所得是刺激,所以,如果你觉得幸福,你就会获得更多的东西,包括工作上更大的成功等。而 A、B、C 都是具体的实物上的,是大众的观点,而非作者的观点。

49. A 【解析】细节题。根据最后两段可知 A 正确,B 正好与作者的观点相悖,C、D 两项文章没有讨论到,所以不正确。

50. C 【解析】推理判断题。依据作者在最后三段的阐述,可知幸福是无条件的,觉得幸福你就会拥有你所想要的,而且还会超出你的想象,所以答案为 C。

Text 2

[文章概述] 本文主要讨论了女性工作和婚姻的问题。

51. A 【解析】词义猜测题。根据句意不难理解 portend 是"预示"的意思。signal"显示";defy"不服从,反抗";suffer from"忍受,遭受";result from"由……产生"。

52. D 【解析】细节题。题干的 the economy slides 等于原文的 economic downturns。根据第一段倒数第二句可知经济低迷时期人们倾向推迟婚姻, 因为双方不能承担一个家庭或者担心更窘迫的日子。D 符合原文意思。

53. C 【解析】细节题。根据第二段最后一句 By raising a family's standard of living, a working wife may strengthen ... and emotional stability.可知答案为 C。

54. A 【解析】细节题。根据第三段第二句可知不能外出工作的妇女会感到被关在笼子里,相当于 A(她们感到被剥夺了自由)。所以答案为 A。

55. D 【解析】主旨推断题。用排除法解题。A 因果颠倒,排除;B 文章从未提及;C 以偏概全;只有 D:女性的外出工作对婚姻的影响因人而异,才准确表达出文章中两种平行的相反观点。

Text 3

[文章概述] 本文介绍了在美国骑车的一些情况与许多的禁忌,以及政府采取的一些措施。

56. C 【解析】细节题。从第一段可知在美国,骑自行车被许多人认为是鲁莽、草率和粗鲁的,他们应该走那些不好的路,应该受到管制。

57. D 【解析】细节题。根据第一段第三句的后半句可知,骑自行车的人应该走路边,而不是走车道,所以答案为 D。

58. A 【解析】细节题。根据第一段第七句 Roads are believed to be designed for cars and not for bicycles, which are tolerated at the pleasure of motorists, who really own the roads.可知答案为 A。

59. B 【解析】猜测句意题。该句句意为:"骑自行车的人行驶在摩托车道容易被追尾,因为自行车没有摩托车速度快。"答案为 B。

60. C 【解析】推理判断题。根据文章第二段各地政府采取的措施可知,这些措施的共同点都是为了保护骑车者的生命安全。

Part B

61. G 【解析】主旨题。介绍猪流感病毒的基本信息。

62. B 【解析】推理题。讲从事和猪打交道的工作的人的危险度。

63. C 【解析】细节题。讲 H1N1 病毒的起源尚未知晓。

64. F 【解析】细节题。讲抗病毒的药在病人出现症状后两天内使用能够发挥到最佳效果。

65. E 【解析】主旨题。讲一些药物尚未获得批准用来治疗猪流感。

Section IV Writing

Part A

本例要求考生写一则道歉信:因考试耽误了编排短剧的任务,故向老师道歉,并申请延期表演。

解题步骤:

第一步:确定题材——道歉信,注意格式

第二步:列出要点——任务没能及时完成的原因;申请延期;保证不会再发生

第三步:列出关键词——apologize; be engaged in; get well prepared; sincere apology, etc.

第四步:落笔成文

October 12th, 2009

Dear Professor Li,

I'm writing to apologize to you that we haven't prepared the play scripts for tomorrow morning. As you know, we have had several exams in the last two weeks, so all of us were engaged in preparing for the exams. After the examinations, we tried to prepare the play scripts, but we just can't get well prepared. So I was just wondering whether we could do it next Wednesday so that we would have a week more to get well prepared.

I promise it won't happen again. My sincere apology again!

Respectfully yours,

James

Part B

解题步骤:

第一步:审题

1. 题型:看图作文

2. 文体:论述说明文

第二步:框架分析

1. 说明漫画内容,点出要点;

2. 针对漫画描述的情况,给予自己的评价或者提出看法。

第三步:列出写作思路

1. 首先简要介绍漫画背景:全球性经济危机给就业造成了很大的影响,很多人找不到工作,大学生甚至 CEO 都处于失业状态;

2. 提出自己的观点:在校生必须更加努力,保持竞争地位,提高自己的综合素质,只有这样,毕业后才能找到理想的工作。

第四步:列出关键词和词组

because of; financial crisis; serious situation; swarm into; potential employer; keep our competitive edge, etc.

第五步:落笔成文

Because of the financial crisis, more and more college students cannot find proper jobs, while many workers have lost their jobs due to unfavorable economic situations. In the cartoon, even CEOs are joining the army in search of jobs. What a serious situation it is!

From this, we can see that today's college students face a situation unheard of years ago. Many students swarm into job market or look every talent fair for potential employers. Hunting a job is of great importance for everyone but now we may have to accept some jobs offered no matter what the job is, which is very dangerous.

As the job market is shrinking, we should take the chance to receive further training to better develop ourselves so that we can keep our competitive edge and find a comparatively good job when the market has recovered or we must think creatively to run our own businisses.

专家预测试题(二)

Section Ⅰ　Listening Comprehension

Part A

1. A　【解析】男士说他梦到的是赢得一场比赛,比赛的奖励是到一个荒岛上去度假。

2. A　【解析】女士首先肯定了自己对舞会的喜爱,但是要和 Tom 确认(check)一下,说明她有可能出席舞会。

3. B　【解析】数字计算题。文中出现 3 个数字,30 岁开始写作,现在 70 岁,所以共写了 40 年。

4. D　【解析】由女士的第一句话可知女士想要的是电池。

5. C　【解析】由女士问男士是否能把他带到车站可知女士是在向男士寻求帮助。

6. C　【解析】女士看了钟说"已经五点了",然后男士说这表快 15 分钟,说明现在是 4:45。

7. A　【解析】根据男士的回答 In spite of my continuous failure, I have already made some progress.可知答案为 A。

8. D　【解析】男士预订房间,时间是 9 月 7 日到 10 月 10 日,根据计算可知,他要住 34 天。

9. A　【解析】男士是要 send a letter(寄信),毫无疑问是在邮局。

10. C　【解析】男士指出 I'm pleased … 由此可知答案为 C。

Part B

11. B　【解析】本文谈到了收音机的普及促进了报业的发展,而电视的普及却使电影院票房降低,没有人到体育馆观看球赛。由此可知,本文在讨论不同媒体之间的关系。

12. A　【解析】Radio and print were not substitutes for each other, but actually supported each other.从而可知,听收音机的人也买报纸。

13. D　【解析】文章提到了,电视的发明,使电影业票房降低:Movie attendance dropped when audience members chose to stay at home and be entertained. 所以答案为 D。

14. A　【解析】文章说当人们可以在电视上看到直播的球赛时,体育场的看台就没人了。由此可知是讲到了电视的另一种影响。所以答案为 A。

15. A　【解析】女士说我在 6 岁的时候写完了我的第一本书,它是关于小动物的。所以答案为 A。

16. D　【解析】女士之所以觉得很幸运是因为 … to be able to support myself by writing …所以答案为 D。

17. B　【解析】女士强调她没有什么预先的计划,而是先有 ideas 之后才在其之上来写书(The ideas come first, so it really depends on the idea that grabs me next!),所以答案为 B。

18. A　【解析】女士回答说:"我不知道这些灵感是哪来的。"所以答案为 A。

19. A　【解析】根据"二手烟是严重威胁公众健康的因素之一(… secondhand tobacco smoke is a serious public health risk.)。"可知答案为 A。

20. A　【解析】此题信息在第三段,即父母吸烟对孩子的影响。选项 B 太绝对;选项 C 不对,因为 children will have a slow lung growth;选项 D 不正确,因为文章没有提到这一信息。

21. B　【解析】根据第四段可知在美国,二手烟每年导致约 50,000 成人死亡。

22. D　【解析】文章提到 separate from the smokers 以及 clean the air in the buildings 还不足以解决问题,但暗示了这也是解决问题的办法,文章又提到建立 smoke-free public areas 的进展,说明这也是积极的解决办法。但文章没有提到是否限制烟草生产问题,所以答案为 D。

23. D 【解析】根据第一句可知在美国散步休闲的人是不多见的,所以答案为 D。
24. C 【解析】在郊区,人行道很少,路况很差,所以车子不得不开得非常慢。所以答案为 C。
25. C 【解析】文章在介绍美国人没有习惯散步,这是美国文化的一部分,书中还解释了其原因。所以答案为 C。

附:听力原文

Section I   Listening Comprehension

Part A

1. **M:** I had a very strange dream last night. I dreamt I won a competition.

   W: Oh, really? What did you win? Money? A new car?

   M: I won a holiday on a desert island. I hope it will come true.

2. **M:** We are having a little party at the weekend. Can you and Tom come?

   W: That sounds nice. Thank you. But I'll have to check with Tom. I'll tell you tomorrow.

3. **M:** So, Jane, how long have you been an author?

   W: Well, Tom, I didn't start writing until I was in my thirtieth, and I'm over seventy now. So goodness, I must have been writing for about forty years.

4. **W:** Excuse me, do you have any batteries? I need some to my radio, because mine isn't working.

   M: Sure. They are over there, next to the pens on the desk next to the bed.

5. **W:** Hello, Jack! Do you think you can give me a lift to the station? I must go there to pick my sister.

   M: I'm terribly sorry, but I can't. I have to be at work by 8:30. I can call you a taxi, though.

6. **W:** Oh, no. It's five o'clock already, and I haven't finished my homework.

   M: Don't worry. That clock is fifteen minutes fast. You still have time to do it.

7. **W:** How are you getting on with your experiment?

   M: In spite of my continuous failure, I have already made some progress.

8. **W:** Good morning, sir. What can I do for you?

   M: Yes. I'd like to have a single room with a bath from the morning of September 7th to the morning of October 10th.

9. **M:** Excuse me! I just need to send this letter the fastest way possible.

   W: Let's see. We have overnight business service. That takes just two days.

10. **W:** Who's your new secretary, Tom?

    M: I'm pleased with the work she's been doing so far.

Part B

11—14

With the introduction of radio, newspaper publishers wondered how broadcasting would affect them. Many feared that radio, as a quick and easy means of keeping people informed, would displace the newspaper industry altogether. Others hoped that the brief newscast heard on the air would stimulate listeners' interest in the story, so they buy the newspaper to get more information. This second idea turned out to be closer to the truth. Radio and print were not substitutes for each other, but actually supported each other. You see, the relationship between different media is not always one of displacement, but can be one of reinforcement. However, this is not always the case. Take television and motion pictures for example, with the popularization of TV, the motion picture industry suffered greatly. Movie attendance dropped when audience members chose to stay at home and be entertained. Likewise, when a football game was shown on the air, the stands were often empty, because fans chose to watch the game at home.

15—18

M: Hi, Miss Rowling. How old were you when you started to write, and what was your first book?

W: I wrote my first finished story when I was about 6. It was about a small animal, a rabbit I mean, and I've been writing ever since.

M: Why did you choose to be an author?

W: If someone asked me how to achieve happiness, step one would be finding out what you love doing most and step two would be finding someone to pay you to do it. I consider myself very lucky indeed to be able to support myself by writing.

M: Do you have any plans to write books for adults?

W: My first two novels were for adults. I suppose I might write another one, but I never really imagine a target audience when I'm writing. The ideas come first, so it really depends on the idea that grabs me next!

M: Where did the ideas for the *Harry Potter* books come from?

W: I've no idea where ideas come from and I hope I never find out, it would spoil my excitement if it turned out I just have a funny little wrinkle on the surface of my brain which makes me think about invisible train platforms.

M: How do you come up with the names of your characters?

W: I invented some of the names in the Harry books, but I also collect strange names. I've gotten them from medieval saints, maps, dictionaries, plants, war memorials, and people I've met!

M: Oh, you are really resourceful.

19—22

Scientific evidence has been building about the dangers to people who do not smoke from those who do. Now the top doctor in the United States says the evidence cannot be argued: secondhand tobacco smoke is a serious public health risk.

Recently Surgeon General Richard Carmona released the government's largest report ever on secondhand smoke. For example, it says nonsmokers increase their risk of lung cancer by up to thirty percent if they live with a smoker.

He noted the added dangers faced by children who have to breathe secondhand smoke. These children are at increased risk for sudden infant death syndrome, severe breathing problems and ear infections. The report says smoking by parents also slows lung growth in their children.

Scientists have estimated that secondhand smoke kills about fifty thousand adults in the United States each year.

The report says separating smokers from nonsmokers or trying to clean the air in buildings is not enough protection. Doctor Carmona noted the progress in establishing smoke-free public places in the United States. Blood tests show that Americans are being exposed to secondhand smoke in fewer numbers and at lower levels since the late 1980s.

23—25

Going for a walk, whether in towns or in the country, is just not part of the American idea. An English journalist who was just walking along the road in Los Angeles was questioned by the police, because it seemed so strange that he should be doing this. Except in town centers, it is rare to find any sidewalk beside a road and some suburban roads are so bad that cars have to travel very slowly, too slowly to be dangerous to children. A person who tries to walk at night may find not only that he is almost hurting his feet on the uneven surface, but also that there are no street lights (the headlights of cars being good enough for the motorist) and that he will be pursued by angry dogs from the houses among which he is passing. The dogs are so unaccustomed to seeing anybody walking that, like the Los Angeles police, they think he must be trying to do something evil.

Section II   Use of English

[参考译文] 从童年到老年,我们都使用语言,把语言看成扩展关于自己和我们周围世界知识的一种手段。人类一开始进化的时候,就像新生儿童无法使用这种有价值的工具。然而,一旦语言发展了之后,人类未来的成就以及文化发展的可能性也随之增加。

语言学家认为,进化使人们具备创造并使用语言的能力。他们声称,我们高度进化的大脑给我们提供了一种天生的语言能力,这种能力在低等有机体上是找不到的。这种理论的支持者声称,我们的语言潜能是天生的,但是,作为儿童时期人脑成长期间的一种功能,语言本身也是渐渐发展的,因此语言形成有着关键的生理时期。

人们目前对这一理论的评价褒贬不一。然而,支持有先天能力的证据也不容否认。事实上,越来越多的学校发现,外语最好在低年级进行教学。接触几种语言的儿童往往能够学会这些语言,而成人一旦自己的母语的语言规则确立之后,学习另一种语言就困难得多。

尽管无法否认语言的某些方面是先天的,但是语言不是在真空中自动形成的。如果儿童脱离其他人便无法掌握语言,这就表明,如果要形成正确的语言,就必须要与其他人进行交流。有些语言学家认为,交流对于人类语言的习得来说甚至比其他任何先天能力更重要。这些理论家把语言视做可模仿的学得的行为。换而言之,儿童学习语言是通过跟自己父母模仿而学的。通过肯定准确的模仿和否定不精确的模仿,父母渐渐地塑造了自己孩子的语言技能。

26. B 【解析】本题考查动词。根据下文(evolution),答案为B。此处意为"当人类刚刚开始进化,他们如同新生儿一样不会运用语言这种工具。"evolved"逐渐发展,进化",符合题意;generate"产生"(及物动词);born (bear 的过去分词)不能作谓语动词;originate"起源",不能用 first 修饰。

27. A 【解析】本题考查形容词。valuable"珍贵的";appropriate"合适的,适当的";convenient"方便的,便利的";favorite"最喜欢的"。语言并不是人类选择的结果,而是人类在进化过程中慢慢发展起来的,对人类来说,应当是珍贵的。所以答案为A。

28. A 【解析】本题考查名词。此处意思是:"语言的发展增加了人类未来的成就和文化进步的可能性。"attainments"成就";feasibility"可行性";entertainments"娱乐";evolution"进化"。所以答案为A。

29. D 【解析】本题考查固定搭配。此处意为:"许多语言学家认为进化使人们产生和具备了语言的能力。"固定短语 be responsible for"对……负责,是……的原因"。其他选项不与 for 搭配。所以答案为D。【知识拓展】"对某事负责": be responsible for something,而"对某人负责":be responsible to somebody。接人或事用的介词不一致,这种现象在译语中比较常见, 如 be strict with somebody,但 be strict in something,be familiar with something 意为"熟悉某事",而 be familiar to somebody 则意为"为某人熟悉"。

30. C 【解析】本题考查动词。根据语法分析,空格后应是一个宾语从句,而 A、B、D 三项后都不能接从句作直接宾语。confirm(确认)+名词;inform(通知) sb.of sth.;convince(使某人确信) sb.of sth.所以答案为C。

31. D 【解析】本题考查动词短语的固定搭配。provide sb. with sth.意为"向(人)提供(物)",所以答案为D。

32. B 【解析】本题考查名词。句意为"高度发达的大脑使我们具备了其他低等动物所不具备的语言能力。"显然,这里是把人和低等动物相比较。organisms"有机体,生物体"。所以答案为B。

33. A 【解析】本题考查名词。句意为"人类的语言能力是与生俱来的,但语言本身也在逐渐发展",所以这种能力应该是潜在的。potential"潜力";performance"履行";preference"偏爱";passion"激情"。所以答案为A。

34. A 【解析】本题考查介词。句意为"语言本身作为童年时期大脑生长的一种功能,其发展是渐进的。"as"作为,当作",合乎题意。like 作为介词的意思是"像……一样"。所以答案为A。

35. B 【解析】本题考查形容词。句意为"语言的发展有一个关键期,人体的成长是生物变化的过程。"biological"生物的";ideological"思想上的";social"社会的";psychological"心理的"。所以答案为B。

36. A 【解析】本题考查名词。句意为"目前人们对'先天论'评论观点不一,但是支持某些天生能力的证据却是确凿无疑的。"reviews"评论";reference"参考";reaction"反应";recommendation"推荐"。所以答案为 A。

37. C 【解析】本题考查副词。作者是倾向于先天论的,这一点可以从 evidence supporting 和 discovering 看出,为了进一步证明先天论是有道理的,作者选择了以学校为例加以说明,因此这里应填一个表示递进关系的词 Indeed(实质上)。所以答案为 C。

38. D 【解析】本题考查文章上下文关系。从下文 young people 与 adults 的对比可以说明,此处意思是"越来越多的学校发现在低年级学外语较容易",所以答案为 D。

39. B 【解析】本题考查固定搭配。通过接触多种语言,孩子们可以学会好几种语言。be exposed to 是固定搭配,意为"接触到"。reveal(显露)sth. to sb.,不符合题意,因本题中的 them 指 languages。其余选项不与 to 搭配。engage in"从事";be involved in"参与"。所以答案为 B。

40. C 【解析】本题考查名词。句意为"一旦母语的规则被深深印入脑海中,成年人就很难再学好另一种语言。"rules"规则,规律";regulations"规定";formations"构成,构造";constitutions"宪法,章程"。所以答案为 C。

41. A 【解析】本题考查连词。从句意思是"语言的某些方面肯定是先天的",主句意思是"语言不会在与人隔绝的状况下自行发展"。前后应为转折关系。所以答案为 A。

42. D 【解析】本题考查动词的被动语态。与人隔绝的儿童不能掌握好一门语言。isolated"孤立的,与世隔绝的";distinguished"区别的,杰出的";different"不同的";protected"受到保护的"。答案为 D。

43. D 【解析】本题考查名词。必须通过与他人交往,语言才能够发展。interaction"相互作用";exposition"暴露";comparison"比较";contrast"对比"。所以答案为 D。

44. A 【解析】本题考查固定搭配。本句中的 this 和 even more basic 分别指代上句的 interaction with other human beings 和 necessary,此处所填词对应上文中的 language development。也就是说,language acquisition 语言习得。appreciation"欣赏,感激";requirement"要求";alternative"转移,转变,转换"。所以答案为 A。

45. C 【解析】本题考查副词。本句功能是以另一种方式解释前文中的 imitative, learned behavior (模仿性的后天行为)。In other words"换言之,换句话说";As a result"结果是";After all"毕竟";Above all"首先"。所以答案为 C。

Section Ⅲ Reading Comprehension

Text 1

[文章概述] 美国准备着迎接世界上最大的足球盛宴,他们有史以来第一次承办世界杯。当全世界有数以百万的人在踢足球时,这项运动在美国才刚刚火热起来。主办方声称这一届的世界杯会成为历史上最盛大的一届。足球在美国仅仅有一百多年的历史,但这项运动是怎样流传到这个国家的?足球在世界其他地方存在多久了?没有人确切地知道。

46. C 【解析】是非判断题。文中第一段第五句提到,足球在美国是发展最快的运动,但没有说在世界范围内是发展最快的运动。所以答案为 C。

47. B 【解析】细节题。根据第二段第一句可知 American football 是在青少年中最为流行的传统运动。所以答案为 B。

48. A 【解析】细节题。根据第三段第一句可知英式足球在美国有 100 多年的历史了。

49. B 【解析】细节题。根据最后一段第一句可知英国是现代足球的发明者。

50. B 【解析】推理判断题。文中最后一段讲述了英国是现代足球的发明国,接下来就应该介绍足球在英国的发展才符合逻辑,所以答案为 B。

Text 2

[文章概述] 本文主要讲述了美国新当选的黑人总统奥巴马成为美国人,尤其是美国黑人

和少数民族的偶像的事情,一定程度上反映了美国的文化特色。

51. D 【解析】推理判断题。第三段说,奥巴马的当选给美国黑人和其他少数民族一个新的国家级偶像,多年来,人们将目光投向运动员和音乐家寻找激励自己的偶像。由此判断应选 D,在奥巴马成为美国总统之前,美国黑人在政治领域没有自己种族的偶像。

52. A 【解析】推理判断题。第七段 Bill Bank 说,年轻的黑人需要在自己社区寻找偶像,这个偶像不是马丁·路德·金,也不是奥巴马,而是离他们的生活很近的人,奥巴马的影响仅此而已。所以答案为 A。

53. B 【解析】猜测题。A 项字面理解,显然是错误的,结合上下文,the relationship 只能和 B 搭配,指"黑人和白人的关系总会有个结果的"。

54. B 【解析】主题大意题。全文讲述美国新当选的黑人总统奥巴马成为美国人,尤其是美国黑人和少数民族的新偶像。

55. C 【解析】推理判断题。最后一段说,奥巴马上任后,举办八国集团峰会时最重要的四个国家的领导人来自中国、印度、日本和美国黑人,这对于世界范围的白人和有色人种都是个很大的心理转变。从这些信息看,其含义是 C,到那时,这重要的四个国家领导人中没有白人。

Text 3

[文章概述] 意大利巴里大学日前开展的一项研究表明,舒适愉悦的环境有助于减轻病人的痛苦。这一发现有力驳斥了认为医院不应该把钱浪费在艺术品装饰上的说法。研究人员相信新的研究会对患者疾病起到新的治疗作用。

56. B 【解析】猜测词义题。根据第一段最后一句... as it suggests a pleasant environment helps patients ease discomfort and pain. 可知答案为 ease(缓解,减轻),而不是治愈、消灭或"增加"。

57. C 【解析】数字计算题。本文提到的艺术家有 Leonardo da Vinci, Sandro Botticelli, Vincent Van Gogh, Pablo Picasso, Anonio Bueno, Columbian Fernando Botero 六人。

58. D 【解析】推理判断题。根据第三段内容可知答案为 D。A 与第四段所叙述的内容不符合;B 与第五段第一句所叙述的内容不一致;C 与第五段中间部分的内容不同。

59. B 【解析】推理判断题。根据本段的最后一句可知托马索教授说:"这些人不是艺术家,所以一些他们认为难看的作品其实都是世界名作。"其言外之意就是只有艺术家才能知道这些看似难看的作品其实都是世界名作。

60. A 【解析】主旨大意题。根据全文内容和研究结果可以知道本题答案为 A。而 B、C 只是其中的一个研究结果中的一部分,不能概括全文。D 范围太大,不能概括全文的主要叙述内容。

Part B

61. E 【解析】细节题。像检查有没有未读邮件或新的短消息等行为都是延迟、拖沓的表现。

62. F 【解析】细节题。讲有过一次推迟执行某个任务的经历,就有可能会有下一次的推迟。

63. C 【解析】细节题。讲我们把应该解决的,最有压力的任务完成,然后我们就可以轻松地享受快乐。

64. A 【解析】细节题。讲完成论文时要注意分解任务使任务更加具有可实现性。

65. D 【解析】细节题。讲没有任何事与永久地延迟那些未完成的任务更令人感觉疲惫的了。

Section IV Writing

Part A

本例要求考生写一则书信:因教室被他人借用只好换教室,于是向老师建议更换地点。

解题步骤:

第一步:确定题材——书信,注意格式

第二步:列出要点——遗憾;教室不可用的原因;提议更换地点

第三步:列出关键词——sorry; be available for; venture to suggest, etc.

第四步:落笔成文

October 15th, 2009

Dear Professor Yang,

I'm sorry to tell you that Room 201 won't be available for us to enjoy the movie next Monday. Someone else has already reserves it. However, the good news is that Room 203 is still available. So may I venture to suggest that we watch the movie in Room 203 instead next Monday?

All of the class are still very excited to learn that we are going to see the wonderful movie you mentioned in class, and they just don't want to miss the chance.

Looking forward with great eagerness to your positive relpy.

Sincerely yours,
David

Part B

解题步骤:

第一步:审题

1. 题型:看图作文

2. 文体:论述说明文

第二步:框架分析

1. 说明图画内容,点出要点;

2. 图画现象发生的原因以及你的感受。

第三步:列出写作思路

1. 改革开放30年来,中国发生了翻天覆地的变化,以人们写信方式为例,说明这种变化;

2. 重点描述图画内容:爷爷那辈不识字,要写信不得不找人帮忙,父亲那一辈是自己写信,而现在,我们已经可以通过手机来联系,而不用再写信了,通过描述、比较可以知道改革开放以来,我国社会取得的巨大进步;

3. 表述自己的感觉、发出呼吁:自豪感,作贡献等。

第四步:列出关键词和词组

the reform and opening up policy; rapid development and advance; take ... for example; keep in touch with; with the development of, etc.

第五步:落笔成文

It is 30 years since China carried out the reform and opening up policy. Great changes have taken place and each aspect of life can give a clear sign of the rapid development and advance in today's China.

Take people's communication for example. In the past, our grandpas had to ask someone who could write for help when they wanted to contact their relatives or friends. As for our fathers, they kept in touch with each other by writing letters by themselves. With the development of science and technology, we can communicate with each other anytime and anywhere by sending instant messages with mobile phones.

As a new generation, we are so lucky to be living in the new century. We're proud of our country and its achievements. So we should cherish the happiness of today's life. Meanwhile, we should put more effort and make more contributions to our beloved motherland to make it more and more powerful and more and more prosperous.

2008年9月全国英语等级考试真题

Section Ⅰ Listening Comprehension（略）

Section Ⅱ Use of English

[参考译文] 网络摄像头是一种数码相机,这种数码相机能够将视觉或者可视图像传给其他电脑用户。网络摄像头的大小和一个高尔夫球差不多,网络摄像头通常放在电脑显示器之上。一旦把网络摄像头与带有必要软件的电脑接口相连。你的现场图像就可以通过互联网的即时信息服务传给一个或多个用户。

　　一只网络摄像头售价大约为50美元。配件好(比如配有高分辨率的图像配件)的网络摄像头品牌更贵。罗技和创新是两大网络摄像头厂商,他们提供各种各样的摄像头,而且包括了相应的软件。传送和接受图像无须额外收费,但是你得注册才能享受到免费的即时信息服务。大家能够在实际时间里看到彼此并听到对方的声音。祖父母能够更经常地看到自己的孙子辈。只要是在近5年内买的电脑几乎都可以使用网络摄像头,而且可以节省长途电话费。

　　如果你没有宽带,即高速电缆调制解调器或者有DSL拨号,那么要下载图像也许要花很长时间,就像放幻灯片而非像放电影那样。虽然实现网络摄像头和电脑对接比较容易,但是学会安装相应软件却要花一定的时间。你必须重新调整相关配置。

　　如果你的调制解调器是56兆,而想跟你联系的人不介意只看到现场拍摄的画面而看不到不完美的图片,那么网络摄像头依然挺有意思。不过,买之前,一定要确保大家都注册获得相同的即时信息服务器。

26. **B** 【解析】本题考查语义的理解。根据空白处后的句子"网络摄像头通常是放在电脑显示器的上面"可知,这里讲的应该是摄像头的大小和一个高尔夫球差不多,所以答案为B。

27. **D** 【解析】本题考查动词词义辨析。根据文意"把摄像头安放在显示器的上面",只有sit最合适,意为"坐落在,安放在某个地方",所以答案为D。rest"休息";remain"保存,保留";stay"停留"。

28. **C** 【解析】本题考查近义词词义辨析。join"参与,参加;附着在……上";attach"连接,衔接";fasten"栓紧,拴住"。而文中提到把网络摄像头连接到电脑的接口上,所以答案为C。

29. **A** 【解析】本题考查形容词词义辨析。live"实况转播的,现场的";living"活着的";lively"真实的,栩栩如生的";lovely"可爱的"。网络摄像头所传送的图像是现场的人或物的活动状态,相当于现场直播,因此是现场的图像,所以答案为A。

30. **A** 【解析】本题考查介词的用法。文中提到利用即时信息服务,可以把图像传递给他人,所以这里应该是一个表示方式的介词,via有"通过,经由"之意,所以答案为A。

31. **D** 【解析】本题考查名词的用法。device"设备", feature"特征", design"设计", attachment"附件,配件"。由such as后举的例子:better picture resolution"高分辨率",可知此处要填入的词是"配件",所以答案为D。【知识拓展】通常such as后为名词或相当的词语的列举,最后用and连接。而for example/for instance往往接完整的句子。此外,such as还相当于like,可拆开用,as后可以接句子。

32. **D** 【解析】本题考查连词的用法。文中提到罗技和创新是两大主要制造商,通常生产各种型号的摄像头,并且配备了必要的安装软件。此处应该选择一个表示并列的连词。所以答案为D。

33. **B** 【解析】本题考查动词辨析。句意为"传送和接受图像都不会额外收费,然而你必须注册免费的即时信息传送服务。"limit"限制"; charge"收费"; registration"注册", rate"等级,价格"。所以答案为B。

34. **B** 【解析】本题考查动词短语。check in"登记"; log in"联机,注册",相当于register; sign up"签字"; draw up"拟定"。这里指注册获得免费的即时信息传送服务,所以答案为B。

35. **A** 【解析】本题考查近义词的辨析。true"符合一定标准的,真实的,正在发生的"; actual"实际的",genuine"非伪造的,非冒牌的";real 强调外表与实质之间的一致性。所以答案为 A。

36. B　【解析】本题考查形容词词义辨析。句意为"通过摄像头,祖父母就可以经常看到自己的孙子辈"。只有 B 选项 frequently"频繁的,经常的"符合题意。recently"近来";realistically"实际地";immediately"马上"。所以答案为 B。

37. A　【解析】本题考查形近词辨析。reduce"减少";reform"改革";remove"移动";retain"保持,保留"。句意为"通过网络摄像头交流,可以帮助我们节省大笔的话费。"所以答案为 A。

38. A　【解析】本题考查语意的理解衔接。文中上句:有了宽带,下句:下载的图像速度仍很慢,可以得知两个分句之间是转折的,although"虽然,尽管,即使",表转折,所以答案为 A。

39. D　【解析】本题考查词义的辨析。此处指图像的下载需要花费很长的时间。waste"浪费时间、金钱等";spend"花费",但是它的主语应该是人,而不是物,只有 take 最适合。所以答案为 D。
【知识拓展】spend, cost, pay, take 都有"花费"的意思,但其用法不一样。cost 主语一般为物,意为"花了,使……丧失";take 一般为形式主语,意为"花去(时间)";pay 和 spend 的主语一般均为人,常见的搭配有:pay for something / somebody,It pays to do something. 做某事还是值得的。spend ... in doing something (其中 in 可省),spend ... on something。

40. B　【解析】本题考查非谓语动词用法。通过上下文可知 resemble 的主语应该是 images,用在分句中应该使用动词的现在分词形式,即 resembling,所以答案为 B。

41. D　【解析】本题考查动词词义辨析。此处指很容易把摄像头连接到电脑上,但是安装软件需要花费一定的时间,四个选项中只有 fix 有"安装"的意思。所以答案为 D。

42. C　【解析】本题考查连接词的用法。文中提到了,如果你拥有了 56K 的调制解调器,所以此处应该选择一个表示假设的连接词,四个词中,只有 if 最合适,所以答案为 C。

43. A　【解析】本题考查动词词义辨析。reach"联系,到达";touch"触摸";know"认识,了解";show"展示,显示"。此处指你想联系的人,所以答案为 A。

44. D　【解析】本题考查连接词的用法。文中提醒读者在买摄像头之前,必须确定双方都申请了同一个即时信息服务器。因此需要一个表示转折关系的连接词,只有 but 合适,所以答案为 D。

45. A　【解析】本题考查动词词义辨析。通过上下文可知,此处指每个人都申请了相同的即时信息器,因此只有 register for 符合题意,所以答案为 A。

Section Ⅲ　Reading Comprehension

Part A

Text 1

　　[文章概述]　劳动赔偿:英国一位雇员因工作压力过大上庭申请雇主对其精神赔偿,此后英国当局采取了相应措施解决员工压力过大的问题。

46. A　【解析】细节题。根据第一段第一句可知兰开斯特夫人由于工作带给她的巨大压力而获得 67,000 英镑作为补偿。所以答案为 A。

47. C　【解析】细节题。根据第一段第二句可知因为工作造成的人身伤害,雇主应该承担相应的法律责任。因此,兰开斯特夫人控告城市委员会的原因是其应该对她的问题负责任。所以答案为 C。

48. B　【解析】推理判断题。兰开斯特夫人因工作造成巨大的精神压力,最终获得精神补偿。由此可知,每一位雇员在因工作遭受精神伤害的时候都有权利获得补偿。所以答案为 B。

49. C　【解析】推理判断题。第一段中提到兰开斯特夫人是第一个因巨大的工作压力而拿到补偿金的人,接着作者指出 it's likely to start a flood of other workers' claims,所以法庭会接触到更多的关于工作压力造成精神创伤的案件。所以答案为 C。

50. A　【解析】推理判断题。根据第二段第五句 ... with no continual, a constant high workload and little clerical support...",第三段第一句 ... Frances Kirkham said she understood the position of

troubleshooter was different from Mrs. Lancaster's precious job. 可知因为前后两份工作截然不同,给兰开斯特夫人带来了巨大的精神压力,所以如果伯明翰委员会打算调换员工的工作,必须确保两份工作的衔接性。所以答案为 A。

Text 2

[**文章概述**] 自主学习:终身学习独立于时间、地点和老师,可以很容易地学到知识,包含生活、学习两部分,可以使孩子学到他们所需要的知识,用他们自己的方式认识世界。

51. B 【解析】细节题。文章第一段开始作者就强调很难给终身学习这个概念下定义,所以答案为 B。

52. B 【解析】细节题。文中第二段最后提到 ... but they haven't really learnt much at least of the official curriculum. 由此可知,学校模式下的学习忽视了正式课程中的某些部分,所以答案为 B。

53. A 【解析】细节题。文中第三段第一句可知,终身学习者认为,如果学习者不被强迫,如果他们认识到了学习的必要性,学习将会变得容易许多,所以答案为 A。

54. B 【解析】主旨归纳题。文中第四段最后一句可知终身学习是一个不断探索、求知、冒险,且不断犯错的过程。即 B 选项里提到的充满了尝试和错误,所以答案为 B。

55. B 【解析】推理判断题。文中最后一段中说终身学习使学习者理解世界,了解文化并与之进行交流,所以答案为 B。

Text 3

[**文章概述**] 纳米技术:新式洗衣机将细小的银粉颗粒沉淀在衣服上,在不注入热水的情况下用以帮助祛除细菌和气味,它代表了纳米科技在家用设施上的广泛应用。整篇文章围绕纳米科技展开,主要以三星公司的 Kim 先生研发的新式洗衣机为例。

56. A 【解析】推理判断题。文中第一段中提到 Kim 把银纳米应用于洗衣机中,制造出了新式洗衣机, 根据第二段最后一句 When he go back to Seoul, Kim applied the principle to washing machines. 可知先生是搞产品开发的,所以答案为 A。

57. B 【解析】细节题。第一段提到纳米洗衣机比普通洗衣机更能除菌除味;最后一段提到纳米产品为三星公司带来了 77.9 亿美元的收益, 因此纳米洗衣机在洁净的同时带来了丰厚的利润。故选 B。

58. A 【解析】细节题。第三段最后一句说返回汉城后,Kim 把纳米技术用到了洗衣机上。所以答案为 A。

59. D 【解析】推理判断题。纳米科技的发展是很有前景的,即 promising。所以答案为 D。

60. B 【解析】主旨推断题。 整篇文章以三星公司的 Kim 先生研发的新式洗衣机为例,围绕纳米科技开展,这篇文章是以一项科学技术在现实生活中的应用为中心的。所以答案为 B。

Part A

[**文章概述**] 本文主要阐述了五个关于什么是幸福的观点。

61. E 【解析】主旨理解题。希瑟迈可依强调遵从某些固定的步骤或者规则是无法找到幸福的。寻找幸福并不像遵守一本如何做的参考书那么简单,幸福必须通过每个人自己的方式才能找到。从而说明世界上根本不存在通往幸福的指南。所以答案为 E。

62. D 【解析】主旨理解题。加里拉塞尔指出幸福与财富并不是成正比增长的。当百万富翁遇见亿万富翁的时候,他会感到很失落。然而,每月只有几百美元的一个工人会成为偏僻山区村民羡慕的对象。从而说明幸福就存在于比较之中。所以答案为 D。

63. C 【解析】主旨理解题。大卫尼文认为真正的幸福是永久的欢乐和自由。为了获得幸福,我们应该远离和排除消极的事物。从而说明自由和幸福是紧紧相连的。所以答案为 C。

64. B 【解析】主旨理解题。乔舒亚帕蒂明确强调幸福取决于一个人自己的决定。从而说明幸福掌握在自己手中。所以答案为 B。

65. G 【解析】主旨理解题。劳拉约翰逊认为幸福就是做自己喜欢做的事情,文中提到了很多事例,例如,热爱写作就努力成为一名新闻记者,在冬天的雪地里滑雪等等。从而说明幸福就是做自己想做的事情。所以答案为G。

Section Ⅳ　Writing

Part A

本例要求考生写一封投诉信:一定要注意语气。

解题步骤:

第一步:确定题材——书信,注意格式;

第二步:列出要点——买了电视机;出现问题;提出退货/换货要求;希望问题能够得到合理解决;

第三步:列出关键词——unfortunately; broke down; look forward to; reasonable amount, etc.

第四步:落笔成文

October 19th, 2009

Dear Sir or Madam,

　Last week I bought a TV set in your store. Unfortunately, your product hasn't performed well, because the TV set did not work properly and it broke down this morning. To resolve the problem, I would like you to return my money back, or change a new one for me.

　I hope you can take some measures to settle my problem, and I will wait a reasonable amount of time before taking further measures to handle this matter. Thank you for taking time to read this letter.

　Looking forward to your early reply.

Sincerely,

Wang Lin

Part B

解题步骤:

第一步:审题

　1. 题型:看图作文

　2. 文体:论述说明文

第二步:框架分析

　1. 说明图画内容,点出要点;

　2. 图画现象发生的影响。

第三步:列出写作思路

　1. 图片描述了很多小鱼缸里的鱼都拼命想游到大鱼缸里,引出一个社会现象:大量农村人口迁往城市,就好像鱼从小鱼缸争着往大鱼缸跳一样;

　2. 这种现象带来了严重的问题:人口拥挤、物资紧张、交通不便、环境污染等。

第四步:列出关键词和词组

　exist; be compared to; in contrast; in order to; migrate into; lack of, etc.

第五步:落笔成文

　The cartoon tells us a serious problem existing in China. The big cities are compared to the big fish tanks, while the small cities are compared to the different sizes of fish tanks. More and more fish have swum into the big tanks. In the end, the big fish tanks are so crowded. In contrast, the small fish tanks become empty.

　In our real society, it is the same situation. In order to look for a good job and earn more money, more and more human resources from the countryside have migrated into the big cities. Unfortunately, the big cities become more and more crowded, the food become less and less and a series of problems have arisen, such as the heavy traffic problem, and the serious pollution problem. In addition, in the countryside, the elderly and the young will not be well taken care of, and the crops will not be grown because of the lack of human resources.

With this in view, the government needs to take corresponding measures to prevent such tragic phenomena from happening.

2009年3月全国英语等级考试真题

Section Ⅰ   Listening Comprehension（略）

Section Ⅱ   Use of English

[参考译文] 美国是一个联邦制国家。每一个州都拥有制订本州法律的权力，比如根据民意，各州可以制订自己的教育政策，收取州所得税，决定最高时速的多少、住房的法典和饮酒的法定年龄。

美国大多数地方，你必须年满21岁才能在酒店、酒吧或者饭店里买酒。在有些州，你可以在杂货店买啤酒。如果一个商店把酒卖给未成年人，那么这个店主人通常会被罚一大笔钱。此外，美国的许多州都有"开瓶法"，其意指人们不得在街上或车内饮酒。如果有人开瓶饮酒被抓住，这个人也许会被逮捕。

不过，尽管美国限酒法律众多，酒的消费问题却是美国和加拿大的一个严重问题。在大学校园饮酒现象明显增加了，这里很多人都没有达到法定年龄便开始饮酒。事实上，自从喝酒法定年龄从18岁提到21岁之后，酒的销售量不降反升。有些人认为，如果就像其他一些国家一样，不设立法定最低饮酒年龄的话，兴许北美年轻人消费的酒反而会减少。

26. C 【解析】本题考查名词的用法。根据题意，美国是一个联邦制国家，各州拥有立法权，应该用 right。privilege"特权"；advantage"优势"；tradition"传统"，都与题意不符。所以答案为C。

27. B 【解析】本题考查列举例子的表述方法。根据题意，美国各州都有立法权，下面就举例说明。应该用 For example，所以答案为B。

28. D 【解析】本题考查动词的用法。根据题意，各州可以根据公众的意见（民意）就教育问题制定政策。应该用 determine，所以答案为D。

29. A 【解析】本题考查动词的用法。根据题意，各州可以征收所得税。应该用 collect，所以答案为A。

30. A 【解析】本题考查名词的用法。根据题意，各州可以决定车速上限，应该用 limit。control"控制"；rule"规则"；regulation"规章"，均不符合题意，所以答案为A。

31. D 【解析】本题考查情态动词的用法。根据题意，在美国大部分地区，年龄必须达到21岁才会被允许到商店等地买酒。这是具有法律强制约束力的，要用 must，所以答案为D。

32. B 【解析】本题考查连词的用法。酒店、酒吧和饭店是并列的关系，要用 or，所以答案为B。

33. C 【解析】本题考查名词的用法。根据题意，任何一家商店给未成年人出售酒精，店主将被罚款，而不是收银员、售货员。owner 体现了人与商店之间的所有关系，而 host 指主人，表达不明确。所以答案为C。

34. A 【解析】本题考查动词的用法。根据题意，任何一家商店给未成年人出售酒精，店主将被罚款，应该用 fine 的过去分词形式表示被动。所以答案为A。

35. A 【解析】本题考查连词的用法。根据上下文可以判断，下文讲述的要比前面的情况更严重。应该用 In addition，所以答案为A。

36. D 【解析】本题考查非限制性定语从句的关系代词。which 指代了前面一句话，所以答案为D。

37. C 【解析】本题考查动词的过去分词短语作后置定语的用法。题意为"任何人一旦被抓到携带敞开的酒精容器将被逮捕。"caught"抓到"，有被当场发觉或被逮个正着的意思，符合题意。exposed"被暴露"；suspected"被怀疑"；detected"被发现"。所以答案为C。

38. A 【解析】本题考查连词的用法。这里为让步关系，应该用 nevertheless 最好。

39. B 【解析】本题考查名词的用法。根据题意,酒的消费在美国和加拿大是一个严重的问题,应该用 consumption,所以答案为 B。

40. D 【解析】本题考查名词的用法。根据题意,问题应该用 problem 而不用 question,所以答案为 D。

41. C 【解析】本题考查定语从句关系副词 where 的用法。根据题意,大学校园是很多还未达到法定饮酒年龄的学生聚集的地方。所以答案为 C。

42. B 【解析】本题考查动词的用法。根据题意,大学校园内饮酒人群的数量在增长,应该用 has increased greatly,所以答案为 B。

43. B 【解析】本题考查 since 用于完成时的用法。根据题意,酒精的销量自从饮酒年龄限制被上调以后不减反增,所以答案为 B。

44. C 【解析】本题考查动词被动语态的用法。根据题意,酒精的销量自从饮酒年龄限制被从 18 岁上调至 21 岁以后不减反增,uplift"提高,抬高",符合题意;upgrade"升级",虽也有提高的意思,但多指提高服务质量、档次等。shift 和 change 都不体现改变的方向。所以答案为 C。

45. C 【解析】本题考查连词 as 的用法。根据题意,一些人相信,如果和其他国家一样,如果没有对饮酒的年龄限制的话,北美国家的饮酒数量应该会减少。所以答案为 C。

Section III Reading Comprehension

Part A

Text 1

[文章概述] 本文主要介绍了 Donald Appleyard 的一个关于交通的调查。分别介绍了 Gough Street 和 Franklin Street 的情况。

46. A 【解析】文章主旨题。第一段第一句介绍了 Appleyard 研究的主要关注点,由 A pioneering study by Donald Appleyard made the surprise sudden increase 可知答案为 A。

47. D 【解析】细节题。由第一段第一句 a sudden increase in crime does 可知答案为 D。

48. C 【解析】段落大意题。第二段里用很大的篇幅描写了 heavy traffic 会带来的问题,比如 danger, noise, fumes 等等,所以第二段的主要目的是指出交通拥挤所带来的问题。

49. C 【解析】细节题。文章最后一段讲到了 the old feeling of community was disappearing,这与 C 选项的 their old community is gone 相符合,属于同义替换。

50. A 【解析】细节题。由第二段最后一句 Most families with children had already left. 这就说明了家长意识到了 Franklin Street 的文化氛围不适合孩子,这与 A 选项符合。

Text 2

[文章概述] 文章介绍了一些关于电子游戏玩家的情况和对电子游戏影响的调查。

51. C 【解析】细节题。由第一段第七句可知不止年轻人在玩游戏,玩游戏的人涉及很广的年龄段。所以答案为 C。

52. C 【解析】细节题。第二段第二句可知像 Xbox 和 PlayStation 这些类型的游戏机是二十几岁人的领域,他们喜欢把自己想象成体育明星和赛车手。所以答案为 C。

53. B 【解析】细节题。第三段谈到 The AOL survey suggests some players are in denial about the extent of their habit.随后就说了人们受到游戏对他们不同程度的影响。可知这些人否认受电子游戏影响。所以答案为 B。

54. A 【解析】推理判断题。由第三段,作者提问 Or is it as harmful as television, pulling people ever further from reality?第四段 But don't think we're all heading into a world with everyone plugged into, if not totally controlled by, his own game. 可推测电子游戏没有电视对人的影响大。

55. B 【解析】细节理解题。由最后一段可知他们认为,玩他们游戏的人比不玩游戏的人更乐于参与到现实活动中。故他们认为他们的游戏是健康产品。

Text 3
[文章概述] 本文主要介绍了鸵鸟以及雌鸵鸟产蛋的特点。

56. C 【解析】细节题。根据第一段最后一句可知由于鸵鸟极长而有力的腿和它巨大羽翼张开而产生的浮力的共同作用,鸵鸟可以以很快的速度跑很长的距离。所以答案为C。

57. A 【解析】推理计算题。根据第二段第一句和最后一句可知鸵鸟一个雨季约产20个蛋,它在其他鸟巢产了8、9个蛋后才回自己的巢里产蛋。所以答案为A。

58. D 【解析】细节题。根据第四段第一句可知鸵鸟孵蛋时只能罩住约20个蛋,故它每次孵蛋都要弄几个蛋出巢。所以答案为D。

59. C 【解析】细节题。根据第四段第三句知对于每只雌鸵鸟来说,他们产的蛋有固定的大小和形状,故分辨自己所产的蛋对于他们来说并不难。所以答案为C。

60. B 【解析】推理判断题。文章最后一段最后一、二句可知,有很多鸵鸟巢都会受到袭击,但因为鸵鸟不但把蛋下在自己窝里,还下在其他鸵鸟的窝里,所以当一个鸵鸟巢遭受袭击时,雌鸵鸟在其他鸟巢下的蛋还可能存活下来。故鸵鸟这样做是为了保护它的蛋。

Part B

61. D 【解析】主旨题。婚姻的关键是心灵的融合。文章中那位女士说丈夫不一定非得赚很多钱,她不一定要找那种有更高成就的人。她所强调的是心灵上的融合。所以答案为D。

62. E 【解析】推理题。找一个精神上亲密无间的伴侣不是件容易的事。从 It takes some trial and error and a pretty long and dedicated search to identify the kind of person who is emotionally matching you ... 可以推断出来。所以答案为E。

63. A 【解析】主旨题。最近几十年内,女孩长大后普遍比以前的女性要更加有竞争力、更强。尽管她们在智力方面的成就会阻碍与男性之间的浪漫爱情的发展,多数女性相信一定会有男性被这些聪明的女性所吸引的。因此,事业上的成功并不是一个劣势。所以答案为A。

64. C 【解析】主旨题。成功包括爱情和工作,因此找到事业与家庭之间的平衡点才是成功的关键。所以答案为C。

65. B 【解析】推理题。选择正确的伴侣才能确保婚姻的稳定。根据 a wise judgment about a partner are more likely to eventually end up in a stable marriage. 可以推断出来。所以答案为B。

Section IV   Writing

Part A

本例要求考生回复一则邀请函:很高兴并且愿意接受邀请。
解题步骤:
第一步:确定题材——书信,注意格式
第二步:列出要点——致谢;接受邀请;询问时间、准备等细节问题;再次致谢
第三步:列出关键词——kind, the schedule, necessary, prepare for, looking forward to, etc.
第四步:落笔成文

October 19th, 2009

Dear Li Ming,

It's so kind of you to invite me to go to your beautiful and well-known hometown together with you, I would like very much to come. But could you please tell me some details about the trip and the schedule so that I can make an arrangement for my schoolwork?

By the way, is it necessary for me to prepare all the things? What are the basic necessities for the trip? Could you give me some suggestions?

Thank you again for your wonderful hospitality!

Looking forward to seeing you soon.

Sincerely yours,
Wang Lin

解题步骤：

第一步：审题

  1. 题型：看图作文

  2. 文体：论述说明文

第二步：框架分析

  1. 说明图画内容，点出要点；

  2. 图画现象发生的危害以及你的建议。

第三步：列出写作思路

  1. 描述图画：人们乱扔垃圾，不注意保护环境；

  2. 分析乱扔垃圾的危害和环保的重要性；

  3. 提出你的建议和解决措施，呼吁人们保护环境，科学发展。

第四步：列出关键词和词组

throw; care for; pay attention to; be in danger; prevent from; pick up; make a contribution to, etc.

第五步：落笔成文

The cartoon tells us a serious problem existing in the parks. Many people throw litters everywhere without caring for the environment. The beautiful scenery is totally destroyed by the rubbish they throw away.

With the development of our economy, people are paying less and less attention to the protection of our environment; as a result, we are facing a severe environmental problem. If we don't protect our environment, our lives will be in great danger. We must take some measures to prevent the situation from becoming worse! For instance, we can pick up litters and put them into the dustins, and we can teach children not to throw the litters casually.

As an old saying goes, "A small act can make a big difference." If everyone makes a contribution to the protection of our environment, I believe our world will be cleaner and more beautiful in the future, where green patches can be easily reached and the blue sky can always be seen clearly over our heads.

第6章

口试真题与提示

口试真题与提示（一）

Part I（3 minutes）

Task: Identifying oneself; identifying things / people; passing on information.

Interlocutor: Good morning (afternoon). My name is ... and this is my colleague ... He / She is just going to be listening to us. And your names are ... and ...? Would you tell me your candidate numbers so I can check them, please? Thank you. (Hand over the mark sheets to the assessor.) First of all we'd like to know something about you, Candidate A, so I'm going to ask you some questions.

Job or study

1. Can you tell me something about your job / study?

  (*Yes, I am a math teacher.*)

2. What do you enjoy most about your work / school?

  (*I enjoy teaching my students math.*)

3. What do you dislike about your work/school?

  (*The great pressure for both me and my students.*)

4. Do you have any future plans?

  (*Yes, I do. I'm going to further my study.*)

Interlocutor: Thank you. Now, we'd like to know something about you, Candidate B, so I'm going to ask you some questions.

Family

1. Could you tell us something about your family?

  (*I come from a traditional Chinese family. My parents are farmers and I am a student.*)

2. What does your family usually do for the weekend?

  (*We usually go walking in the quiet country road.*)

3. Do you enjoy it? Why?

  (*Yes, because we can keep healthy by walking and enjoy the country life.*)

4. What do you think of living together with your parents?

  (*We live together harmoniously, and I appreciate it very much.*)

Part II（3 minutes）

Interlocutor: I'd like you to talk about something for three minutes based on the information given below. Try to imagine the situation as if you were one of the three. I am going to listen. I'd like you to discuss the life in a students' dormitory.

Candidates: (Approximately 3 minutes.)

(*Candidate A: In this picture we can see there are four students are in the dormitory.*

Candidate B: Yes, and it is already more than 10 o'clock at night. But one student is still listening to the radio and the other two students are playing cards, laughing and shouting.

Candidate A: The student in bed just can't fall asleep, I'm afraid. He is turning again and again in bed. But the other students simply pay no attention to him. They simply go on with what they are doing.

Candidate B: I think since the students have to share a dormitory, they must think of others. The students who are playing cards and listening to the radio at night should be considerate.

Candidate A: Yes, how nice it would be if we could do everything as we like. Sometimes we will hurt others and can't get along well with them.)

Interlocutor: That's right. Let's stop here. Thank you. (Retrieve the picture sheet.)

Part III (4 minutes)

Interlocutor: Now, I'd like each of you to talk on your own for about one and a half minutes. I'm going to give each of you a different picture and I'd like you to talk about it. Candidate A, here is your picture. (several students are pulling at one end of a rope with great efforts.) Please let Candidate B have a look at it. (Hand over the picture to Candidate B.) Candidate B, I'll give you your picture in a minute. Candidate A, I'd like you to describe the picture and tell us what you think about it. Remember you have only about one and a half minutes for this, so don't worry if I interrupt you.

胜利，需要步调一致

Candidate A: (Approximately one and a half minutes.)

(*What a vivid picture it is! As can be clearly seen from the picture, a group of people are taking part in a tug of war. All of the team members are pulling at one end of a rope with effort with hot sweat rolling from their foreheads. They are full of confidence in winning the contest.*

The picture says a lot to us. It teaches us that only if a group of people keeps in step with each other, they will probably achieve more remarkable success. But if they get out of step with one another, they are certain to fail. So we can draw a conclusion that concerted action alone lead to victory.)

Interlocutor: Thank you. (Retrieve the picture.) Candidate B, is there anything else you would like to say about the picture?

Candidate B: (Approximately 30 seconds.)

(*There are a lot of examples to illustrate the picture. The most obvious one is the case with the war on SARS in 2003. At that time the whole country was plagued by SARS and all of it are under the leadership of our government, all walks of life in the society were mobilized and were united as one.*

Hundreds of medical workers in different hospitals across the country took part in this war. Many medical apparatus and instruments were sent to the epidemic stricken areas to rescue patients with SARS. Soon we won a great victory over the disease. In short, solidarity and cooperation are of great importance.)

Interlocutor: Thank you. Candidate B, here is your card.

(A boy was reading when his parents were caring him.) Please let Candidate A have a look at the picture. (Hand over the picture to Candidate A.) I'd like you to describe the picture and also tell us how you feel about the picture. Remember you have only about one and a half minutes for this.

Candidate B: (Approximately one and a half minutes.)

(*This drawing shows us a funny but realistic situation: a young boy who wears a thick pair of glasses is sitting on a tall chair, reading a thick book hard. Two other books are laid on the tall desk in front of him. The poor boy seems to become dizzy from his continuous hard work. The boy even fails to notice that his shoes have fallen onto the floor. His mother is squatting down on his left to help him put on the dropped shoes and says with a satisfied smile, "My son, you do not need to do anything else. You just study hard to become a VIP one day." At the same time, his father is standing on his right with a plate, feeding him with a spoon patiently.*

　　From the picture, we can tell that nowadays many students study with an incorrect purpose. Their parents expect them to study for money and fame instead of gaining knowledge. They are frequently forced to follow their parents' words and told to care about nothing except for study. In this way, their parents actually have deprived them of the opportunities to deal with problems independently and thus such children tend to become lazy and incapable of coping with practical problems. Their worldview has been twisted and in most cases, they are frail and cannot withstand failure bravely.)

　　Interlocutor: Thank you. (Retrieve the picture.) Candidate A, is there anything else you would like to say about the picture?

　　Candidate A: 〔Approximately 30 seconds.〕 (*From my point of view, parents should not expect too much of their children and should not be too practical and money-oriented. Instead, they should help their children form a correct attitude towards study and give them helpful instructions to real success.*)

　　Interlocutor: Thank you.
　　(That is the end of the test.)

口试真题与提示(二)

Part Ⅰ (3 minutes)

Task: Identifying oneself; identifying things / people; passing on information.

Interlocutor: Good morning (afternoon). My name is ... and this is my colleague ... He / She is just going to be listening to us. And your names are ... and ...? Would you tell me your candidate numbers so I can check them, please? Thank you. (Hand over the mark sheets to the assessor.) First of all we'd like to know something about you, Candidate A, so I'm going to ask you some questions.

Hometown

Either: (for candidates from other provinces)

1. Where did you live before you came here?

(*I lived in Guangdong before I came here.*)

2. How long have you lived here?

(*I have been here for 2 years.*)

3. How do you like it? Why?

(*I like it very much, because the weather is nice and the city is very clean.*)

4. Do you think you will live here forever? Why?

(*No, I have to go back in the future, because my parents want me to.*)

Or: (for candidates taking the examination locally)

1. Do you live near here? Where is it?

(*Yes, it is...*)

2. What do you think are the good points about living there?

(*The living conditions are perfect here.*)

3. How do you usually go to work / school? Why?

(*I go to work by bike. Because it is cheap and convenient.*)

Interlocutor: Thank you. Now, we'd like to know something about you, Candidate B, so I'm going to ask you some questions.

Family

1. Could you tell us something about your family?

(*I come from a traditional Chinese family. My parents are farmers and I am a student.*)

2. What does your family usually do for the weekend?

(*We usually go walking in the quiet country road.*)

3. Do you enjoy it? Why?

(*Yes, because we can keep healthy by walking and enjoy the country life.*)

4. What do you think of living together with your parents?

(*We live together harmoniously, and I appreciate it very much.*)

Part Ⅱ (3 minutes)

Interlocutor: Now, I'd like you to talk about something for about 3 minutes. I'm just going to listen. I'd like you to imagine that you are going out for an evening's entertainment.

[Place picture sheet (including pictures of different sports: 1. pop music concert; 2. Peking Opera;3. ballet dancing; 4. piano playing) in front of candidates.] Talk to each other about the sort of entertainment you like best. It is not necessary to agree with each other. You have only about 3 minutes for this.

Candidates: (Approximately 3 minutes.)

(*Candidate A: Hi, Jake. What do you want to do this evening?*

Candidate B: I want to have some entertainments.

Candidate A: As far as I know, there are many performances these days. There is a pop music concert, a Peking Opera performance, a ballet dancing show and a piano performance.

Candidate B: I like pop music very much. I would go to the pop music concert. A famous band holds it. I believe everyone will be cheerful and even crazy there.

Candidate A: Perhaps you are right. But I'd rather go to the piano performance instead. It's really enjoyable to listen to pieces of beautiful music composed by those many great musicians.

Candidate B: Well, I hope you enjoy yourself this evening then.

Candidate A: Thank you. The same to you.)

Interlocutor: Thank you. (Retrieve the picture sheet.)

Part Ⅲ (4 minutes)

Interlocutor: Now, I'd like each of you to talk on your own for about one and a half minutes. I'm going to give each of you a different picture and I'd like you to talk about it. Candidate A, here is your picture (an old mother is holding her university son). Please let Candidate B have a look at it. (Hand over the picture to Candidate A.) Candidate B, I'll give you your picture in a minute. Candidate A, I'd like you to describe the picture and tell us what you think about the picture. Remember you have only about one and a half minutes for this, so don't worry if I interrupt you.

Candidate A: (Approximately one and a half minutes.)

(*How vivid and accurate the picture is in describing one of the most serious social problems concerning college students in China! As is shown in the picture, a college student, held in his mother's arms, is comfortable, whereas his mother, sweating, carries him with great difficulty.*

It is widely known that high tuition fees, plus lodging and other expenses, have become a heavy burden for university students' parents, many of whom are farmers or laid-off workers. Parents' worries also come from the heavy dependency of today's college students, many of whom are bookworms depending on their parents for everything. Some of them even send clothes home for their parents to wash. In my opinion,college students should be educated to stand on their own two feet. And government and education institutes should also help to relieve the parents' economic burdens.)

Interlocutor: Thank you. (Retrieve the picture.) Candidate B, is there anything else you would like to say about the picture?

Candidate B: (Approximately 30 seconds.)

(*Fortunately, some measures have been taken. For example, banks distribute loans to students; u-niversities cut down charges for poor students and provide them with part-time employment. As a result, we have witnessed some improvements but still there is a long way to go.*)

Interlocutor: Candidate B, here is your card (a man decides to quit smoking). Please let Candidate A have a look at it. (Hand over the picture to Candidate B.) I'd like you to describe the picture and also tell us how you think about it. Remember you have only about one and a half minutes for this.

Candidate B: (Approximately one and a half minutes.)

(*The young man in the picture is a smoker and we can see he is deciding to quit smoking because he throws the whole pack of cigarette out of the window. But before the pack touches the ground, he hurries down the stairs and grabs the pack just in time. Though he has made up his mind, he still can't give up smoking. I think smoking is a bad habit, no matter how hard it is, we should get rid of it.*)

Interlocutor: Thank you. (Retrieve the picture.) Candidate A, is there anything else you would like to say about the picture?

Candidate A: (Approximately 30 seconds.)

(*From the picture I see that it is easy to make a decision but it is hard to carry it out.*)

Interlocutor: Thank you.

(**That is the end of the test.**)